OUT OF THE
FLAMES

About the Author

Stacy Lynn Miller is a late bloomer as an author. She's a retired Air Force officer, having spent twenty years toting a gun and police badge, tinkering with computers, and sleuthing for clues as an investigator. She's a proud stroke survivor, mother of two, tech nerd, chocolate lover, and terrible golfer...with a hole-in-one. When you can't find her writing, she'll be golfing or drinking wine (sometimes both) with friends and family in Northern California.

You can connect with Stacy on Instagram @stacylynnmiller, Twitter @stacylynnmiller, or Facebook @stacylynnmillerauthor. You can also visit her website at stacylynnmiller.com.

OUT OF THE
FLAMES

STACY LYNN MILLER

BELLA
B O O K S
2020

Bella Books, Inc.
P.O. Box 10543
Tallahassee, FL 32302

Printed in the United States of America on acid-free paper.

First Bella Books Edition 2020

Editor: Medora MacDougall
Cover Designer: Judith Fellows

ISBN: 978-1-64247-132-8

Acknowledgments

To Jacky Abromitis and the authors at LesFan, a place for fanfiction writers to test their wings, I owe my inspiration. If not for the hundreds of stories I read there, I would've never thought I had a story in me to tell.

To Cameron MacElvee, whom I met at LesFan and now call a friend for life, I owe my motivation. She set the bar for eloquence and quality storytelling. After reading my first wing-spreading attempt, she became my biggest cheerleader with a single sentence: "You have a very good shitty first draft." Translation: "All first drafts are shitty, but your shit has promise." She encouraged me to take my writing seriously, learn proper craft, and believe I could be published one day.

Because of Cammie, I found the Golden Crown Literary Society Writing Academy. Their outstanding volunteer staff and faculty taught me how to breathe life into my storytelling. One incredible instructor stood out. To Karelia Stetz-Waters, I owe my confidence. After nailing a homework assignment, her four-word reply in capitalized bold print marked a shift in how I looked at myself. She wrote, **"YOU ARE A WRITER!"** From that day, I believed.

To Ann Roberts, my Academy mentor and queen of the markup, I owe my final transformation. Her uplifting guidance made it all click. Besides helping me understand the importance of word choice, she drilled into me the concept of point of view…forty-one times.

Ann's faith in me and personal recommendation led to Bella Books signing me as a debut author. Thank you, Ann, and thank you, Linda and Jessica Hill, for taking a chance on this unknown and letting me tell my story to a broader audience.

To Medora MacDougall, my editor and champion of the Oxford comma, I owe my optimism. Her critical eye and persistent search for the dreaded dangling modifier put the final polish on this story. She and the final product we produced made me believe this journey was worth the never-ending eyestrain and countless sleepless nights.

To my local writing critique group, Laura, Ray, Kelly, and Tamie, whose weekly feedback helped mold that shitty first draft into something worth reading, I owe my determination. Their collective honest advice sprinkled with a dash of love gave me the willpower to see this through.

To Barbara Gould, my best friend and plotting partner in crime, I owe my new life's path. From that first all-day plotting session at my kitchen table, tacking sticky notes to the sliding glass door, to weekly "what do you think" hour-long phone calls, her humor and undying friendship brought me and this story to life.

Finally, to my family, who put up with a year of microwaved burritos and takeout as a dinner fallback option, I owe a debt I can never repay. They gave me the time, space, daily encouragement, and monthly maid service I needed to never give up. Their unconditional love made this dream come true.

I am forever grateful to everyone who had a hand in this journey. If not for each and every one of you, *Out of the Flames* would've remained a vague thought. Thank you doesn't seem nearly enough, but here goes. Thank you!

Dedication

To Jerry Waren.
My dad and role model.
He taught me what it means to be strong.

PROLOGUE

Manhattan Sloane had a secret: all the other thirteen-year-old girls fawned over two male classmates, Hotty Scotty and Beefcake Jake, but she didn't. In grade school, boys were fine to play with, but none ever made her want to do silly things to get their attention. At every opportunity, like tonight, she hung around Finn Harper, a cute tomboy who made her heart hammer so hard her chest hurt whenever she looked her way.

Why her and not a boy? Something had to be wrong. Right? Should she tell anyone? A resounding "no" screamed in her head. *Whatever you do, don't let Finn find out.*

Most girls from her junior high honor choir had already filed out of the well-lit auditorium through the side door and gone down the steps to go home with their parents. All except her and Finn. In the adjoining classroom, Sloane stalled as long as she could at the semicircle of student desks by primping her long brown hair and fumbling with the contents of her book bag. Out of excuses, she slipped on her prized dark blue jean jacket, slung her backpack over her right shoulder, and ambled toward the door. She hoped to hear Finn's voice or catch a glimpse of her hazel eyes as she left.

As Sloane reached the exit, Finn's sweet, silvery tone stopped her in her tracks. "Looks like we're the last two again."

Sloane's heart fluttered, waking the butterflies in her stomach. She didn't expect anything more than Finn's casual smile and "see ya," followed by their mutual post-practice stair counting. Making it worse, as Finn strained to put on her cropped brown leather jacket, it pushed out her blossoming chest. Sloane thought she'd faint. *What's wrong with me?*

Finn extended her hand, inviting Sloane to take it. "Walk out together?"

Sloane had daydreamed at least a dozen times about holding that hand, though, in her dreams, she didn't have the sweaty palms she had tonight. When she took it, its warmth and softness reminded her of her blanket fresh out of the dryer. Then in an instant, her eyes rounded like hockey pucks—she had a crush. Those butterflies swarmed harder, churning the chicken nuggets and shoestring fries from lunch.

Finn tugged, but after Sloane inhaled the citrus scent of her short blond hair, her feet froze to the floor. She'd conjured up rows of orange trees in her head and wanted to breathe them in for hours. *Say something you idiot*, she told herself, but Finn had her tongue tied in a knot the size of one of those oranges in her brain.

"You okay?" Finn looked into her eyes.

With one glimpse at those hazel eyes, the taste of breaded chicken bubbled up in her throat. Before she recycled her lunch on the tips of Finn's denim blue sneakers, she snapped out of her stupor. *Think of something. Anything.*

"Can we wait a few minutes?" Sloane shuffled her feet. "I gotta go out with my parents tonight, and these dinners always end in disaster."

"I can't. My dad will kill me if I'm late again." Finn squeezed Sloane's hand, signaling her heartfelt apology.

Though the euphoric moment would soon end, she held on to the hope they'd have another chance to hold hands after tomorrow's practice while they talked about this and giggled about that. Then a lump formed in her throat. How could she hide the fact she liked Finn the way other girls liked boys? *Ugh. Something is wrong with me.*

"I get it."

Soon they emerged from the auditorium and stood at the top of the concrete steps. *Good, no Dad,* Sloane thought. No doubt tonight's dinner with her grandmother had Sloane's father all worked up. From the lone lamppost illuminating the area, Sloane's mother waved her over.

"I gotta go." Finn waved at her father as he gestured to her from several feet away. "Count?"

"Sure." A surge of boldness spurred Sloane to give Finn's hand a squeeze of her own. Simultaneously, she and Finn stepped down and counted each stair. "One, two, three, four, five, six."

At the bottom. Finn released Sloane's hand. "See ya tomorrow, Sloane."

"See ya, Finn." Sloane's chest tightened when their fingers slipped apart. After Finn walked away, she wished tomorrow were already there. "Tomorrow," she whispered to herself.

"You certainly took your sweet time, Manny." Sloane's mother hunched her shoulders through a button-down thigh-length dark wool coat.

"I hate it when you call me that." Sloane rolled her eyes at the root of her insecurities. Her first name brought on endless teasing about her boyish clothes and mannerisms from the seventh-grade ruling class. To get through it, she counterpunched, pointing out that when those girls were older they were going to have to have regular liposuction to satisfy their inevitable middle-aged vanity.

"I'm sorry, honey. I've been calling you that since the day you were born. It's a hard habit to break."

"But all the girls call me a tomboy, and that nickname makes it worse."

"Would you rather I call you Manhattan?"

"God, no. That's ten times worse." Sloane rolled her eyes again. The fact she was conceived in Times Square on New Year's Eve would haunt her for the rest of her life.

"I'm sorry, honey. I'll work on the Sloane thing, I promise." Her mother chuckled when she rubbed Sloane on the shoulders. "We better get going. Your father will be furious if we're late."

The uneasiness of the night to come replaced the exhilaration of Finn's hand in hers while she walked to the family sedan. "I bet he's already smoking in the car."

"You know how he gets before these evenings with his mother. It helps him relax."

"I know. Let's get this over with." Sloane groaned at the prospect of an evening of polite awkwardness when her mother hurried her along.

Sloane had predicted correctly. Inside the family car, the pungent smell of fresh cigarette smoke filled the cabin. The gift on the front seat forecasted an obligatory birthday dinner with her grandmother filled with faked friendly greetings, superficial pleasantries, and a shouting match as the main attraction. One thing puzzled her, though. Sloane never understood why her father disliked her grandmother so much, nor why she saw her only twice a year. All they told her was that he grew up without a father. During nights like this, Sloane was glad her mother had no other family and no opportunity for full-on drama.

After he doused his Marlboro, Sloane braced herself for his short temper. Luckily, he turned to her mother. "There was an accident on the freeway." He glared at Sloane in the rearview. "And we're already late."

Hello to you, too, Dad. Geez. Instead of firing back, Sloane matched his glare and shot daggers at the salt-and-pepper hair cropped tightly around his ears. The school had scheduled choir practice on her grandmother's birthday, not her, and arguing would only make him mad—something to avoid tonight.

"It'll be fine, Daryl." Her mother placed a calming hand on his arm. "Take the back road and catch the freeway at the Dam Road in San Pablo. We should make it to San Francisco in time, but I'm sure they'll hold our reservation if we're a few minutes late."

After a few grumbled words, he drove off. Its many twists and turns made the back road tricky enough to drive during daylight. Tonight, the fog had settled into the hills and hung on every curve, the absence of streetlights making the way murky. Her mother had taken this road at night dozens of times, but not this fast. When her mother gripped the passenger grab handle after a sharp turn, Sloane considered asking him to slow down but thought better of it.

After minutes of tense silence, her mother turned in her seat toward Sloane in the backseat. "How was practice? Will you girls be ready for next week's concert?"

Sloane relaxed. *Thank God.* With something to take her mind off her dad and the upcoming evening, she perked up and replied at a fast clip. "It was great. Me and Finn are singing ABBA's 'Take a Chance on Me,' and we're really good."

"Ooh, I love that song."

"Sing it with me, Mom."

"Sure." A warm smile formed on her mother's lips.

Sloane loved hearing her mother's melodic voice. Her mother had told her as a toddler that singing soothed her to sleep at night and eased her awake the next morning. By the time she entered school, Sloane had sung along with her every day before her father came home from work, making it their special time.

"You take the background on the first verse. On three." Sloane counted down and began the verse. Her mother joined with the mesmerizing background lyrics.

Her father squirmed in his seat, not unlike his reaction whenever their singing interrupted his concentration when he brought work home. Before they finished the first verse, he glanced over his shoulder at her. "Enough!"

Sloane hushed and glared at him. *Geez, it's only singing.*

Two diffused beams of light emerged around the corner in the misty fog. The oncoming lights moved into their lane, or vice versa, she couldn't tell, but they were on a collision course.

"Dad!"

He whipped his head around and jerked the steering wheel. Their car launched into a fishtail, throwing Sloane against her door with a forceful thud. She clawed the air for her mother's hand. After her father slammed the brakes, the car turned on itself.

What's happening? Every detail came into sharp focus. Her eyes fixed on nothing, yet everything at the same time. Oddly, motion around her slowed as if someone had flipped a strange switch. Her eyes focused on her window while it scraped the road surface. There must have been a screeching sound, but she couldn't hear it.

The world turned again, and the road disappeared. The top of the car hit the asphalt in a dull thud, but she didn't hear it either. While her hands braced her fall to the roof, her backpack joined her hands there. It made no sense—the outside world had turned upside down.

Everything bent again, and the road reappeared. She twisted her head so her eyes could follow her mother's long brown locks and necklace as they floated in the air. Glass shattered, but Sloane couldn't hear the crack. The chunks of glass and contents of her mother's purse joined the hair and necklace in a midair dance.

Something held Sloane in place when the car rolled again and kept her from sliding. Nothing made sense except that the world had turned upright.

The ground fell out beneath them, and everything slanted downward. When the dancing glass fragments flew back toward her face, she blinked to dodge them.

Then came a jolting stop.

The seat belt hugged her. A sharp pain radiated across her chest and abdomen and forced air from her lungs. When she inhaled, a severe ache radiated in her chest, forcing her to take shallow breaths. She winced.

Sloane tried to get her bearings, but her heart pounded in her ears and reverberated with every beat. She recognized the copper taste of blood in her mouth. Then the faint scent of gasoline reminded her she was in a vehicle. Though the car pointed almost straight down, something had suspended her in midair. Her mind was still fuzzy; it made little sense.

Seconds later, a dim glow from the engine compartment provided enough light to see her seat belt held her in place. The car had come to rest in a deep trench not wide enough for it to lay flat. In the front seat, her parents' heads slumped forward.

"Mom…Dad?" When no one answered, she cried out again, this time meeker than the first, "Mom…Dad?"

Her father groaned and raised his head.

She hoped. She prayed. "Dad? Is Mom…?" But she couldn't say the words too horrible to think.

Her father stretched out a bloody hand toward her motionless mother. When he nudged her, she groaned. When he shook her shoulder, she moaned again and raised her head. Alive. She was alive.

"Cathryn?" Blood dripped from his lips.

"Manny?" her mother slurred.

When Sloane took in a rattled breath, her throat constricted. "I'm okay, Mom."

"Can you move?" Her father struggled to push up the steering column.

After slinging her legs to one side, Sloane tugged at the seat belt holding her in place. "Yeah, I can move."

"See if you can get your mother out." His wince signaled considerable pain. "I'm pinned in."

Bracing herself with one hand against the front seat, she released the seat belt with the other. Once free, she pushed her upper body over the top of her mother's seat. She gasped at the sight of her mother's legs trapped by pieces of metal. Flames had peeked out from the wrecked engine, shedding more light on her surroundings. She discovered her father's legs were similarly pinned.

"Oh, God." Sloane ripped at pieces of metal near her mother, slicing her hands on the sharp edges.

Her mother, more alert now, glanced toward Sloane. "It's no use, Manny."

Heat rose from the flames. Sloane's heart pounded in her ears as she tried again to free her mother from the tangled sections of plastic and metal. "I can do it. I can do it." Blood streaming from her hands, she pushed and pulled.

Shards of glass protruded from her mother's hand; blood oozed down her arm. "Listen, Sloane. It's no use. Go. Save yourself."

The flames grew. Sloane needed to get out, but she couldn't leave without them. "I can't, Mommy, I can't." She pulled again on the mangled pieces. "I can't leave you."

"She's right, Sloane. Please go." Her father turned soft eyes on her.

Sloane blinked. They'd both called her Sloane.

She tried the passenger door and then another. Neither budged. The forward window on her mother's side had shattered, making it the only means of escape. Reality set in. She kissed her father on the forehead. "I love you, Daddy."

"I love you, sweetheart."

It broke her heart. This was the first time she'd said those words to him in years. Either he was always working or she didn't care enough to say them. Now it was too late. One tear after another rolled down her face when she turned. She'd told her mother those words every time they said goodbye. Now they seemed not nearly enough. Sloane's lips quivered as she kissed her mother's forehead. "I love you, Mommy."

The flames grew more substantial as heat and smoke filled the cramped space.

"Hurry, Sloane. Hurry," her mother pleaded.

Sloane pulled herself over her mother's trapped body and through the rough opening. When she reached for her mother again, she choked, and the billowing black smoke blinded her for a moment.

"No, baby, get away. You have to get away." Her mother pushed her back.

"But—"

"Run, Sloane. Run!" Her father's scream served to push her further back.

She glanced once more at her mother to memorize the smile on her face. Even through the blood and torn flesh, her mother's beauty left her speechless. Then as the smoke rolled heavier, her mother mouthed the words, "I love you."

Sloane stumbled down the path of the trench as fast as she could, but sobbing and pain slowed her down. Every step from the hot twisted mess took her one step closer to becoming an orphan.

She clawed her way up the edge of the embankment toward the pavement. She glanced up the highway. Maybe there'd be a passing car. Where was the other driver?

Horrid, high-pitched noises pierced the air, sounds like nothing she'd ever heard before, like an animal trapped in sure death. Sloane glanced back as flames engulfed the car. Her mother's arms flailed to the beat of her screams. In an instant, fire consumed her.

Sloane shrieked. "Mommy!"

After advancing a few steps, she stumbled and lifted her head, horrified at seeing her mother's fiery silhouette thrashing back and forth still. An explosive ball of fire concussed toward her and hurled bits of metal into the air. They turned into pinballs bouncing off the trees. Heat scorched her skin, and bright light forced her eyes shut to the horrible truth.

When she shook off her daze, only fragments remained of the burning car, leaving nothing identifiable as human. Another image of her burning mother choked the air from her lungs. A second explosion sent another wall of heat toward her. She scurried back up the embankment and slumped to the ground.

"Don't leave me, Mommy," she whimpered, and her wet tears fell to the charred earth.

CHAPTER ONE

Eighteen years later

Ends of long, tousled, bleached-blond hair tickled Sloane's nose awake along with the rest of her. The rare warmth in the air reminded her that a few weeks remained of San Francisco's tepid summer. Her eyes fluttered open to a dark apartment bedroom furnished with only a rickety dresser, the bed she had stretched across, and the tall, naked blonde next to her. As she extended her long legs across the lumpy mattress, a predicament became clear. Should she ignore her engorged ache or the words whispered into her ear right before falling asleep? She decided on neither.

Sloane had a type, and this one fit the bill perfectly, ideally suited to quench her physical needs and nothing more. Or so she had hoped. After a month of hookups, Sloane thought Michelle knew the score—no commitments, no emotions, just sex. Saying "I love you" broke the rules.

Maybe it had been said in the heat of the moment, or perhaps it was the alcohol talking. If so, they'd be able to return to their unattached entanglement. If not, Sloane's only option was cutting her loose. But not before she took care of her immediate problem.

She ran a finger up the edge of Michelle's toned leg, hoping that would be enough to wake her. When that didn't work, she went for the gold, dipping a hand between that leg and the other to find the patch of short, coarse hairs she'd delighted in hours earlier.

Michelle's legs opened wider. A naughty grin appeared on her face, though her eyes remained closed. "Again?"

Sloane hoped this wouldn't take long. "Gotta start my first day as a detective off right, don't I?"

Michelle's eyes popped open. "Not before I know we're on the same page."

"I think we are." Sloane inched her own tall, athletic body lower until she could take in Michelle's musky scent. "You go first. Then me."

"Not that." Michelle sat up against the headboard, her chin dipped to her chest. "I'm falling in love with you, Sloane. I need to know I have a chance with you."

And there it is. Sloane released a heavy sigh into the rumpled sheets. Every time she found great sex, this happened.

After joining Michelle against the headboard, she picked at the options of how to say goodbye this time. Should she choose the "I warned you this would happen" approach? Or should she go with her tried-and-true "settling down" line? One would leave no room for Michelle to mistake it was over, and the other would let Michelle down gently so Sloane could still frequent her neighborhood tavern in relative peace.

"I'm not ready to settle down, Michelle." Sloane bent her knees up and dangled her forearms over them.

Michelle slapped a section of the mattress and flung her feet to the floor. "Uncle Dylan warned me this would happen."

"He did, huh?" Until now, Sloane wasn't sure if those two talked beyond family and the daily operations of his pub.

Michelle scurried to find her clothes. "He warned me you were unobtainable."

Sloane pulled her back to bed. When Michelle crossed her arms and pulled out her pouty face, Sloane decided a conciliatory tone was called for. "He knows me and that my job makes it impossible to consider settling down."

Even that was a lie. No one knew the real Manhattan Sloane. She let no one get close enough to find out, especially lovers. She was a magnet for heartache and death, so avoiding deep connections seemed like a prudent thing for everyone. Dylan, her only friend and primary bartender—one having everything to do with the other—only knew what Sloane let him see: an aloof orphan accustomed to being alone who married her job the first day she pinned on the badge.

"He knows you better than his only niece," Michelle harrumphed.

"What do you expect? I live a block away and have seen him almost every day for the last eighteen years."

Michelle raised her chin toward the ceiling as if searching for a better explanation. "Was the sex not good enough?"

"God, no." She and Michelle had kept it interesting by weaving daring into the lineup. The image of Dylan's now broken office chair snuck up on her, along with a mischievous grin. "Sex is great with you, but I can't give you anything more."

"I blew my chance with you, didn't I?"

"That's just it." Sloane pulled Michelle's chin toward her. "No one has a chance with me."

"It's time for you to leave, Sloane." Michelle's nostrils flared before she jerked her head toward the window.

Sloane considered giving Michelle a gentle touch or a soft apology but feared she'd lose an arm for her effort. Instead, she dressed and closed the door behind her, thinking she should have gone with "I warned you this would happen."

* * *

Today, newly minted Sergeant Manhattan Sloane traded in her seven-point sterling silver badge for a gold one. For six years, she served and protected the City by the Bay, and like every other patrol officer, she'd had her share of assigned partners. She'd considered each a good cop who brought his or her own unique skills and personality to the job. The weightlifter had her back more than once during bar disturbances. The budding lawyer quoted chapter and verse for every violation to throw against a perp they didn't care for. And the second-chancer spoke the language of every hooker and drug addict they came across. Today, she drew Eric Decker as a partner, a tall, brawny seasoned narcotics detective about three years her senior.

For her first assignment as a detective, she'd requested homicide, but the brass saw fit to send her to narcotics. Just as well, she figured. Her old beat, the Mission District, sat at the center of San Francisco's drug world and had primed her well for it.

As she rode to her first scene in a weathered unmarked sedan, nerves didn't bother her, but she couldn't say as much for her uncomfortable new gear. Whenever she leaned over, despite her thin, athletic frame, the adjuster of her shoulder holster poked the underside of her breast. She must've tweaked it twenty times this morning. The holster differed from the Sam Browne belt she'd worn around her waist for years, and it would take getting used to. She did, however, like the variety of options now available for styling her dark brown hair. She opted to wear it today in a loose bun low on the neck—a refreshing change of pace from the high bun or ponytail required in uniform.

"Don't wear formfitting jackets." Eric shifted his glance from the road and then back again. "It won't rub as much."

She pulled at her dark off-the-rack jacket, grumbling about having to update her entire wardrobe. "This'll get expensive."

"I'll introduce you to my tailor." Eric snickered. "He knows how to let the side out just enough for your holster and still make you look good. Plus, he gives first responders fifty percent off."

Must be a good tailor. The dark blue pinstriped suit he was wearing fit Eric like a glove and played well with his business-cut light brown hair.

Eric pulled up in front of the mid-century apartment building, one of several in the neighborhood that showed its age. The boarded-up windows, weed-lined sidewalks, and smog-stained façades housed a good swath of the city's drug community.

He turned off the engine and rubbed his clean-shaven face. "I suggest you listen and learn. The CSIs can get a little territorial."

Sloane's antenna went up. *Listen and learn because I'm a rookie detective or because I'm a woman?* Years ago, while studying criminal justice at San Francisco State University, she first saw him at a college job fair and didn't get the impression he would treat a woman differently from a man. As a uniformed officer, she'd run into him several times at crime scenes and considered him fair-minded and above petty notions. Maybe she'd given him too much credit.

"If you think I can't handle myself, why'd you request me as a partner?"

"I asked for you because when I first saw you at that career fair, I saw something special in you. Was I wrong?"

"No, you weren't." Bragging wasn't her thing, but she needed to set the tone.

"I didn't think so. You're a good cop and street smart. You know the difference between the law and justice and that the two don't always mean the same thing." He gently laid a hand on her shoulder like her mother used to do when she taught her a desperately needed lesson. "Look, I know you've worked plenty of drug labs as a uni, but I don't want you to step in it your first day."

Maybe she'd doubted him too soon, so she gave him a nod. "Fair enough."

Once past the crime scene van and two patrol cars parked curbside, she approached the uniformed officer guarding the scene perimeter.

"Hey, Holland."

Officer Holland scanned her from head to toe before his eyes settled on the gold badge dangling from her neck chain. "Good to see you moving up in the world, Sloane."

"Thanks." She grinned. Rising from the ranks came with a set of responsibilities, the most important of which was to represent the rank and file with distinction. His nod of appreciation meant she'd earned his respect. "Did you roll on this?"

"Yeah, a small lab to cut your teeth on." Holland's chuckle turned Sloane's grin into a broader smile.

"Nice work." Unsure whether he'd given her a jab or vote of confidence, she patted him on the shoulder and passed by.

The call sheet said a citizen had complained about the smell, and two officers stumbled across the makeshift meth lab. Sloane had discovered at least fifty of these during her time on the streets, but instead of securing the scene and observing today, she would investigate it for clues.

She'd seen it all before. Small or large, Crime Scene Investigations approached each lab in the same fashion. Technicians donned full chemical suits and respirators and disappeared inside, while the team leader managed the command post and logged in evidence from a safe distance outside. She and Eric headed there.

"Santos, what do we have?" Eric pushed back the flaps of his suit coat and rested both hands on his hips.

Santos turned, pushing back her chem suit hood and shaking loose shoulder-length caramel-blond hair, a contrast of light brown and butterscotch streaks. "Hey, Decker. Who's the rookie?"

"Avery Santos, meet Manhattan Sloane, my new partner." He shifted his glance to Sloane. "While you were back in kindergarten getting your department cert, Santos transferred from Ingleside and took over the CSI Lab at Bryant."

Sloane's breath hitched when she looked at Avery's eyes, hazel in color with rings of light green surrounding a cluster of rays the color of golden honey. They transported her, frozen, to somewhere in her past. *I've seen those before, but where? When?* She prided herself on never forgetting a face, and she knew she hadn't in this case. But those eyes were a different story. Answers eluded her, but she couldn't shake the feeling those eyes were meant for her.

A jab to her ribs knocked Sloane back to the present. After forcing a smile, she took her hand, shook it, and mumbled a word similar to "hey."

"I'll need that back." After several awkward beats, Avery pulled her hand away from Sloane's as if shaking off a film of goo. "Nice to meet you, Manhattan."

"Sloane, just call me Sloane."

Damn it, Sloane. For once, you come across a beautiful woman who won't run when she finds out you're a cop, and you act like a lovestruck teenager. Just stay focused on your first case.

"Sooooo…" Avery turned her attention back to Eric, "definitely not a professional lab."

Sloane scanned the evidence Avery had collected. Dried, dark gunk coated most of the items, and they had a distinct chemical scent. Lithium batteries, empty Pepsi bottles, lye, Drano, coffee filters, and several other items meant only one thing.

"Tweaker lab." Sloane's confidence spilled into a cocky smile. She'd run across enough meth-heads to recognize one of their filthy kitchens.

"Rookie's done her homework." Avery turned back to Eric, her voice tight with impatience. "As I was saying, definitely not a professional lab. Most likely a tweaker built it for personal use."

Sloane *had* done her homework. In addition to her own personal experience on patrol, she had studied dozens of case files to familiarize herself with the local drug culture. Eager to impress, she scanned the evidence table again. "Where are the mason jars? Sometimes tweakers hide them in the walls."

"Look, hotshot, you need to stay in your lane." Avery's daggers hit Sloane between the eyes. "Or do you need me to tell you that the best place to find the tweaker who built this lab is on Ellis Street?"

I'm such an idiot. Every one of her words had come across as arrogant. To be safe, Sloane mumbled some compliant response and kept her mouth shut for the rest of the walk-through.

The drive back to 850 Bryant had Sloane stewing in her juices and a grin plastered on Eric's face. After parking in the police garage, he turned to Sloane. "I think that went well, don't you?"

In a loud thud, she bounced her forehead off the dashboard and grunted. Never had she acted like such a fool, not as a rookie on patrol, and never in front of a beautiful woman. That was it; that performance pretty much assured that she'd blown her chance with the woman who had her spellbound at first sight.

* * *

The following day, Sloane barreled through her townhouse's front door and thumped down the stairs to the bottom-floor bedroom.

From the living room couch, a concerned voice rang out. "Where's the fire?"

"Sorry, Nana. I have a date." At least she hoped it was one.

Not two hours earlier, Sloane's heart had raced and her mouth had gone dry when Avery stopped her outside the squad room and said, "I'd like to make up for biting your head off yesterday. How about you let me buy you a drink after work?"

"O—kay." Sloane's response had made her sound like a pitiful tongue-tied teenager.

"How about Eddie's?" Avery's smile had brightened when she parted her lips, telegraphing an interest in more than drinks.

Perfect, a cop bar. Sloane would be in her element. The only hitch—she had enough time to change but not enough to shower following a late afternoon scuffle with a junkie.

After skidding across the wood floor in her room, she sifted through her closet and dresser, searching for something casual yet appealing. The moment she picked out an item, she discarded it in a huff, leaving a misshapen pile on her bed. "Too casual. Too plain. Too baggy. Too revealing. Too…just too."

"Try your favorite Levi's." Her grandmother appeared in the doorway, winded from her climb down the stairs. "And that light purple sweater you wore when you took me to the movies last week."

"Genius." Sloane snapped her fingers and glanced toward the door, where her grandmother stood gripping her cane. That fragility accompanied by a look of determination reminded Sloane of the days following the accident. In less than a month, her fear of having to live with the woman her father had such problems with turned out to be pointless. "Nana, you shouldn't be down here. The doctor said no stairs after your last stroke."

"I've survived a lot worse, and I'm not letting a few stairs keep me from finding out about this date."

"You're so stubborn, Nana." *You survived because I found you in time. Next time you may not be so lucky.*

Without time for an argument, she shoved at the mound of clothes and patted the corner of her bed, presenting an inviting temporary resting spot. "At least sit."

Her grandmother parked herself at the nearest corner before taking in a restorative breath. "Now, who is this woman?"

Sloane changed in a flash. "Just someone from work."

"She must be special if you're already this worked up."

Sloane paused. The women she dated in the past never had her dumbstruck at every turn, but this one did. Avery had the potential of holding her attention beyond the attraction, and now that she'd slowed down enough to consider that, it troubled her. Someone would get hurt. Her cautious side warned her to turn back, but the image of those haunting hazel eyes pulled her forward.

"It's just a date, Nana." Her energy now tempered to a slower pace, a quick brush through her hair, and Sloane was ready to go. She turned and posed. "How do I look?"

"Perfect, honey. Now, help this old woman up the stairs before you go."

The short drive to Eddie's hadn't calmed Sloane. At the bar, Avery's formfitting jeans and a blue and white striped button-down blouse caught her attention. Her breath hitched again at the pleasing mix of light and dark hair against dusky skin—a combination she hadn't encountered before Avery. *Get it together. It's just drinks.* After swallowing her nerves, she maneuvered through the standing-room-only cop crowd and joined Avery, who had sat at the bar.

"Hey." Sloane's nerves manifested in a shy, soft tone.

Avery turned and scanned Sloane up and down. "Glad you made it. You look nice."

Polite observation, or was she checking me out? No matter the case, it made her feel sexy.

"You look great too." Appreciating the lines of Avery's trim jean-clad legs crossed at the knee, she took a seat on the neighboring barstool.

Avery swung around, her expression turned serious. "I'm sorry I was a jerk yesterday." Masking part of a frown, she sipped on her cocktail. "I was having a bad day. Hell, I've been having a bad month, and I took it out on you."

The bartender popped over and laid a napkin in front of Sloane's spot at the bar.

"I'll take another vodka gimlet, and she'll have…" Avery turned to Sloane for the answer.

"Scotch on the rocks." After the bartender scurried off, Sloane shook her head, unwilling to let Avery take the blame. "I overstepped. Let's chalk it up to first-day jitters." *Or more accurate, Avery jitters.*

"I'm normally not that snippy."

"Is the job testing you too?" Relieved when her much-needed drink arrived, Sloane sipped on the scotch to take the edge off yesterday's embarrassment and tonight's nerves.

"Nothing I can't handle." Avery downed the rest of her current drink before accepting her next. "Breaking the glass ceiling sometimes ruffles a few feathers. I'm bound to get cuts and scrapes along the way."

"Been there, done that. You're bruising the egos of the old male guard." Before Sloane realized it, she'd squeezed Avery's hand. "And I'm sure my weak attempt to impress you didn't help."

"I've learned to lick my wounds." Avery sipped on her drink as if savoring its pain-relieving effects. "And outperform anyone who gets in my way."

"Amen. I do the same." Blushed cheeks, Sloane remembered cockiness had almost ensured that this "just drinks" didn't happen. She lightened her tone. "Or at least I try to."

Sloane shifted on her stool and raised her glass. "Tell you what, apology accepted."

They clinked glasses.

Avery leaned forward until her lips settled inches from Sloane's ear. "Thank you." Her silky tenor hinted more at seduction than regret.

This is more than just drinks. Sloane's stomach fluttered, competing with a tightness in her chest. *You're right, Nana. This one is special.* Under any other circumstance, she'd turn and run, but Avery had captivated her since her first mumbled word. This woman would test Sloane's resolve.

"Are you hungry?" Sloane hoped she was... *No commitments,* she reminded herself. "Would you like to get dinner?"

Avery checked the time on her cell phone. "I'd love to, but I have a teenage daughter at my apartment who's helpless in the kitchen." The creases at the bridge of her nose became more prominent as if she'd said too much for a first date.

A teenager? Avery can't be that old. "How old is she?"

"Fourteen." Avery released a long breath. Sloane's curiosity must've been a good sign.

Fourteen for Sloane meant fending for herself with TV dinners or microwaved nachos when her grandmother worked late at the school. She couldn't let this beautiful woman worry about her daughter on a first date.

"How about we pick up something for all three of us? My treat." Sloane topped off her proposition with a toothy smile.

Avery matched Sloane's smile. "I'd like that." She suggested they stop at a deli across the street from Eddie's and then walk the few blocks to her place. Arms filled with two bags of soup and sandwiches, they settled into polite chitchat. "Why did you become a cop?"

"When I was a teenager, my parents died in a car crash, and a police officer helped me. Bernie later died trying to save someone else, so I joined to honor him."

Avery's curiosity both pleased and upset her. With rare exceptions, the women Sloane dated found the exit after learning she worked as a cop and those who didn't never stayed long enough to find out why. But Avery did. That alone made her special, though the knot in her stomach reminded her why she avoided the question. Sloane held back the fact that Bernie died trying to help her again. Death followed her. The best thing she ever did was to bury her past.

"I'm so sorry about your parents." Avery rubbed Sloane's arm with her free hand.

Friendly compassion or something more? Sloane couldn't tell. She stopped her stride and met Avery's gaze, searching for a sign of interest. Avery's shy smile answered her question. *This is a date.*

"I've never done this with a woman." Avery steered her eyes toward Sloane's lips, licking her own.

Unsure if Avery was gay or experimenting, Sloane resisted the urge to kiss her. In her younger days, she'd kissed her share of thrill-seeking straight married women, but she swore off that years ago. "Tell me one thing?"

"What?"

"Are you married?"

"Widowed. He died in a military training accident." Avery kissed her on the cheek. Her lips lingered as if she were dipping her toes into a pond for the first time. After pulling back a fraction, she whispered, "I've always been attracted to women but never acted on it until now. And before you ask, no, I'm not looking for a one-night stand."

"I'm not looking for anything long-term." For her own preservation, Sloane had to say it. If her instincts were right, she would need the out.

"Let's just see where this goes." Avery curled her nose and sniffed. "Do I smell cherry?"

"Slushy shower with a junkie today." Warmth flushed Sloane's cheeks. "You like?"

"I do." Avery's smile grew, and the promise of something more to come floated in the air.

* * *

The way Sloane's jeans hugged her lean, athletic form and how her brown curls fell on her shoulders to frame her high cheekbones had caught Avery's eye during their "just drinks" date two weeks ago. Except for the long hair, her features resembled those of her dead husband. Man or woman, she realized, she had a type. As if her looks and matching cool and sexy tomboy fashion of jeans and tees weren't enough, Sloane's mix of playfulness, intelligence, and kindness had her hooked. Being hooked didn't mean she was ready for Sloane to reel her in though.

Despite six dinner dates, including two at little cafés and taverns only locals knew about and just as many coffee dates, Avery was still waffling. At least a dozen times her and Sloane's blood-pumping near-kisses had her wondering if she'd ever forget her upbringing and dive in. Sloane deserved a medal for her patience and her unending reassurances—"It's okay, whenever you're ready…"

With each passing day, goodbye kisses on the cheek had gotten longer and more dizzying and light caresses on the arm had turned into increasingly long, full-body hugs. Each time, Sloane's body had buzzed with arousal. Every inch of Avery's had too, especially at their last encounter, but her Catholic guilt had her running for the door before she could succumb to it.

Endless fantasies about women since adolescence had Avery convinced that she was going to hell. This thing with Sloane, though, had her thinking hell was a small price to pay to make all her fantasies come true.

Sloane had introduced her to the Tap days ago. Its faded Formica tabletops created a far from trendy atmosphere, but Sloane was enamored with it and called it her second home. The cluttered walls plastered with light wood paneling and mirrored beer signs made the place cozy. If Moe's Tavern on *The Simpsons* ever existed in real life, this would be it. However, the distinct smell of cooking grease reminded her the Tap offered food as well as liquor. Dylan's lunch and dinner menu offered several dishes she wanted to sample, and tonight, she had his Southwestern egg rolls on her mind.

Dylan delivered their shared plate and wiped his hands on his lightly stained white apron. "Since you're the only ones left, I'm getting ready to close up for the night, ladies."

"Would you prefer us to take it to go?" Sloane asked. Avery hoped he'd say no. Alone was perfect for what she had in mind.

"Take your time." He waved his hand as if her suggestion was preposterous. "I already turned off the sign. I'll be in the back cleaning the grill. When you finish, close the door behind you, and I'll put the bill on your tab."

"You're the best, D." Sloane gave him a wink.

Avery rubbed her hands. "Ooohhh, I've been thinking about this all day."

"Me too." Sloane's wistful voice made it clear food wasn't the only thing on her mind.

Last night's goodbye kiss on the cheek had Avery imagining Sloane's lips against hers, guessing what flavor she'd find when she dipped her tongue in for the first time. The corners of her mouth inched up, hoping that first taste would be Southwestern egg roll.

They dug into the food. While Avery's eyes widened at the spicy combination of tastes, Sloane's first bite resulted in an epic struggle with a long string of cheese, drawing giggles from both.

"Here, let me help." Avery reached up and broke off the end of the cheese closest to the egg roll. In midair, she rolled it around her index finger until she reached Sloane's lips. "Open wide." Her tone turned husky.

Their laughter came to an abrupt stop.

When her gaze settled on Sloane's eyes, she recognized a sexual hunger, the same one overwhelming her. It made her feel like a virgin, begging for that first magical kiss. After Sloane opened her mouth, she eased her finger in and grazed her tongue, sparking a sudden pulse between her legs. Sloane wrapped her lips around the finger, causing her to shudder at the warm, moist sensation. All the teasing and flirting of the last few weeks had come to a head. By the time she removed her finger, shallow breaths had dizzied her. She didn't have to hope Sloane felt the same; she saw it on her face. Her whole body ached to feel Sloane's lips against hers.

Avery brushed her lips against Sloane's. In that fleeting moment when their lips met, all her childhood teachings melted away. All the fantasies she had about kissing, touching, and making love to a woman were on the brink of coming true. What would Sloane's kiss feel like? Would it be like a man's, forceful and possessive, or would it be like her own, tender and trusting?

Air couldn't fill her lungs fast enough. She pressed her lips against Sloane's, expecting her to take control. But she didn't. Sloane relinquished it. The kiss was on Avery's terms. Pressing harder, she moaned at the electricity lighting her body and thought she heard Sloane moan too.

She'd wanted to taste her for days, but only now found the courage. Caressing Sloane's cheek, first with one hand and then two, she parted her lips a fraction and gave light brushes and tender licks. Kissing never felt like this before, had never curled the toes in her sneakers. And it obviously was supposed to.

Sloane wrapped a hand around the back of her head and pulled when she opened her mouth further. The moment their tongues bumped against one another, blood rushed to Avery's center, producing a powerful ache. *Hell, my ass. This is heaven.*

Their tongues danced, sharing the taste of egg roll, for how long, she couldn't be sure, but when she ended the kiss, different music was playing in the background. She fluttered her eyelids open and whispered. "Wow."

"Wow is right." Sloane still had her eyes closed, but the look of pure satisfaction on her face had Avery wanting another kiss.

CHAPTER TWO

A door slam punctuated Reagan's point—she didn't like Sloane. She'd acted this way since the first night Sloane had picked up Avery for dinner and greeted her with a kiss at the door. That kiss left no doubt Sloane was a suitor, not a friend or colleague. Avery had suspected having a woman come calling had thrown Reagan for a loop, and all she needed was time. But after almost a month, nothing had changed. In her core, Avery was sure she hadn't raised her daughter to be judgmental about such things, so something else had to be at play.

After pushing away her lunch dish, Avery slumped her head against the crook of her folded right arm resting on the kitchen tabletop. Thinking back, she realized Reagan had reacted the same with the three men she dated seriously enough in the last six years to consider initiating the daughter test. Today, Avery got the distinct feeling Reagan would reject anyone she brought home, effectively dropping a dilemma in her lap. She was falling in love with Sloane, of that she was sure, but Reagan's acceptance, or tolerance at best, was a deal-breaker. What was she supposed to say to a moody teenager without making it sound like an ultimatum?

"I should go home." Sloane's voice had a soft, understanding tone but did little to soothe Avery's frustration.

Sloane's leaving was the last thing she wanted. Thanks to a teenage sleepover, sixteen hours earlier at this very table, weeks of slow, hesitant exploration had culminated in an eruption of desire. The passionate kisses and caresses she'd come to expect over the previous weeks had built into irresistible knee-buckling foreplay.

In every intimate encounter before, Sloane had gestured or asked for permission to take things a step further. But last night, Avery took control, begging for skin-to-skin contact. Sloane quickly swept the Chinese takeout boxes from the table, a mess Avery didn't fret over until morning. Within seconds she had invited Sloane to take a breast between her lips, eliciting a reaction that sent her into a heat that lasted for hours.

Though that blissful discovery had ended well before breakfast, Avery hadn't prepared herself for goodbye. She'd never felt more in tune with her own body, nor more connected to another. She extended a hand that Sloane instantly took. "I don't want you to leave."

"Staying will make things worse."

Avery reluctantly walked her to the apartment door and said goodbye, but not before gliding her fingertips beneath Sloane's shirt and over the smooth skin encasing her taut back muscles. One last blood-pumping kiss took minutes before Avery could bring herself to close the door behind her lover. "Lover." She liked how it sounded.

Avery leaned against the cold, smooth door, still sensing the tingling in her lips and elsewhere. Her only regret about last night was that it took her so long to work up to it. How could sex be that good? How could she experience one climax after another and the desire for more never stop? Her only answer was Sloane. She was who Avery had waited a lifetime to meet.

Avery now had only one hurdle—Reagan. What to do with a teenager bent on tanking any relationship she dared introduce to the mix? Having been so much like Reagan at that age, Avery decided on the only approach that had worked on her when she rebelled in her youth.

After gathering the appropriate weaponry, Avery marched to Reagan's bedroom door and knocked. In response to the muffled "go away" coming from the other side, she turned the knob and walked through. She'd done enough to announce herself.

Inside, every new under-five-dollar makeup or skin product under the sun cluttered the dresser. The nightstand had a bit more open space, but empty plastic drink cups had multiplied like rabbits in the spring. The floor was not much better; Avery would have to speak to Reagan about using the carpet as a laundry basket. At least she'd clustered the anthill piles of clothes in the corners.

Reclined against the headboard, earbuds lodged in each ear, Reagan ignored her mother's invasion and focused on the laptop screen balanced between her raised knees and belly. The battle of wills had begun, and each of them would have to be armed.

Avery sat on the edge of the bed and extended to Reagan her choice of weapons. "Chocolate or vanilla?"

Reagan's expected scowl morphed into a temporary ceasefire. "Chocolate."

Ice cream never failed to create a lull in their skirmishes, no matter the topic or intensity. The key was to let Reagan make the first overture of surrender. Like so many times before, the heat from their earlier argument cooled after several bites.

Reagan's spoon clanked against the edge of the bowl to lap up her diminishing supply of ice cream. "I don't like her."

"What don't you like about Sloane?" The lack of a straightaway response convinced Avery that Reagan's objection wasn't about Sloane but something deeper. "This is about us, isn't it?" A corresponding deep sigh confirmed her suspicion. "What are you afraid of?"

"Of it not being just you and me anymore."

Avery retrieved their bowls and placed them on the nightstand before reclining against the headboard next to Reagan. "What do you think would change if Sloane spent more time with us?"

"We wouldn't have times like this when it's just the two of us."

"Do you remember in sixth grade when Deni let Shellie hang out with you two after school?"

"But that's different."

"How is it different? You resisted the addition and were so mean to Shellie those first few weeks."

"I thought being friends with Shellie meant Deni didn't want to be friends with me."

"And how did that work out?" Avery paused at Reagan's dispassionate shrug. "You three are best friends now. My spending time with Sloane doesn't mean things between us will change. It might make it better. All I ask is that you give her a chance."

"If I agree, does it mean I can get more ice cream?"

Reagan's playful shoulder nudge meant they'd formalized a truce. Maybe this thing with Sloane had a fighting chance.

* * *

Sloane had escaped to the Tap for a much-needed drink. The ice cube melting at the top shifted against the glass tumbler, mesmerizing her as it slid further into the amber liquid. The glass and its contents had remained untouched since Dylan placed the double scotch in front of her ten minutes ago.

For as far back as she could remember when a relationship lasted longer than a month, it meant trouble—the expectation of commitment. Case in point Michelle, though she didn't consider that dating. With all her exes, once a woman used the word love, she walked away, and until now, she had never looked back.

Against her better judgment, it had been five weeks since her first date with Avery, and she couldn't bring herself to stop. Everything about the woman intoxicated her, and she needed it more each day. Sure, Avery had a stubborn streak, but only when she needed it. She had a fiery side too, but only when someone got her defenses up like Sloane had when they first met. To Sloane, both traits made her even more addictive. No one, not Michelle, not her first lover, had ever gotten this deep under her skin. It terrified her.

Dylan's plump, white hand glided into view from behind the bar, wiping down its glossy top with a white cotton towel. She raised her gaze and studied his receding dark hairline. Making up for the lack of hair on top, he'd grown it out and styled it into a salt-and-pepper man bun in the back. Surprisingly, it looked good on him.

"You haven't touched your drink yet," Dylan announced over the piano riff of Journey's "Don't Stop Believing" as he adjusted his grease-stained white apron. "What's got you so gloomy, young lady?"

"She said, 'I love you.'" Sloane gripped the tumbler and swigged, feeling the burn from her throat all the way to her stomach. After slamming the glass back on the bar, she chastised herself for hanging on too long. A few flicks of her finger signaled her order for a second round to soothe the knot in her gut.

"Ah." Dylan stopped tending to the bar top and prepped her drink. "And you walked out."

She hung her head. "You know I'm not ready to settle down."

That worn-out line, as real as the day was long since college, no longer had meaning. She'd only ever looked for sex, fun, and more sex and had avoided falling in love at all cost. Now she had—there, she finally admitted it: she was helplessly, can't-live-without-you, in love with Avery Santos.

Now what? She had no clue, which is why she ran. The moment the words "I love you" flowed from Avery's lips, she wanted to say them too, and that was a horrible idea. Wasn't it? It was her own damn fault. At what point should she have called it quits? Maybe before their third date, a cozy picnic at Crissy Field on the soft, expansive green overlooking the bay. Or maybe before the fourth, a tandem bike ride through the lush pathways of Golden Gate Park. No, those outings didn't take her to the point of no return, but making love to Avery did.

Their first time marked Avery's first encounter with a woman, and the lead-up to it both excruciated and exhilarated

Sloane. Unsure who was more nervous when the time came, she took the lead, slow and gentle, not unlike how she bedded virgins before. But Avery's unbridled curiosity sent her over the edge. For hours, Avery touched, tasted, and memorized every inch of her in more than a sexual awakening, a spiritual one.

Trouble had found Sloane, but she couldn't walk away.

"It's a shame." Dylan replaced her drink with a fresh one. "Avery's perfect for you."

Sloane could only nod. Dylan had known her since the day she moved in with her grandmother a block up the street. That first night in town, as the Tap's cook and bartender, he whipped up greasy, yet delicious, burgers and fries for her and Nana along with delivering fascinating conversation. Over the years, Sloane had had no other friend but this kind ex-hippie. She'd brought most of the women she dated into the Tap, and he had made sure Sloane knew that in his opinion Avery outstripped the lot.

Dylan looked over Sloane's shoulder. "Don't look now, but it looks like someone is here to convince you otherwise."

"Shit." Not in the mood for an argument, Sloane downed her sweet liquid courage to steel herself for the storm brewing behind her.

Without a single word, Avery sidled up to the bar and sat on the neighboring stool, a shoulder's width away. Even from that distance, Sloane felt the silent pull. Her heart told her to take Avery into her arms and tell her it was all a mistake, that she loved her too. But her head screamed, "Stick to your guns, or we'll both get hurt."

"My usual, Dylan." Avery shot him a nod.

"Coming right up." While mixing Avery's vodka gimlet, Dylan didn't say a word—a first for him. Once he pushed it across the bar to her, he scurried out of the way like a soldier ducking for cover out of the line of fire.

Avery had yet to look at Sloane. Instead, she sipped on her drink as if she would nurse that thing until closing. Only the unbearable silence between hurt lovers remained.

As she experienced with past girlfriends, Sloane expected if not tears, an angry outburst, but this silent tactic was much worse. She waited, but Avery continued to sip on her drink. The quiet drowned out every other sound in the room.

"I'm sorry." Sloane's meek voice matched her loss of spirit. Doing the right thing never felt so wrong.

"Sorry about what?" Avery took one more sip before placing the glass on the bar. In slow motion, she faced Sloane. Her eyes reflected neither anger nor heartache, but curiosity.

"For hurting you." Sloane averted her eyes.

"You're hurting yourself, but for the life of me, I can't figure out why."

"It's complicated."

"You're just full of clichés." Avery's snicker signaled her frustration. "Next, you'll tell me it's about you, not me. I deserve an explanation."

Avery deserved much more, but what was she supposed to say? "You'll end up dead, so let's call it quits now?" She'd do better with an old, worn-out line, but she couldn't bring herself to that. Her defenses had already weakened.

"Like I said, it's complicated." Sloane swirled her drink, refusing to make eye contact again.

"Bullshit. That is such a cop-out. I have news for you, Manhattan Sloane. I'm not giving up on you." Avery ran a gentle fingertip down Sloane's cheek, sending a chill from her face down to her toes—stronger than anything she'd encountered. The pull had Sloane rolling her head into Avery's palm, a sign her resolve had cracked.

Avery leaned in and pressed their lips together, and to Sloane's surprise, she didn't fight it. Avery drew her closer, the kiss becoming magnetic and drawing Sloane in deeper. With each shift of their lips, Avery's pull grew stronger. Soon she would be at the point of no return.

"I can't." Regret laced Sloane's voice.

"Whatever it is," Avery pressed their foreheads together, "let me help you."

"I want to but—"

"No buts. I'm in this for the long haul. I know you love me. I can feel it." Avery searched Sloane's eyes. "If you can tell me you don't love me, I'll walk out that door and out of your life forever."

Fear paralyzed Sloane. She could neither speak nor run. Maybe fear didn't handcuff her, but the realization she had found a woman she couldn't walk away from did.

"I'm afraid." Sloane's voice was soft, shaky.

"So am I." Avery grasped Sloane's hand and entwined their fingers. "You're the first one I've let in after Reagan's father, and it terrifies me to love you this much."

"You don't understand. I'm not afraid for me, I'm afraid for you."

"I'm sure you've left a trail of broken hearts in your wake, but—"

"That's not it. There's…" Sloane had carried this stupid anxiety for almost twenty years, and the one time she tried to explain it to her grandmother, she'd bungled it. "There's a lot I haven't told you about my parents' accident."

A gentle stroke of Avery's hand down her arm both soothed and encouraged her. Where to begin? She'd never spoken of the horrors for good reason. Though she'd locked away the unbearable parts, her parents' screams still haunted her every night. "I was in the car. I saw them…" Her voice trailed off, unable to speak the entire truth.

Avery rose from the stool and pulled Sloane into an embrace. Her warm arms shielded Sloane like a blanket from the cold, dark secret that had chilled her all these years. Sloane knew at that moment her days of walking away were over.

* * *

Sweaty palms. Soft velvet.

Sloane groped the small red box in her coat pocket, focusing on the objective for the evening. She couldn't recall a day when her nerves had her more on edge, not her first day wearing the badge, not her and Avery's first date. Reliving the sweet memory of their first kiss as they walked to the Tap, she barely noticed when they entered their favorite tavern.

"Sloane?" Avery tugged on her hand.

"Huh?"

"Our table, it's free."

"Oh, sure, let's sit."

You're the best, D. Sloane had it all worked out, right down to Dylan making sure their favorite table remained unoccupied when they walked in. She continued to fumble with the velvet box in her pocket, reciting in her head the words she'd prepared for tonight. Once seated, she signaled Dylan, his cue to send over their usual drinks.

"You seem distracted." Avery nudged her on the shoulder.

"Just thinking about our first kiss." Sloane focused her full attention on Avery as she slung an arm, sweaty palm and all, across the back of Avery's chair. "It was right here at this table."

When their breaths mixed, Avery stared at Sloane's lips and magnified her seductive timbre. "As I recall, I had to take the lead."

Sloane's tongue ached for the familiar taste of Avery's mouth. It could wash away the frustrations of the day and stir the pangs of desire with ease. She brushed her mouth against her lips. "You told me on our first date—"

"That wasn't a date."

"It was for me." Everything about that slushy-tinged evening had screamed first date to Sloane. "You told me you'd never kissed a woman, so I waited for you to make the first move. But I gotta tell you, those were the two most agonizing weeks of my life."

"Really?" Avery raised a single eyebrow. "What about the two weeks we waited to make love after we kissed?" She added a wink.

Their drinks arrived, and Sloane rubbed her chin. "You're right, second worst."

Their heart-pounding make-out sessions those first few weeks had frustrated her beyond anything she'd experienced. She ran mile after mile and took one cold shower after another to quell the arousal each encounter awakened. Neither of which worked. And when they finally made love, the reality far surpassed the fantasies.

Avery kissed her like she did at the bar the night Sloane had walked out on her. That night marked the moment Sloane began her slow crawl out of the dark, lonely hole she'd been in since the accident and the day her nightmares about it and death subsided. Tonight, with the love of a good woman, she tucked away her fears.

In one swig, she downed the last bit of courage she needed. When she cupped Avery's hand with both of hers, all the jitters disappeared.

She cleared her throat. "Avery, these past nine months have been incredible beyond words. Before I met you, I was just going through the motions. The only things important in my life were my job and my Nana. Then you came along. Every time we kiss, you fill a small hole in my heart. Every time we make love, I feel a part of me I thought was long dead come to life. When Nana died last month, I thought I would slide back into that black hole, but I didn't—because of you."

Sloane paused when Avery placed a second hand on hers and squeezed.

"You held my head above water until I could swim on my own, and for that, I am forever grateful. That's when I knew how much I loved you. You and Reagan have become the reason I wake up every day, and I can't imagine a life without the two of you in it."

She pulled the small dark red velvet box from her pocket and bent down on one knee. Opening the lid, she exposed her mother's vintage engagement ring, a single diamond flanked by two white gold infinity symbols. *You'd love her, Mommy.*

Avery threw a hand over her mouth and gasped.

"Avery Santos, would you do me the honor of becoming my wife?" Sloane had her nodding before she finished her question.

Moisture pooled in Avery's hazel eyes. "Yes, I'll marry you."

Sloane's face beamed, streaked by tears. Her world shifted with those words. Fear no longer had a hold on her. Nine months with Avery had erased almost nineteen years of believing she was meant to be alone. After sliding the ring on Avery's finger, she pulled her into a long, passionate kiss.

Sloane broke the kiss and turned toward Dylan behind the bar. He hit his busboy in the ribs with an elbow. When she scanned the rest of the pub, she found every gaze there had landed on them. "She said, yes!" The room erupted into cheers and applause. "Drinks are on me!"

* * *

"I feel like I'm letting you down." Eric sipped on his beer before returning it to the top of Sloane's favorite table. "You should've let me throw you a bachelorette party."

"I would've sprung for the stripper." Dylan raised his own beer, prompting Eric to raise his again. They clinked glasses.

"I don't want a party, and I especially don't want a stripper." Sloane patted Dylan's shoulder and threw Eric a lopsided grin. "Besides, who would I invite? You and Eric are my only friends, but he doesn't count because I have to work with him. I'm happy spending my last night as a single woman here at the Tap with the two of you."

"I thought Avery was stopping by?" Dylan leaned back and rubbed his prominent belly through his black Journey T-shirt.

"She should be over soon. Reagan needed help putting the finishing touches on her new room at the townhouse before we go on our honeymoon." Sloane inspected her empty scotch glass. "I'm ready for another one. How about you guys?"

Dylan offered to get it, but Sloane waved him off. "I gotta hit the ladies' room. I'll get them. Besides, they're all going on Eric's tab."

When she returned to the main dining area, she bellied up to the end of the bar. The bartender approached moments later with a not-so-innocent smile on her face. "What can I get the hottest cop in the city?"

"Chivas…on Eric's tab." She gave Michelle a cautious smile. After Sloane cut her loose last year, Michelle ignored her—until the day Avery walked into the Tap on her arm. After that, her flirting became relentless and had had Avery facing off with her more than once.

"Top shelf? Must be a special occasion." Michelle positioned herself so Sloane had a decent view of her cleavage.

"It is. I'm getting married tomorrow." Sloane added a serious hint to her voice to avoid a repeat of the last few months.

"Married, huh? That's some lucky lady." Michelle's shoulders slumped. "Let's get you that scotch."

Michelle moved Dylan's old stepstool in front of the scotch section of the top-shelf bottles before turning to Sloane. "Mind spotting me on this old thing? I don't trust it."

Sloane scanned the room for someone else to lend a hand, but the four or five beers Dylan had downed had him in no shape to help. "Why don't I get it for you?"

Michelle wagged a finger. "Uh-uh, Uncle Dylan's rules. Customers never touch the liquor."

"Sure, hold on." Sloane shrugged.

Michelle moved up the few steps with Sloane right in front to steady the stool. Taking her time, she bent enough to give Sloane a good view of her bottom. When she descended, she tipped a little to the right. Accidental or not, Sloane couldn't let Michelle fall.

"Whoa, there." Sloane grabbed Michelle by the hips. "You could've hurt yourself."

Chivas bottle in hand, Michelle wrapped her arms around Sloane's shoulders and then her neck. Before Sloane could object, she laid a hot, steamy kiss on her lips.

Sloane hesitated. Was it reflex? Some echo of her player days? Whatever the reason, that wasn't her anymore. She tried to pull away, but Michelle held on tight. She pried Michelle's hands from her neck and stepped back.

"Michelle, I'm flattered, but I'm getting married. Just pour me that drink."

When Sloane turned around, she saw Avery, frozen a few steps away. She expected her fiery eyes, but Avery's were etched with disappointment. She turned and marched out of the Tap at a fast pace.

"Avery!" *No, no, no, no, no!* She chased after her, leaving Michelle, Eric, and Dylan in the dust. Once out the door, she turned toward her townhouse. With only the faint glow of an outdated streetlight to illuminate her path, she squinted and spotted Avery trotting away. "Wait, Avery, wait!"

This can't be happening, not now. In less than twenty-four hours, she hoped to marry the one perfect thing in her life. Her swirling head told her she had to fix this before it spun out of control. When Avery picked up speed, she did the same but faster. She closed the distance between them and caught Avery at the doorstep of the townhouse.

Avery fumbled through her right hip pocket. The house key Sloane gave her snagged on the fabric of her jeans. "Damn it."

Winded, Sloane positioned herself between Avery and the door. "Please, talk to me."

When Avery turned her head away and leaned against the wall, Sloane pressed her palms against the stucco on either side of Avery's head.

"The silent treatment? Okay, just listen." She expected a tongue lashing, but Avery's silence meant she wanted to pull away. "I want you, only you. Michelle was her usual flirty self, which I ignored. What you saw was her throwing herself at me, which I deflected."

"Deflected, my ass." Avery gave her a death stare. "It looked more like a solid catch. If you still want to fuck around with your ex, you're not ready to get married."

A hard, lumpy swallow followed her thought of losing Avery over this. Sloane matched Avery's intense stare. "Are you done?" Cold silence. "First off, she is not my ex."

"Okay, fuck buddy."

"Fair enough, she was my fuck buddy. The optimum word being *was*, meaning in the past. I have no desire to fuck around with her. The only desire I have is to marry you tomorrow and then make love to you until you pass out. But first, I'm spending the next few hours gargling because that kiss she planted on me tasted nasty."

Avery grinned, a sign Sloane had cracked her icy façade.

"Second, I promise never to touch another woman like that again." Sloane leaned in closer. "I'd like nothing more than to kiss you, but I love you too much. I can't let you get this nasty taste in your mouth."

Avery's smile beamed in the darkness. She pushed Sloane back with a finger. "Gargle for ten minutes. Then we kiss."

CHAPTER THREE

One year later

A plume of heated air wafted down from the ceiling vent, tickling the fine black hairs on Sloane's outstretched arm atop the comforter. It nudged her out of peaceful sleep. She opened a single eye to gauge the time. The room was still dark; she had at least a few minutes before the morning alarm.

Dressed in only a cotton tank and boy shorts, Sloane scooted toward the center of the bed, landing her breasts and knees against the warm body sleeping next to her. Tunneling her hand beneath the covers, she swept the skin under her wife's tank top until she found her target. Every part of her drew Sloane in, but touching Avery's breasts stirred both of them. Inching closer, she massaged the supple flesh and laid soft feathery kisses along her wife's neck. She received the response she'd hoped for—a faint, drawn-out moan.

"Happy anniversary, Avery." The softness of her whisper matched that of the blanket covering them.

Avery craned her neck and flipped her ruffled hair to the side. In a soft, hushed timbre, words tumbled from her lips.

"Happy anniversary, Sloane." She rolled over and entangled their legs, pressing their bodies together. "I love you."

Sloane ran a hand up Avery's leg, over her bikini briefs, and settled on the taut muscles of her back. In between kisses, she lowered her voice into a husky, staccato rhythm. "I…love… you."

Every memorized flaw and blemish of Avery's toned bronze body combined to make her perfect. When she was angry, Avery's hazel eyes turned to fire and her tongue sliced her to pieces. A small price to pay. Because when they were making love, those eyes had a hunger in them that made her feel ever so sexy and that tongue had a precision that rocketed her into ecstasy.

She ran her tongue along Avery's full, round lips and teased them until they invited her in. The taste of morning ignited a spark. The heat grew, forcing her inner walls to contract. Avery had every part of her revved up and ready to take and be taken.

Their bodies rolled and rocked, and their hands began a slow, familiar exploration. Each pushed fabric out of the way and created new areas of exposed skin. Both tongues continued to dance as the first predawn light broke through the window.

After slipping a hand under the waistband of Avery's shorts, she caressed the light hairs underneath. Her voice dripped with hunger. "Baby, spread your legs."

Beep, beep, beep, beep… The alarm shrieked at them from across the room.

She buried her face in the crook of Avery's neck. "I hate that damn thing."

Avery pecked Sloane on the lips and guided her hand back out. "Sorry, babe. You know I'm a sound sleeper." She jumped out of bed, but not before tossing Sloane a suggestive wink. "I'll see *you* in the shower."

After throwing the covers to the floor, Sloane raced to the bathroom, Avery's teardrop-shaped bottom teasing her every step of the way.

The smoky voice of Rihanna and the sharp thudding of knives bouncing off a chopping board floated through the bright kitchen. Sloane wielded the chef's knife like Rachel Ray and chopped bell pepper, onion, and tomato into perfect cubes. Her grandmother had passed along this skill and insisted on sharing the first meal of the day, a tradition Sloane missed since she died. After Avery and her daughter moved in, Sloane resumed the custom, and breakfast became family time in the Sloane-Santos household. No "grab and go" toaster pastry would do.

She and Avery worked side by side in their small, updated kitchen. And like most days as newlyweds, they ran late. While Sloane chopped, Avery prepped the egg mixture for their quick go-to morning meal. When either reached for this or that, fingers brushed against the other's arm or a thigh slid against the other's backside while swaying to Rihanna's "Love on the Brain" in a perfected seductive dance.

Reagan entered the room with her backpack in tow. At sixteen, she mirrored her mother in almost every way: athletic, hazel eyes, and dusky skin. If she kept her dark blond hair a half-foot longer, Sloane would swear they were sisters.

Reagan chuckled when she scanned the kitchen counter. "Migas again? Good to see the honeymoon phase isn't over yet."

Avery's cheeks turned the color of the tomatoes Sloane had been chopping before she grabbed the dish towel from her shoulder and tapped it against Reagan's butt. "That, young lady, is none of your business."

"It is when I can hear you from my bedroom." Reagan rolled her eyes.

Avery's blush turned redder, which she followed by giving Sloane a glancing hip check when she maneuvered toward the refrigerator.

Amused at their playful banter, Sloane snickered and swatted Avery on her bottom too. Before she came along, it had been just mother and daughter; Reagan was two years old when she lost her father. Since then, not one man Avery dated had had the qualifications to pass the daughter test. Neither did Sloane at the start. But she stuck it out, and now Reagan included her in the fray.

To eat their migas and fruit, the three took their traditional seats at the sleek dining table for four near a wall of windows overlooking the back deck. Not a single cell phone or newspaper distracted them from the panoramic view of the morning fog receding to reveal the dark, choppy waters of San Francisco Bay. Their conversation touched on school, volleyball practice, boys, work, and the anniversary party occurring later that night.

"The Tenneys are driving in from Reno for the party tonight, right?" Sloane clicked off in her head all the moving parts of the day before their big night. Getting Avery's former in-laws settled in was the last item.

"Yeah. They'll crash in our guest room and head back Sunday," Avery nodded.

With a naughty expression, Sloane whispered into Avery's ear so only she could hear, "Someone will have to be extra quiet tonight."

Avery pointed to herself and then to Sloane while mouthing, "Me? You."

A broad satisfied grin encircled Sloane's lips. Earlier, the tiled shower had formed a perfect echo chamber, proving Reagan's point—the honeymoon phase had yet to end.

"Do you think Grandpa will bring his Mustang? I wanna practice driving a stick on the hills." Reagan pushed the remnants of her food around her plate, acting as if her question were nothing.

"Oh, honey, driving on the flats in his 'Stang is one thing. Taking his baby out in the hills is another." Avery laughed as if Reagan had asked to borrow the crown jewels for a night on the town. "I don't think his blood pressure can take another one of your clutch-grinding sessions."

Sloane checked her watch. Just enough time to get to work. She gulped down the rest of her coffee and grabbed her suit jacket from the back of her chair. "We gotta go."

After adjusting her shoulder holster and badge, she secured her Sig Sauer service sidearm. "You got cleanup today, young lady," she reminded Reagan.

Avery popped one last strawberry in her mouth, placed her dishes in the sink, and filled her to-go coffee mug at the countertop machine. "Reagan, remember you're expected to make more than an appearance at our party tonight. Your grandparents want to spend time with you, not just serve as your driving instructor."

Reagan rolled her eyes again. "But Deni and Shellie invited me over for…uh…a pizza sleepover. Do I have to stay for the entire party?"

"Honey, I told you—" Avery started.

Sloane nudged Avery and whispered into her ear, "Let her go. The last thing a teenager wants to do on a Friday night is spend it with a bunch of old farts."

Avery rolled her eyes, an adorable quirk she and Reagan shared. When Avery pulled out her pouty lips, Sloane had won the argument before it even started.

"One hour, young lady." Avery wagged a finger at Reagan. "You give your grandparents one hour. Then you can go."

"Thank you." Reagan kissed her mother on the cheek and then mouthed "thank you" to Sloane.

Sloane tossed Reagan a wink and pulled Avery along by her coat sleeve. On their way out the front door, she yelled, "Have a good day at school. See you at the Tap."

* * *

Sloane rolled up to the parking garage at 850 Bryant. The security arm rose, one of the few things that worked as advertised in the sixty-year-old dilapidated building. After weaving her SUV through the multilevel underground garage, she passed through a secondary security barrier into an area designated for SFPD only.

After backing into a slot, she kissed Avery on the lips. When she tried to pull away, Avery used her tongue to rim the circumference of her lips. Sloane rewound the memory of their morning shower and how Avery used that tongue. She was soaked with arousal. *Every time, every single time.*

Their ragged breaths mixed. Windows fogged. *I could make love to you right here.* Sloane pulled back and fought the urge to put the car in drive, return home, and do just that. "Don't get me started or I'll be late for my meeting with the DEA."

"A little something to tide both of us over until after our anniversary party tonight." Avery's smile hinted at much more to come.

Sloane blew out a long breath to tame the tiger roaring inside her. She slammed her head back against the headrest, unsure how she would concentrate on work. *Damn.*

"Babe?"

"Yeah?" Sloane turned toward her.

"You and Reagan… I'm glad you two are finally close."

"I love her like she's my own."

"That's just it. I want Reagan to be yours. What would you think about adopting her?"

Sloane stretched her smile to the corners of her eyes, her teeth lighting up the dark interior of the car. Avery made parenting look so easy, but Sloane had quickly learned that came with years of experience. Before she fell in love, being a parent never crossed Sloane's mind, but after a year of living with Reagan, she embraced the responsibility. A long road awaited, but she welcomed the challenge. "I'd love to."

Avery threw her arms over Sloane's shoulders and pulled her into a hug. "You've made me so happy."

Minutes later, hand in hand, they exited the elevator on the sixth floor. Their offices were only yards apart, but their work rarely had them in each other's company. Avery turned left toward the Crime Scene Investigations Unit, and Sloane turned right. When their footsteps forced them to let go, their fingertips grazed until the last possible moment. They'd have to wait until the end of their shifts to touch again.

Sloane passed through the glass doors guarding the Investigations Bureau. The open floor design sectioned off by groups of 1960s industrial-style metal desks gave the area a sense of outdated, semi-organized chaos. The Narcotics Unit was housed in the far corner, a blessing and a curse. Because it was nearest to the windows, the space offered the best views of the city. It also had the disadvantage of being underneath the seventh-floor men's bathroom, notorious for its leaky pipes. Overall, 850 Bryant had the distinction of being the city's worst shithole.

As Sloane approached her desk, her gaze fell to a bucket on the floor, sitting dangerously close to her chair. She hoped that what had just hit the prepositioned pail was a drop of plain water and not something worse. Her eyes tracked the water to its source in the ceiling and to a rust-stained panel that was threatening to release another drop.

She leaned over and gave the container a tentative sniff. "Shower or john?"

"Shower." Eric recrossed his ankles atop his desk, his nose buried in a case file.

"Phew." It had taken days to get the stench out after last month's not-so-rosy leak. "Looks like it's gonna be a good day."

Their lieutenant opened her office door. "Decker. Sloane. My office."

"Or maybe not." Sloane would rather go through a root canal than sit through the next meeting. The last time the DEA visited their building, they said, "We're here to help" and then promptly stole one of her and Eric's hard-worked cases.

"I hope that douchebag Prickhead isn't here."

"Prichard. His name is Prichard." Eric kicked his feet from his desk. "But you're right. He is a douchebag."

She shrugged and followed him into their boss's office. Lieutenant Morgan West maneuvered around her metal desk, revealing her button-down white blouse and black suit. The black helped hide her middle-age pooch. She wore several tailored outfits, but this one Sloane liked best against her wavy, collar-length graying blond hair.

"Decker. Sloane. You remember Special Agent in Charge Nate Prichard?" Lieutenant West gestured toward Nate.

Damn, Prickhead again.

Prichard, a paunchy bureaucratic fifty-something whose pasty skin matched the white shirts he always wore, had brought a lackey with him this time. Standing near the narrow, sun-filled window, a second agent, wearing a dark designer suit, took in the limited view of the bay, her back to the room. Her shoulder-length dark blond hair and slim shape appealed to Sloane.

"Of course." Eric shook Prichard's hand.

Sloane peeled her gaze from the woman to shake Nate's hand.

"Let's get started." Prichard turned toward the window. "Harper, you ready?"

"Yes, sir." The woman, Harper, kept her gaze focused out the window for a moment longer.

Sloane froze at the familiarity of that voice. The woman turned. Her hazel eyes and light skin were unmistakable. Sloane's breath hitched, her heart pumping like that of a thirteen-year-old again. The name rolled off her lips as if she'd seen a ghost. "Finn."

"I'd like you to meet Assistant Special Agent in Charge Finley Harper. I recently brought her over from the Oakland office." Prichard extended his hand toward Agent Harper.

In a confident stride, Finn took the few steps toward the small conference table buttressed against the front of West's desk and closed in on Sloane. She'd grown a good foot since they last saw each other, ending up only a few inches shorter than Sloane. She smiled when she extended her hand. "It's good to see you again, Sloane."

It is you. Sloane had dreamed about those eyes for years. Soft green tones encircled a pale rust-brown inner ring only visible in the bright light. Those kind eyes hadn't changed since she last peered into them.

The cute tomboy had ripened into a polished, feminine woman, not that different from Avery. Her high cheekbones had lost the roundness of youth, and her lips had filled in with the plumpness of maturity. The tailored suit coat signaled her breasts had as well.

When Sloane slid her hand into Finn's, a warmth spread up her arm and settled in her cheeks. Her blush turned into a tender smile to match Finn's. "It's good to see you again, Finn." A poke in the ribs from Eric's elbow. "Yes…well…shall we start?"

After taking their seats, she caught Finn sneaking a glimpse at her. *She feels it too.*

Finn pulled a small, clear plastic evidence bag from her folio and passed it to Sloane and Eric. The writing on the front showed agents had seized its contents two days ago in Oakland.

Concentrate. Back to business. After chastising herself, Sloane turned the bag over to the see-through side and inspected the contents, holding it up to get a better look with the light. "What is it?"

Finn's smile disappeared when she shifted to professional mode. "It's called Kiss, a new form of Ecstasy. Very potent, very cheap, and very much in demand in Alameda and Contra Costa counties."

The half-dozen small, bright pink chalky pills resembled a heart-shaped Valentine's Day candy with an imprinted pair of a woman's red lips on one side. The dangers this new drug posed to high schools alarmed Sloane.

"Are they saturating the market just above cost?" She had seen this before. Gangs often flooded a community with a new drug by offering it pennies above manufacturing cost to create a demand for it.

Finn accorded her a nod of respect. "You know your stuff."

"I had a good teacher." She glanced at Eric and gave him a wink.

"So, what brings you to our side of the bay?" Eric had that skeptical look on his face that he always got when he suspected a setup.

"The chemical makeup of these pills match ones we found in San Diego, Los Angeles, and Vegas. It seems—"

"Cartel."

When Finn's lips curled upward into a small, almost seductive smile at her remark, Sloane realized she'd done two things. She had been right and she had impressed Finn. *Is Finn flirting?*

"Correct." Finn's expression turned serious. "We suspect this involves the cartel or a similar organization. While the pills found in the other locations aren't exact duplicates in terms of appearance, they are an exact chemical match."

Sloane darted her eyes back and forth and settled on a widespread, well-funded operation as the only explanation. "So, you think the cartel has set up distribution in these locations?"

Finn leaned forward. "Yes. That would explain the chemical consistency, but not the slight differences across multiple states. That remains a mystery."

"And you think they've set up distribution in our city." Eric matched Sloane's curiosity.

Finn shifted her gaze from Sloane to Eric. She pointed at the evidence bag on the table. "The teenager who had this said he bought it at a club in the Mission District."

Sloane glanced at Eric with eagerness. The Mission District was her old beat, and she knew the business owners and prominent residents like they were neighbors. After six years on patrol, she'd built a roster of snitches there so large it rivaled that of any seasoned detective.

She turned to her boss. "I want in."

Prichard cleared his throat, signaling his intent to take charge. "You misunderstand, Sergeant Sloane. We're not asking for your help. This is a DEA case that overlaps multiple jurisdictions. We just want you to be aware of this new drug, and if you come across it, call us, and we'll do the rest."

And there it is. Prickhead. Sloane shot daggers at him. "You expect us to—" She stopped when Eric covered her hand with his own.

"You got it." Eric nodded. "Can you send us some pics of the other versions of Kiss you've come across? We need to know what we're looking for."

Sly. She and Eric had been through this before with the DEA. Eric taught her during their first encounter to give the impression of cooperation, even if they had no intention of following through with it. She had no intention of handing over another case to the fucking DEA.

Prichard stood and buttoned his suit jacket. "Harper, make sure they get whatever they need."

"Of course, sir." A slight grin built on Finn's lips.

Still bothered by Prichard's brush off, Sloane exited first and made a straight line for her desk. Not halfway there, something grazed her arm. She turned.

"My God. Manny Sloane." Finn had a wistful smile on her face. "It's been what? Twenty years?"

That silver-toned voice and a sense of nostalgia made Sloane forget Prichard had pissed her off. Then when Finn gave her what lasted too long to be a friendly hug, she melted into her thirteen-year-old arms. *Is she gay?*

Although Sloane broke the embrace, Finn kept her hands on Sloane's arms. "I always wondered what happened to you, Sloane. I wouldn't have guessed you'd become a cop." Her smile faded. "I'm so sorry about the accident and your parents. It must have been unbearable."

"It was." Those two simple words didn't describe the horror she'd witnessed. She couldn't...wouldn't find the words.

Prichard emerged from Lieutenant West's office. "Harper, we need to go."

Finn raised a hand toward him, gesturing "one minute" before turning to Sloane. "Let me text you those pictures."

Before Sloane could suggest otherwise, Finn grabbed the iPhone out of her hand and typed. Finn handed back her phone before silencing her ringing phone in her back pocket. "Now, I can send you those pictures, and we can catch up," she added a faint wink.

Sloane's lips turned upright, and her cheeks felt warm again. *Definitely gay and definitely flirting.*

On his way to his desk, Eric passed by Sloane and Finn and coughed loud enough to wake a sleeping bear. Not at all subtle. Sloane adjusted her shirt collar, damp from nervous perspiration. "I gotta," she pointed at her desk, "get back to work."

The disappointment in Finn's eyes mirrored her own hope for more time to make up for twenty lost years. If asked to describe what she was feeling at that moment, Sloane wouldn't know where to begin. She'd never experienced it before. As far as she could tell, it was a mix of nostalgia, infatuation, sadness, teenage giddiness—and fear.

"I'll send you those pictures within the hour." Finn glanced down at the tops of her black pumps and back at Sloane. "It was nice seeing you again. Let's catch up soon." She gave Sloane one more hug, turned on her heel, and caught up with her boss at the elevator.

When Sloane returned to her desk, Eric spun around in his chair. "What the hell was that?"

Get a grip. Focus on Avery. Guilt clawed at Sloane and forced out a long breath. Today of all days! She shouldn't compare her wife to her first crush. After removing her suit jacket, she threw it over the back of her chair. "I knew her in junior high school. Nothing to worry about."

"Didn't seem like nothing. You forget I was with you the day you met Avery. I saw the way you looked at her. It was the same way you looked at Harper just now."

"I was *not* looking at her like that." She sat down, resenting the truth in Eric's accusation.

Eric scooted a little closer. "Don't screw this up, Sloane. Avery is the best thing that happened to you, besides drawing me as a partner." He grinned, but for only a second. "I didn't serve as your best man to watch you throw it all away a year later."

After all these years, Finn had rattled Sloane. She admitted to herself the hug had lasted too long, but there was something more. She tried to convince herself this meant nothing, that she and Avery would be fine, but her gut told her nothing would be the same again.

"I won't screw this up. I took a stroll down memory lane, that's all."

A chime from her iPhone alerted her to a new text message. After checking the incoming pictures from Finn, she texted back, *Thanks, Finn.*

The memory of the last time they were together as kids rushed into her head, frothing the migas she had for breakfast. Before she spewed them and the mounting guilt she was feeling in the bucket aligned under the leaky pipe, she pointed toward the squad room doors. "I gotta hit the restroom."

She walked to the empty bathroom down the hallway at a swift pace. With both palms, she leaned against the sink counter. Not two hours earlier, the woman in the mirror had tucked away her painful past and prepared breakfast with her wife as if making love. She splashed water on her face to wash away the guilt and the memories of the little girl who suffered through something so awful she'd never told another soul. Not even her wife.

CHAPTER FOUR

After six weeks, stacks of moving boxes still lined two of the four walls in Finn's bedroom-size den, taunting her about the impermanence of her new living arrangements. Since she'd moved into her partially furnished Market Street condo, anything that didn't find a home in other rooms somehow migrated into this one. She only braved the growing mess as a last resort, such as tonight's mission to locate a spare charging cable for her cell phone.

After a frustrating search through the many boxes still unpacked, Finn finally found the charger. "There you are."

Tussling with three or four cords, she untangled the one she needed. She began restacking the boxes, this time putting consideration into their order.

The doorbell rang, interrupting her futile attempt to organize the chaos. A growl in her stomach reminded her of the food delivery service she'd called earlier, so she left the boxes for later and answered the door.

"You haven't called in days." The tall, sexy brunette at the door was dressed in an expensive skirt and business jacket and had a designer Saffiano leather tote slung over her shoulder. Her elbows were set wide against her body, fists planted on both hips.

"It's called space, Kadin." Finn kept a hand on the doorknob and debated whether to invite her in. When she carried out the last of her things from their shared Oakland apartment the previous month, they exchanged harsh words, with Finn receiving the bulk of them.

Kadin's eyes softened when she reached into her tote and pulled out an old coffee mug. "You forgot this in the dishwasher."

The cartoon picture of a frog and the words "Homework makes you ugly" brought a smile to Finn's lips. She'd stopped using the faded and chipped cup most days, pulling it out only on special occasions the last few years to preserve its message. Her mother gave it to her the day she moved into the dorm at Stanford, a not-so-subtle reminder for her studious daughter to have fun in college. Following her mother's death from breast cancer in her junior year, the mug became a reminder for Finn to live up to her mother's dreams for her.

"Thank you." When she took the mug into her hands, the bad blood between them faded into the background. "I don't know what I would've done if I lost this."

"I know how important it is to you."

A teenage boy dressed in his delivery company's purple shirt and cap appeared in the corridor behind Kadin. He held up a brown paper sack the size of a toaster oven. "Delivery for Finn."

"That's me." She held up an index finger and turned her attention back to Kadin. "Come in. Let me take care of this."

Finn handed the young man a five-dollar tip after signing for the charge. With food in hand, she closed the door. She found Kadin gazing out the dining room window.

"Have you eaten? I ordered plenty." Finn placed the sack on the table and unpacked its contents.

"Incredible view." A wistful tone suggested Kadin's disappointment in the fact that she didn't share its beauty with Finn on a daily basis.

"It is."

Finn recognized the look on Kadin's face. The orange glow of the Bay Bridge's final span stretching across the dark, choppy waters of San Francisco Bay had captivated her. Finn's condo provided a much more picturesque view than the Lake Merritt apartment she and Kadin had shared for nearly two years. Overlooking the shipyards, it was a space they had settled on while vowing to upgrade once a certain unit became available. That never happened.

Finn joined her and offered her a plastic-wrapped set of knife and fork. "Hungry?"

"Famished." Kadin accepted Finn's white flag, as temporary as it might be, and forced a smile. Finn had seen that smile before. It suggested regret.

After choosing this and that to fill their paper plates, they settled into light conversation, avoiding until now the subject that precipitated the pause in their relationship.

Kadin stabbed her last piece of orange chicken, and with the familiarity that two years of dating and living together brought, asked, "How's work?"

Finn raised her head. Kadin's unintended missile found a soft spot. The work had been a point of contention for years, first with her father and then with Kadin following a dicey raid.

"Busy."

Done with talking, Finn flicked her napkin on the table. She couldn't tell Kadin that once she left 850 Bryant, she had had Manhattan Sloane in her head all day. Nor could she mention that for hours on end, she had relived the exhilaration she had felt on the day she held Sloane's hand twenty years ago. Sloane wore a wedding ring, for God's sake. She had no right to think or feel any of those things.

"You still resent me, don't you?" The hurt look on Kadin's face told Finn moving into this condo hadn't helped their differences move along.

"We've been over this a hundred times." Finn fell back into her chair and released a long, frustrated breath, running both hands through her hair.

She took the San Francisco position, a desk job over the fieldwork she loved, to assuage her girlfriend's fears. At first, she didn't mind. The promotion came with a significant pay raise, but later politics came into play, and she had since regretted her decision.

Kadin's gaze fell to the table. "I'm sorry you hate your job, but I'm not sorry you're safer."

Finn wrapped a hand around Kadin's. "I get that, but I can't plan my life to please you and Daddy."

A deep sigh from Kadin. "I know."

"I love you." Finn gave her hand a gentle squeeze. "I just don't know if I can live with you again."

Moisture filled the lower rims of Kadin's eyes. "I hoped leasing this place would be temporary."

"So did I." Finn brought Kadin's hand to her lips and kissed its back. "Stay tonight."

The kiss they shared gave Finn the answer she'd hoped for.

* * *

At lightning speed, Sloane changed into her casual tomboy outfit of boot-cut jeans and a white T-shirt covered by a pullover light blue sweater. *Ah, just in time for my favorite show.* Stretched across the solid gray cotton comforter, nestled against the bevy of paisley-patterned gray and white throw pillows at the head of the bed, she had the perfect view of her wife.

Clad only in panties and bra, Avery bounced across the wood floor from closet to dresser to bathroom, gathering pieces for her outfit. Every turn and bend fed Sloane's sexual fantasies, forecasting they'd be later than they already were.

"Tell me again why we're going to a party on our first anniversary instead of spending it in bed?" Debating the topic may have been Sloane's ploy, but drawing out Avery's dressing routine was her ultimate goal.

Avery glided to the bed. "Because I was swabbing for blood at a crime scene instead of dancing with you at our wedding reception." She kissed Sloane on the lips. "I want to dance with you tonight."

It took only a single taste of Avery's lips to make her forget about the dozen guests waiting for them at the Tap. Unable to wait until after the party, she grabbed Avery's arm and pulled her onto the bed next to her. Shifting on top, she pushed up the fabric of her wife's bra and took a breast into her mouth.

This is the only body I want... This is the only body I need.

Avery moaned...what Sloane wanted to hear. Avery writhed...what Sloane needed to feel.

Her hands roamed and stoked the embers that had smoldered since that kiss in the parking garage this morning—and since her unexpected encounter with Finn Harper.

Whether out of desperation or uncontrolled lust, she surprised herself with her next move. Rising to her knees on the bed, she leaned her bottom down to her heels. After grabbing the thin waistband of Avery's thong, she ripped it off and discarded it to the floor. Sloane inched Avery's core up, angled the pool of arousal toward her, and drank and quenched her thirst.

Soon they lay side by side with Avery struggling to catch her breath, her body flushed from Sloane taking her over the edge again and again. In between breaths, Avery uttered, "Where... the hell...did that come from?"

Sloane told herself it was to nourish their connection, but she knew better. Sex was her way of coping with the fact she didn't have an answer for Avery, only a burning question. *Why haven't I told you about Finn?* Avery made her constant nightmares disappear. Why wouldn't she tell the woman she loved, the woman who eroded her stupid, idiotic fears, about Finn?

She couldn't voice the growing, gut-wrenching doubt. *Are you enough?* After rolling over, she threw an arm and leg over Avery. Sloane's face nuzzled against the soft skin between her neck and shoulder. "Thank you."

"For what, babe?" Avery ran a hand up and down her back, sending shivers down Sloane's spine.

Sloane moved her head to rest on Avery's breast. "For making me believe I'm not meant to be alone."

* * *

Hand in hand in a half-jog, they giggled every step of the way to the main door of the Tap, where Avery grabbed Sloane by the elbows. "I'm your only dance partner tonight, okay?"

Sloane wrapped an arm around her waist, pressing their bodies together. Her lopsided grin meant her playfulness was front and center. "Marking your territory?"

Avery was. Bryant may have been a big facility, but it was small in terms of gossip, especially when Todd, her second in command, was involved. If she had delivered those damn forms herself to Narcotics today instead of sending the office gossip mill, she would've avoided the subsequent stares and hushed conversations.

"That was no innocent hug, I tell you," Todd had finally fessed up after Avery threatened to spike his coffee mug with bowel prep when he least expected.

"If my wife was having an affair, I'm sure she wouldn't flaunt it in front of a dozen crusty detectives gunning for her."

Marking her territory tonight was a distasteful natural reflex. She didn't doubt Sloane desired her. Their pre-party delay went a long way to prove that. Though, in the back of her mind, she knew fifteen years of one-night stands and short-term relationships hadn't prepared Sloane for marriage. And Todd's blathering made Avery question whether she was enough for Sloane. She tried to not let her mind go there, but she wondered if Sloane still craved the variety.

"Since I missed out on our wedding day, I want every dance with you." Avery pecked her on the lips.

Sloane traced a finger down her cheek. "Only with you."

Once inside, Avery checked the time—an hour late. Not too bad even for them, but it didn't slow down their guests. They'd already dug into the food without them and appeared to have put a healthy dent in their bar budget.

Eric spotted them first and raised the drink in his hand. "You made it."

Other guests joined in a cacophony of greetings. "Heeeey. 'Bout time. Come up for air? Thought you'd miss your own reception again."

She and Sloane made their way around the room and greeted the small crowd of mostly coworkers and friends. Then she gave Sloane a light tug on the arm.

"Caleb and Janet are here." Sliding her hand into Sloane's, she guided them to a corner table.

"There you are!" Caleb flapped his arms in the air, knocking his aviator-framed eyeglasses off the bridge of his nose. He caught them before they passed the final button on his blue plaid shirt. He looked sharp tonight. Janet must have dressed him because the green stripes on the shirt matched his green twill pants.

"Glad you two made it down." Avery hugged Janet and then Caleb.

"Wouldn't have missed it for the world." Janet's rounded cheeks glowed against her bright smile. Combined with her new short graying haircut and sleeveless blue dress, she looked great. "Any excuse to see you three again."

"You may regret it if Caleb takes Reagan out for another driving lesson." Sloane gave Caleb a sympathetic pat on the shoulder.

Caleb laughed and rubbed what little gray hair remained on his head. He turned toward Reagan, who was seated next to him and pursed his lips. "No hills."

Reagan pumped her fist at the prospect of driving the cherry-red Mustang again, even though he'd put hill driving off-limits. The gesture drew laughs from everyone at the table, especially Avery. She never imagined thirteen years following their son's death, the Tenneys would still treat her like a daughter, not a former daughter-in-law they had to endure to spend time with their only grandchild. And since Avery came out, they treated her better than her own parents. "It's a sin," her mother had cried. "You're no daughter of mine," her father had lashed out. But not the Tenneys. Caleb and Janet only asked, "When do we get to meet her?"

Dylan popped by, pointing a curious finger back and forth between Sloane and Avery. "The usual for you two?"

"That'll be great." Sloane offered him an appreciative nod.

Avery enjoyed her vodka gimlet and catching up with Janet, but out of the corner of her eye, she noticed Reagan was typing furiously on her smartphone every few minutes.

Sloane whispered into Avery's ear, "Wanna grant Reagan her parole?"

"I was thinking the same thing." Avery gave her a smiling nod and turned to Reagan. "Honey, I know you love spending time with your grandparents, but you shouldn't keep Deni and Shellie waiting." She turned toward the Tenneys. "They have special plans tonight too."

"Go, have a good time, Reagan." Caleb added a smile. "We'll get in that driving lesson before we head back up the mountain."

"Are you sure?" Reagan was horrible at feigning concern, and if the expressions on the faces at the table were an indication, she had convinced no one she wanted to stay.

"Go have fun." He waved her off.

Reagan picked up her things and kissed her grandparents goodbye.

Avery reminded her, "Text me when you get to Deni's and be home by ten for breakfast tomorrow, all right?"

After Reagan agreed and took off in a cloud of dust, Sloane whispered into Avery's ear, "Nicely played."

Moments later, when one of Avery's favorite songs played, Sloane stood and extended a hand to her. "Dance with me."

After taking her hand, Sloane guided her to a spot near the center of the room and wrapped a strong arm around her. She slung her arms over Sloane's shoulders and pulled their bodies close, settling into a smooth, swaying rhythm. Like so many times before, when she was in her wife's arms, the rest of the world, along with her regrets about her parents, blurred into the background.

Syncing her breaths with Avery's, Sloane pressed their foreheads together and mouthed the words of The Beach Boys' song, "God only knows what I'd be without you."

In the arms of the woman she loved, celebrating their first wedding anniversary after making love with a hunger that should've put her in a coma, Avery still had her doubts. She thought Sloane's only secrets involved her parents' accident, but now two more nagging questions tempered her mood: *Who was that woman today, and why haven't you told me about her?*

Sloane kept her promise. She met all attempts to pry them apart with a polite "no" and danced every song with Avery as her only dance partner. When the evening came to a close, Eric tried one last time and tapped Sloane on her shoulder. "May I cut in?"

After she continued to dance, he cleared his throat and tapped her shoulder again. Avery raised an eyebrow and snickered. "Are you just going to ignore him?"

"Yep." She tightened her arms around Avery. "He had his chance with you a long time ago."

"You're still holding that against me?" Eric put his hands on his hips. "I asked Avery out one time before you even met her, and she shot me down flat."

Avery struggled to keep a straight face when Eric threw his hands up and walked away, laughing. "You know, he only asked me out as a mercy date. He felt sorry for me after the way his old partner tried to man-splain things."

"Peter Rook is a chauvinistic pig. I'm glad he retired." Sloane pulled Avery in tighter.

"Then you came along, and I took it out on you on your first day."

"I was an ass."

"I was crabby, which is why I asked you out for a drink the next day."

A mischievous grin grew on Sloane's face. "Guilt can be a good thing."

Do you feel guilty, Sloane? Is that what brought on tonight's passion?

After the song ended, the opening guitar riff of Journey's "Lights," Tap's traditional closing song, played. Steve Perry's distinctive voice filled the room, along with the off-key voices of dozens of patrons. "When the lights go down in the city…"

Avery crooned without asking Sloane to join in.

"I never sing," Sloane had told her within a month of their first date, and that was all it took. Something in her voice and expression told her to never ask again.

When the song finished, they continued to hold each other until Dylan tapped Sloane on the shoulder. "Last call, ladies."

They stepped apart and discovered that all but Caleb and Janet had left. "Janet looks great tonight." Sloane pitched her chin toward the Tenneys.

"She's down thirty pounds since they visited in the spring." Avery scanned Janet's much thinner body from across the dance floor. "I haven't seen her wear that dress in years. I think she's teasing Caleb."

Sloane laughed, pulling Avery along. "We better rescue them."

"Ready to go back to our place?" Avery focused on Janet's tired face, her chin propped up by an upturned palm and bent elbow resting on the table.

"Hours ago." Caleb helped his weary wife out of her chair.

"I'm sorry," Avery slipped her arm in the crook of Janet's. "You should've said something."

"Nonsense." Janet tried but failed to hold back a yawn. "It's a joy seeing you so happy and in love. I just wish your own parents could see how happy Sloane makes you."

"You know how they are. Homosexuality is a sin. They still refuse to have anything to do with me unless it involves something they want." Avery's voice cracked when she wiped a stray tear.

She'd made her choice—Sloane over her parents. Most days, she put up a good front and pretended their lost affection didn't matter. But when her birthday and Christmas came and went without them, it hurt more than Avery expected. Her only solace was Sloane, holding her until she fell asleep, reassuring her she'd made the right choice.

Sloane rubbed Avery's back and whispered, "Let's go home, baby."

CHAPTER FIVE

"*Save yourself, Sloane.*" *Shards of glass protruded from her mother's hand; blood oozed down her arm.*

The flames grew. "I can't, Mommy, I can't." She pulled on the mangled pieces. "I can't leave you."

The flames grew more substantial, and heat and smoke filled the cramped space.

"Hurry, Sloane. Hurry," her mother pleaded and pushed her back. "Run, Sloane. Run!"

A bright flash…darkness…silence.

Sloane woke with a jolt, drenched in sweat, and her heart pounding so hard her chest ached. *What the hell?* It had been nearly two years since she had a nightmare about the accident. Not since falling in love with Avery had her past haunted her, and now that it had, she didn't know what to make of it.

A quick glance to the right confirmed her wife, inches away, hadn't awoken. She licked her lips, but her parched mouth failed to wet them. As softly as she could, she slung her legs over the side of the bed. In the dark, she tapped her fingertips along the top of her nightstand until she located her iPhone. Nightmares or not, as a detective, she remained on call twenty-four-seven, and that meant wherever she went, so did her phone.

After wiping her damp brow with the back of her hand, Sloane padded down the dark hallway. When she reached the living room, two small dots of lights, one red and one blue, along the wall on her left, came into focus. The flat-screen television and satellite box standby lights signaled her to make a quick turn to her right toward the dining room window. When she did, the hundreds of distant amber and white lights dotting the Oakland Hills came into view.

Once in the kitchen, she filled a glass with tap water. The digital clock on the microwave to her right above the stove read two o'clock. She hadn't been asleep long. The vivid nightmare had her wide awake now, so she settled into a chair at the dining table, mesmerized by the lights twinkling across the bay.

The nightmare still troubled her. Convinced Finn's sudden reappearance had triggered it, she struggled to figure out why this particular nightmare had reappeared. When she was a young girl, this variation of the accident had popped up several times—but only when fear gripped her.

"What am I afraid of?" Sloane asked herself.

She searched the cityscape's twinkling man-made Milky Way for an answer. Her thoughts bounced between Avery and Finn. Only yesterday, she celebrated their anniversary, yet she had spent half the day thinking of Finn. That bothered her.

Sloane clenched her jaw to tamp down the regret bubbling in her throat. How would've things turned out if her childhood fears hadn't sucked her in? Questions fired in her head like a machine gun. Would she have found Finn and dated? Made love to her? Gone to college with her? Gotten married? Had children? Would she have become a cop and Finn a DEA agent?

Sloane couldn't change the past, but she could control what she did today. She shook her head to throw aside all thoughts and regrets about Finn. "I won't fail you, Avery."

After a deep yawn, she glanced at the oven clock again. Twenty minutes had passed, and the need for sleep had returned.

She downed the rest of the water and returned her cup to the sink.

Reagan's ringtone pierced the silence. Even before thumbing the iPhone screen, she sensed trouble.

"Reagan? What's wrong?"

"Sloane," Reagan's voice cracked between sobs. "Something happened, and Deni and Shellie are sick… It's really bad."

"Where are the Scotts? Did they take the girls to the emergency room?"

"Umm…They're in Vegas. It's a long story. An ambulance picked up Deni and Shellie. I'm at the Firepit, and the police are here. Can you pick me up and take me to the hospital?"

Sloane bit inside her cheek, resisting the urge to ride her for sneaking off to a nightclub. "What happened?"

"I don't know, but I think they took X."

Her temples throbbed at the word X. She and Avery had drilled into Reagan's head the dangers of drugs. She knew better. Sure, Reagan had gotten into the occasional mischief, but this had overdose written all over it, and in her experience, that seldom ended well.

"I'm waking your mom."

"Wait, please don't. Can you just come?" Reagan's begging tone had no effect.

"No, Reagan, I can't. Your mom needs to know. I have one question."

"What?" Reagan's meek voice trailed off.

"Did you take any drugs?" Sloane closed her eyes to listen to her tone, hoping she'd say the right words.

"No, I didn't. I swear. I was too afraid."

Sloane had encountered hundreds of people on drugs, and Reagan's voice and intonations had none of the earmarks. Still not the time for a lecture. "Okay. We'll be there soon."

Seconds later, she turned on the light at Avery's bedside and placed a hand on her wife's shoulder. "Baby." Avery didn't wake. This time she shook her shoulder. "Baby, wake up. You need to wake up."

"What?" Avery's eyes opened slowly and her voice was groggy.

"Reagan is safe, but there's been trouble, and we need to get her."

Avery popped straight up and rushed her words. "What happened?"

"I'll tell you on the way." Sloane hurried her wife out of bed.

While Avery dressed, Sloane woke up the Tenneys. She kept the details vague and explained they might not be home by breakfast.

As Sloane drove toward the Firepit in the Mission District, she and Avery exchanged not a single word, too tense to speak. She slid a hand off the steering wheel finally and cupped the hand Avery had been tapping against the center console. "We'll get through this."

"I hope so." Avery tightened their fingers, easing their shared worry.

Sloane pulled in front of the Firepit next to two patrol cars, which were angled against the sidewalk with their overheads flashing, a sign the scene was still fresh. She displayed her badge to the patrol officer guarding the main entrance, and he directed her to the main floor.

Sloane had never liked this club. Besides attracting an array of drugs, its fire-themed décor made her uncomfortable. Projected images of flames dancing on shimmering wall curtains combined with colored uplighting and downlighting washed the room in an assortment of gold, red, and orange. The resulting illusion—fire engulfing the club.

The expected earsplitting, brain-numbing music had stopped, and most of the patrons had filed out. A dozen staff members in their club uniforms huddled at three tables, and two police officers remained questioning witnesses near the bar, including Reagan.

"Mom." Reagan ran up and wrapped her arms around Avery.

"Honey, what happened?" Avery curled her arms around Reagan.

Sloane pulled the uniformed officer aside. "Hey, Perry, I don't want to step on your toes, but that's my stepdaughter. What do we have here?"

"Looks like multiple overdoses, one male adult and two female juveniles." Perry showed Sloane an evidence bag. "The male vic had this on him."

Sloane inspected the contents, a single small pink pill in the shape of a heart with a pair of women's lips imprinted on it. "Damn it," she mumbled. "Is she involved?"

Perry shook his head. "Dispatch reported she's the one who called 911. Your daughter said she was the designated driver and consented to a search. She's clean. I've finished her statement so I can release her into your custody."

"Thanks, Perry. I'll take it from here."

Sloane redirected her attention to Avery and Reagan. Their conversation appeared contentious and one-sided. However, Reagan took her mother's tongue-lashing well, nodding in agreement to whatever Avery said.

Once Avery finished doing her mother thing, Sloane joined them. Reagan's slumped posture, dipped chin, and crossed arms told Sloane Avery had laid into her enough. "Let's go to the hospital."

Sloane ignored the standard zombie-like emergency room Friday night crowd, bypassed the check-in queue, and approached the head nurse's station. She flashed her badge. "Three ODs rolled in."

The nurse checked her computer terminal. The grimace on her face meant things had turned bad. "They're still working on one patient, but you can see Nurse Raj at station two."

Sloane turned back to Reagan's pale face and placed both hands on her shoulders. "Stay here with your mom. I'll be back as soon as I can."

Sloane weaved through the overcrowded, chaotic emergency room. She'd seen it all before. She sidestepped several gurneys in the hallway filled with addicts sleeping it off and a high school football player with a temporary splint on his arm. Staff darted to and from the exam rooms, and paramedic radios squawked. When she turned the corner at station two, she approached Eric while he talked to a battle-weary nurse. *I knew he'd beat me here.*

"This is my partner, Sergeant Sloane. Can we talk to the girl yet?"

"She's still a little groggy, so keep it short." Nurse Raj adjusted the stethoscope strung around her neck.

"You got it." Eric turned to Sloane. "Two were DOA." He placed a hand on Sloane's arm. "I'm sorry, Sloane, but Shellie didn't make it. Only Deni Scott survived."

Her knees turned weak, and her throat choked back a gasp. A regular fixture at their house, Shellie had had dinner with them a few days ago, with her and Reagan laughing and doing makeup. Anything but homework. Sloane straightened her back and placed her hands on her hips to steady herself.

Eric turned gentle eyes on her. "I can handle this."

"No, I need to do this. Give me a minute." Sloane shook her head and cleared the lump in her throat before turning to Nurse Raj. "I know both of the girls. I'll make the notifications."

Reagan's best friend had died, and now she had to tell her. More importantly, Gus and Fabiola's daughter had passed away, and she had to tell them Shellie wouldn't be coming home. And not because of some accident or horrible disease, but from a stupid decision to experiment with Ecstasy. No matter how much she'd welcome pawning this off on Eric or some uniformed officer, the responsibility rested with her.

After Raj nodded and returned to her station, Sloane turned to Eric. "Let's do this."

She slid back the curtain guarding the emergency room cubicle. Half-asleep, Deni didn't appear at all like herself with puffy, bloodshot eyes and ashen skin.

"Hi, Deni." Sloane used a comforting tone. "I'm so relieved you'll be okay."

Deni fought to prop herself up on the bed and reposition the arm that had the IV lead attached to it. "Mrs. Sloane…I…I…"

"Deni, I need you to tell me the truth about what happened tonight." Sloane kept her tone soft and calm. "Reagan tells me you and Shellie scored X at the Firepit. Is that right?"

Deni turned her head away. When she didn't respond, Sloane pressed. "Look, Deni. This isn't you girls cutting class.

This is serious. Shellie died." Deni sobbed, her body trembling, but Sloane didn't let up. "I know this is hard, but I need the truth. Who sold you the X?"

"A guy at the club. He goes by the name Diego."

Sloane had heard the names of a hundred drug dealers, but not this one. This had to be someone Finn was tracking. "Had you bought from him before?"

"No. I got his name from a friend at school." Deni shook her head.

"Okay, Deni. I believe you. Can you describe the X?"

"They were little pink heart-shaped pills with lips on them."

Eric turned toward Sloane and gave her a nod. They were in sync.

"Did Diego have a name for the X?"

"Yeah, he called it Kiss."

An ache formed in the back of Sloane's throat. Kiss had claimed its first victims in her city, one of them a family friend. This had become personal. Sloane had to work fast. She needed to get a jump on Diego before the DEA got wind of him.

While questioning Deni, she learned two things: Diego had been selling Kiss out of the Firepit for at least a month, and it had taken two pills each to put her in the emergency room and Shellie in a body bag.

After an emotional phone call to Deni's parents, she and Eric searched for Avery and Reagan in the waiting area. When her gaze met Avery's, she shook her head from side to side, telegraphing she had alarming news to break.

She stopped and pulled on Eric's coat sleeve. Her subdued tone underscored the personal nature of this case. "There's no way I'm handing this over to the DEA."

Eric nodded. "Wasn't planning to. We'll bring Diego down ourselves."

Satisfied they had each other's back, Sloane closed the distance to her family. After rubbing Reagan on the arms, she tossed her chin toward several empty chairs across the room. "Why don't we sit?"

Avery wrapped an arm around Reagan and guided her to an empty chair.

Sloane followed, dreading what she had to say. "Honey, I have bad news. Deni is recovering and will be fine, but Shellie… She didn't make it. She passed away before they got her to the hospital."

Avery gasped and covered her mouth.

"Noooooooo!" Reagan fell into her mother's arms.

Avery and Sloane offered several words of comfort, but nothing eased their daughter's pain. No stranger to death, Sloane understood soothing words had little effect. Reagan needed a jolt to get past the initial shock.

"It's all my fault…I should have stopped them," Reagan called out.

Sloane kneeled in front of her. Familiar with the overwhelming power of guilt, she lifted Reagan's chin with her hand. "Look at me."

Reagan focused on Sloane's eyes.

"This is not your fault. They made a choice. They knew the dangers of experimenting with drugs. I made sure of that. I won't lie and say you shouldn't have tried to stop them because you should've. But even if you did, knowing those girls, there was no guarantee they would've listened. So don't put all of this on yourself."

Reagan fell into her arms in tears.

Sloane had made several death notifications, but none where she knew the victim and her family. Each time she became more familiar with the process: be clear and concise and say the word "dead." Reactions varied, but most included surprise that the police were at the door, the shock of the news, the hope Sloane had made a mistake, and finally, the horror when reality set in. During it all, Sloane needed to remain detached. She feared that would be her downfall in this case.

At the apartment door, Sloane raised and then lowered her hand several times, searching for the courage to turn the Rodriguezes' world upside down. She dreaded to think whenever they remembered this day, the day they lost their child, the image of her would forever burn in their memories.

Eric waited. He'd taught her to not rush this important and somber job. "You got this," he whispered.

After tucking away her trepidation, she knocked on the door. At six o'clock on a Saturday morning, Shellie's mother should be home and her father should be getting ready for work.

The door opened, and like so many times before, Fabiola greeted her with a smile. "Morning, Sloane. It's early, even for you."

"Is Gus still here?" Sloane asked, unable to return the smile.

Fabiola glanced back over her shoulder. "He's finishing breakfast."

"This is my partner, Eric Decker. May we come in? I need a word with you both."

"Uh...sure." When she let them pass, Fabiola's raised eyebrows and shaky voice told Sloane she suspected there was a problem.

Family pictures littered the walls of the entryway, most of which marked special events in Shellie's vibrant life: birthdays, holidays, and school portraits. Sloane took in as many as she could.

Seconds later, a voice boomed from the kitchen. "Sloane! What brings you here this early? Have our girls gotten themselves into trouble again?"

Sloane swallowed the lump in her throat when she entered the decades-old kitchen because the mood in the room would soon change. "Gus. Fabi. Why don't we sit?"

"You're scaring me, Sloane." Fabi's face turned pale. "Did something happen?"

"Yes, Fabi, something did." Sloane squeezed her nervous hand. "The girls were supposed to be at a sleepover at Deni's house, but they snuck out to a club."

Gus threw his napkin on the plate with his half-eaten breakfast and rose from his chair. "Did they go drinking? I warned her if she did that again, I'd ground her for life."

"Mr. Rodriguez, please. Let's sit back down." Eric used a calm voice to cajole him into returning to his seat.

"Yes, Gus, they went drinking last night." Sloane paused until Gus stopped squirming in his chair. "When they were at the club, Deni and Shellie bought Ecstasy from a local drug dealer."

Gus and Fabi lowered and shook their heads.

"Were they arrested?" Fabi asked.

Sloane ignored the question and the chill in the room, bracing herself for her next words. "Both girls overdosed and were taken to Bayside Hospital. They did everything they could, but Shellie didn't make it. Shellie is dead."

She'd said the three essential words.   There'd be no mistaking what Sloane had said and what it meant. Their only child would never come home. No more birthday parties for Sloane and her wife to attend. No more school pictures for their daughters to exchange.

At first, no one made a sound. Fabi covered her mouth with both hands and gasped for air.

Gus shook his head. "It's a mistake. This has to be a mistake."

Both stared at Sloane as if hoping for a sign it wasn't true, but none came.

Reality hit them in the gut. Fabi rocked in place and wailed. Her screams and moans ripped Sloane's heart in two. Gus jumped to his feet and paced, pulling at his hair. He repeated, "No, no, no, no, no."

Sloane and Eric stayed until a circle of friends joined Gus and Fabi's side. Once they walked out the door, Sloane was certain no amount of time could heal a wound that deep. She stopped and clenched her fists. "I don't care how we do it. I want that son of a bitch Diego."

CHAPTER SIX

The Firepit had been at the center of drugs sold in the Mission District for years. On more occasions than Sloane could count, she'd dealt with its owner, Jimmy Chiang. He may have been a smart businessman, but he skirted the law. Though she couldn't prove it, the report of the officers first on scene convinced her he'd ditched the security equipment and tapes from last night.

Sloane and Eric needed more information on Diego, and given the right incentive, the Firepit's sleazy owner could provide it. She waited until noon when delivery trucks made their rounds to this nocturnal business, also the hour when Chiang traditionally counted the previous night's take.

With the front doors locked, Sloane and Eric turned down the adjoining alley. Walls of aged red brick, dotted with patches of cracked and peeling red and pink paint, rose on either side like a fortress. Rusty fire escapes jutted from the flat planes and cast small shadows in the midday sun.

They negotiated a passage wide enough for only a single delivery truck to pass by scattered crates and trash cans. Sloane tiptoed through a minefield of puddles. Water? The odor led her to believe otherwise. Once at the service door, she rang the bell located to the right of the door.

Minutes later, a young, scruffy male worker with a slight build groused as he opened the door. "Dude, you're early. I was on the shitter."

Sloane held out her badge to catch him off guard. "Thanks for the overshare."

With a single hand, Eric shoved the now trembling worker against the open door, towering over him by a good six inches. He straightened the young man's collar. "You need to take a coffee break down the street. Half an hour should do it."

The young man nodded, ran down the alley, and splashed through urine puddles along his path. Eric chuckled at his handiwork.

Sloane raised an eyebrow. "Sometimes, I think you enjoy your job too much."

Eric craned his neck out the door to catch one last glimpse of the man and then laughed again. "I think you're right."

Sloane's grin disappeared, replaced by a set jaw and narrowed eyes, a look that warned people to stay out of her way.

Eric wiped the smile off his face and delivered a curt nod. "Let's do this."

She led the way from the receiving area deep into the club. The small office off to the side was empty, so she pushed through to the main dance floor. Bright overhead white lights had replaced the dancing wall flames and fiery orange glow from earlier this morning and only one person occupied the room.

"Jimmy…Chiang." Sloane intended her slow, deliberate pace to capture his attention as she closed in on the bar.

Chiang, a stout, aging Chinese American, was dressed in his signature purple, silk long-sleeve shirt and a pair of polyester pants a few shades darker. He appeared unfazed by Sloane's sudden appearance and continued to tally the previous night's sales receipts atop the bar.

In a slight accent, he spoke as if he expected visitors from the police. "Good afternoon, Sergeant Sloane." He shifted his stare over her shoulder. "Sergeant Decker. Following up on last night?"

"Now, we wouldn't be doing our job right if we weren't." Sloane matched Jimmy's playful tone.

"Well then, how can I help two of San Francisco's finest?" Chiang rolled up the sleeves of his silk button-down shirt and returned to his task of counting.

"Let's cut the crap." Sloane rested an elbow on the bar and leaned against it. "I can have health and safety inspectors and anyone else I can think of here within an hour. They'll shut your club down for months while they sort things out."

Chiang finished stacking the receipts in perfect order, placed them in the cash register drawer, and closed it. He turned his attention back toward Sloane and Eric. "What do you want?"

Glaring into Chiang's eyes, she leaned her face a foot from his. "The girl who died last night was a friend. And don't try throwing me some bullshit like 'I had no idea.' Nothing goes on in this club without you knowing about it. Diego sold her the X. I want Diego."

Eric kept his position.

Chiang glanced at Sloane's and Eric's resolute postures. "And if I give you what you want?"

"You mean besides not being arrested as an accomplice after the fact?" Sloane turned stone-faced, slamming a fist atop the bar.

Eric stepped forward, right behind Sloane to back her up. "We'll find Diego one way or another, and we give out only one get-out-of-jail-free card."

Chiang twisted and cracked his neck. A nightclub owner didn't need two dogged detectives, hellbent on disrupting his business until they got what they needed. "I may have overheard where Diego likes to conduct business when he's not here." Chiang waved his arms open wide, reminding Sloane of the empty room. "Would that give you what you need?"

"If it pans out." Eric shrugged, not making any promises.

"I hear he likes to do business with the twinks in the Castro." Chiang shrugged his shoulders. "They have to stay thin somehow."

* * *

With their only lead in the Castro, they were hot on the trail of Diego. Sloane and Eric concentrated their surveillance on the handful of clubs where twinks scored crank and their predators snatched up Ecstasy. Armed with a rough suspect sketch based on Deni's description, Eric camped out on one street in an undercover sedan, while Sloane took surveillance along another.

For five days, they watched gay men and their suppliers come and go, none of which resembled Diego. Sloane picked at the shoulder holster digging into her breast, something she hadn't done in several years. Everything about this case had her uncomfortable.

The sun had her stakeout in the aging unmarked sedan teetering on unbearable for hours. The broken air conditioner endlessly recirculated the same warm air and had her tongue stuck to the roof of her dry mouth on several occasions. Only the AM/FM radio worked in this heap from the PD lot.

She welcomed any distraction from her baking thirst and switched on the radio. When ABBA's "Take a Chance on Me" played through the speakers, she froze, her fingers still wrapped around the knob. The lyrics repeated on a loop, every word pounding her head, gripping her in a chokehold of the memory of her mother singing this song with her on the night of the accident. As she recalled the swerve of the car, pressure built in her chest like a kettle set to boil. By the time she remembered the bright fireball that had consumed her innocence along with her parents, sweat beaded down her cheeks.

A voice came through her dash-mounted phone, but she couldn't decipher it. The sound grew louder until it brought her back to the present, prompting her to turn the radio off. "Eric?"

"You okay?" Concern cut through his voice.

"I'm fine, just thirsty." She shook her head to clear her thoughts.

"Are you sipping every five?"

"Yeah, but the sun's beating down on the windshield, and the A/C isn't cutting it."

Eric had taught her the cardinal rule of stakeouts—limit your liquids. A good detective always focused on her target and never let calls of nature get in the way.

"Crybaby," he half-chuckled.

"You're in the shade. Who you calling a—" Sloane stopped. A man who fit Diego's description was approaching the club from the opposite direction wearing dingy street clothes common to the local gangs. "Hold on, I think I got something." She checked the suspect sketch one more time. "That's him."

"On my way."

In less than a minute, Eric dashed across the street and into view and behind the suspect. Sloane gestured at Eric, identifying their moving target. After Diego passed a cross street, a principal avenue of escape, she exited her car and closed the distance between them. Needing him to turn and run, she didn't conceal her movements or intentions.

When Diego locked eyes with her, he froze. When the fight-or-flight instinct kicked in, he pivoted 180 degrees on his heel and took off, running right into Eric's side-stretched club of an arm. In two steps, Eric had him clotheslined. His feet rocketed in the air, and he landed his ass flat on the sidewalk with a loud thud.

"Oof!"

Eric stared down at him as he writhed on the ground in pain. "Going somewhere, Diego?" His voice contained a little too much delight.

Sloane narrowed in on Diego and grabbed him up by his jacket collar. "Gotcha!"

* * *

As the senior detective, Eric usually took the lead during interrogations, but not this time. With a personal stake in this case, Sloane had every motivation to get it right. She'd proven herself a skilled interrogator, so he gave her the show.

She'd had Eric cuff Diego to the metal table in the dead center of the small room almost half an hour ago. To enjoy the show, she retreated to the other side of the two-way mirror. Diego didn't disappoint. He squirmed in his chair and pulled at the cuffs on what must have been an achy arm, but she had yet to see the cue she needed.

The interrogation rooms at 850 Bryant were like those in any of the others around the city—with one minor exception: they stunk. While the brass had situated the narcotics section underneath the men's seventh-floor bathroom, they'd located the interrogation rooms under the women's. It had the same problem: leaky pipes.

A clerk walked in with the results of Diego's background check. Using his fingerprints, the FBI's National Crime Information Center unearthed a rich arrest record from grand theft auto to possession with the intent to sell. The lack of convictions told Sloane that he had a gang or cartel affiliation or some cop had him on their snitch roster. Since his name didn't pop on any SFPD list of paid informants, she leaned toward the former. She'd have to figure out which at the onset and adjust the direction and tone of her questioning on the fly.

"Looks like the pump is primed." Eric's half-cocked grin meant the fun was about to begin.

Sloane raised her glance. Diego's face had turned a slight shade of green at the not-so-faint sewer odor that never went away. "Let's get this party started."

Eric gave her a single fist pump.

With an aura of being the woman in charge, Sloane strode into the room. After she sat in a metal chair across from Diego, Eric joined her in the nearby chair. She didn't need to, but she flipped through Diego Rojas' record jacket as if to familiarize herself with his criminal history and then slammed it on the table. After laying out a small evidence bag, she pointed to an item taken from Diego's pockets when she and Eric took him down on Castro Street.

"You know what this is?"

Diego shrugged.

"This is your ticket to the execution chamber." Sloane took in a sharp breath, remembering the shock and horror on Gus and Fabi's faces when she told them their little girl had died.

Diego puffed his chest and spoke in a slight Hispanic accent. "You need to make a phone call."

With that one sentence, Diego answered Sloane's question. If he were well-connected, he would have kept quiet and waited for his benefactor to send a lawyer. A phone call meant he had the backing of law enforcement as a snitch. She'd step on someone's toes if she didn't make that call, but she didn't care. Her goal: put a needle in his arm, not hand him over to another cop.

"The only phone call I'll make is one to take your measurements for a casket. Your Kiss is the kiss of death. Two of your customers from the Firepit died."

After pulling out morgue pictures of the two victims, she pointed to them one at a time. "This is Michael Wong. He was a UCSF senior studying to be a dentist. He was weeks away from being the first one in his family to graduate from college, but now that will never happen."

She pointed to the next picture. "This is Shellie Rodriguez. She was only sixteen and the only child of a city bus driver and an elementary school teacher. Now they'll never see their little girl finish high school."

Diego stared at the pictures. His lumpy swallow told Sloane he had a speck of remorse—or a healthy fear of the consequences.

"I have an eyewitness who says you sold them Kiss..." Sloane pointed to the evidence bag, "...which is an exact match to the pills we found on you." She was guessing there, but the law allowed cops to lie to suspects, and she did it with refined expertise. "That, my friend, is what we call a slam dunk."

Diego swallowed hard again. "You need to—"

Sloane flew to her feet before slamming her hand on the table. "I don't need to do a damn thing."

Eric rested his hand on Sloane's shoulder. "But you do, Diego. If you cooperate, the DA might take the death penalty off the table."

Someone from the observation room pounded on the two-way mirror three times, their boss's signal to stop the interrogation. Sloane's eyes shot up toward the mirror. Her brow furrowed when she fixed her stare on Diego again. *Son of a bitch.*

He leaned back in his chair with a smug look on his face, interlocking his fingers with his arms behind his head.

"I'm not finished with you." Sloane pointed a stiff finger at Diego, wishing it was an executioner's bullet.

After snatching up the evidence and files, she stormed out of the room with Eric. When the door closed, she searched out Lieutenant West and waved her hands in the air. "What?"

"We have a problem," West said.

"What kind of problem?" Eric knitted his brow.

The exterior door opened. Finn Harper walked through, dressed in another tailored business suit. The DEA was the last thing Sloane needed.

"Fucking great!" Sloane rolled her eyes and threw her hands up again. With the DEA here, that meant West had kicked her case up to the Feds.

"My hands are tied." West released a frustrated breath. "They're taking the case."

"Taking it?" Sloane turned to Finn, her eyes narrowed. "How'd you even know he was here?"

Finn blinked. "NCIC."

Sloane slammed the folder on a desk. If this were true, it meant the DEA had flagged Diego's record to alert them if anyone ran his name or prints. "Well, ain't this grand. You knew about him and did nothing? Now two people are dead because of you."

Finn squeezed the bridge of her nose and blew out a long, deliberate breath before saying, "It wasn't my call."

Sloane craned her neck left and right to look behind Finn. "So, where's Prickhead?"

"Prichard?" Finn earned a chuckle from Eric.

"That's enough, Sloane." Lieutenant West's narrowed eyes meant Sloane had reached her limit. "The DEA is taking jurisdiction, and we need to bounce him."

"Whoa, whoa, whoa." Eric put up his hands in a stopping motion. "What do you mean, bounce him?"

"We need to let him walk for the time being." Finn ended her statement with a sigh.

Sloane snapped her head toward Finn. Veins popping in her neck, she narrowed her eyes.

"Define 'time being,'" Eric said, stepping forward before Sloane could do anything more to earn their boss's rebuke.

"I can't tell you that." Finn turned toward Sloane and shook her head. Disappointment laced her voice. "I don't have a choice. I wish I did, but we've been trying to penetrate Los Dorados for months."

"Are they the ones who've been manufacturing and distributing Kiss in NorCal?" Sloane's words were sharp as knives. "Why didn't you mention that before? Oh, that's right, you didn't ask for our help. You gave us just enough information for us to be your whipping boys after doing your job."

Finn squared off against Sloane, toe-to-toe, face-to-face. "This goes way beyond your city, Sloane. This stretches from Vegas to San Francisco. Every time we get close to linking someone to Kiss, they end up dead. I found Rojas. He's my asset. He's the only one I've been able to flip. So, like it or not, we can't risk tanking the investigation when we're close to identifying who's bankrolling the entire operation. He needs to walk for now."

"So says Lord Douchebag."

"Sloane." Eric placed a hand on her shoulder.

"That's it, Sloane!" West's face turned red and she clenched her jaw. "You need to go home. Now."

"Look, Sloane," Finn changed her expression to a softer one and touched Sloane's arm. That touch sent tingles up Sloane's arm, and for a moment, her anger subsided. "I want to put everyone responsible for those people's death behind bars just as much as you do."

"They're not just people. Their names are Michael Wong and Shellie Rodriguez." Sloane's eyes blazed with fury. "Say it… Michael and Shellie."

Sloane waited for Finn to repeat their names, but she never did. She expected more from her. This case had nothing to do with some junkie who OD'd in an alley or a sleazy motel room. It had everything to do with a sixteen-year-old high school girl who ate at Sloane's dinner table and rode in her SUV to volleyball games. About a girl who'd been friends with her stepdaughter for years.

She clenched her fists, and her voice took on a resolute tone. "Shellie was a friend, and I don't care what Prickhead says, Diego Rojas is going down for this." Before she left, she turned back. "One way or another, he's going down."

CHAPTER SEVEN

The metal door lowered after Sloane pulled her SUV into the townhouse garage. Her body ached as much as her heart, and falling into her wife's arms would serve as the perfect end of a bad day. Yet she remained at the wheel. Once she walked through that door, she'd have to face her failures of the last several days. She had let Diego slip through her fingers, and on one too many occasions, Finn had had her thinking about missed opportunities.

After swallowing her pride, she dragged herself up the steps leading to the main floor and into the shroud of sadness smothering her home. The absence of music and teenage giggles made for a strange silence.

"Avery?" she called out.

Not finding her wife in the living room or kitchen, she spotted a glass of scotch, neat, on the dining table—Avery's signal that she'd escaped to the deck. Before opening the sliding glass door, she grabbed the tumbler of amber liquid and sipped. The burn assured she'd have numbing relief in a few short minutes.

Outside, Avery sat in her favorite chair, facing the waning sunlight and sipping on a vodka gimlet. "Hey." That one word from Avery sounded forced.

Bloodshot eyes and rosy cheeks meant she'd been outside drinking for a while or crying again. Either way, their daughter's depression following Shellie's death had triggered it.

"Hey, you." Sloane honeyed her words to mask her fatigue and then kissed her on the lips.

Once Sloane firmly settled into her usual chair, the cool light bay breeze comforted her for several minutes while a cargo ship lumbered in and out of view. When the day numbed, she reached out for Avery's hand, hoping her wife's smooth, slender fingers would suffice until she could take her into her arms.

"I don't know what I'd do if I lost Reagan." Avery's voice trailed off, revealing the same anguish Sloane had battled all week. If not for Reagan heeding her badgering about the dangers of drugs, they'd be planning Reagan's funeral, not attending one.

"We're lucky, so damn lucky." They'd dodged a bullet. Gus and Fabiola's faces when reality finally sunk in flashed in Sloane's mind, making today's turn of events sting even more.

Avery gave her hand an extra squeeze.

"I caught the son of a bitch today." Sipping more of her scotch, Sloane expected her indifference to confuse Avery.

"Diego?" Avery dropped her hand and whipped her head around. "You caught Diego?"

"The DEA rolled in and bounced him." Sloane didn't break her stare at the bay and downed the rest of her drink.

"They what?" Avery leaped to her feet, forcing Sloane to shift her gaze. Her expression begged Sloane for an explanation.

Between Shellie's death, Diego's release, and Finn's reappearance, tension continued to build in Sloane's shoulders. One drink wasn't nearly enough to ease it. Clenching her jaw, she pushed herself out of her chair. "I'm going for a second round. Want one?"

"What do you mean they bounced him?" Avery stayed on Sloane's heels all the way to the kitchen and their makeshift bar.

"Just that." Sloane poured half a shot, but when her hands shook, she put the bottle down. She formed a fist with one hand while gripping her drink extra tightly in the other. "Get this. He's their asset, and they let him walk. For the time being, she said."

"Who's she?"

"Fucking Finn Harper." Sloane threw her glass in the sink, shattering it into a dozen pieces. Finn had her worked up, but not only about Diego. Her past had wormed its way out of the box she'd locked it in the day Avery said "I love you," and now as she tidied up after herself, gathering the fragments, she questioned her choices.

"Leave it." Avery came up beside her and placed a gentle hand on hers.

Sloane dipped and shook her head. "I'm sorry." Between Finn and the case, something had to give.

"It's only a glass, babe." Avery ran a reassuring hand down her back.

"It's not that." Sloane dropped the pieces in the sink and then rested both hands on the edge of the counter, elbows locked. She'd failed at her job and had failed her wife in a way she'd only begun to understand. She turned and searched Avery's eyes for redemption. "I failed you and Reagan and Shellie's parents."

"You've failed none of us." Avery rested both hands on Sloane's cheeks. "You'll make this right. You always do."

"But—"

"No buts."

God, I love this woman. She kissed Avery, slowly at first, letting the softness of those lips take over. After wrapping her arms around her wife's waist, she pulled her body tight. If anything could right today, making love to Avery could. Sex always did that for her. She reached down and hoisted Avery onto the kitchen counter. Her kisses became more intense as a desperate instinct ignited. She needed to dispel every doubt.

After Sloane lifted Avery's blouse over her head and threw it to the tile floor, she attacked the clasps of her bra. Her kisses deepened, with her tongue darting in and out, barely tasting the lime from Avery's gimlet. Sloane removed the bra and discarded it. Almost rabid in her hunger, she latched onto a breast and sucked and massaged at an unfamiliar pace. She clawed at Avery's leggings and panties until she'd removed every stitch of clothing.

"I need to feel you." Her hungry growl gave Avery little warning before she plunged two fingers deep inside. Her lips, tongue, fingers, and hips all worked in unison to expel the demons tormenting her. She funneled her anger into each thrust and pushed past her perceived failures. Driving her own center into Avery's leg, she worked them both into a heated frenzy.

In too short a time, Avery's walls clamped down like a lion's jaw on its prey, hurtling them both over the edge. Sloane kept her hand in place, and with each pulsating wave, Avery siphoned the rage and confusion from her body.

Legs wobbling, Sloane lacked the energy to pull Avery from her precarious position atop the counter. Instead, she rested her head against Avery's chest, rising and falling to the deep gasps filling her lungs.

You must be a magical creature. Only magic could jettison all of Sloane's anger and doubt.

"How do you do that?"

"Do…what?" Avery's words came out between ragged breaths.

Sloane's legs now stronger, she lifted Avery down and held her limp, naked body against her. "How do you make everything better?"

"Simple. I let you ravish me until neither of us can stand." Avery pulled back enough to give Sloane a satisfied grin. "Though I think I get the better end of the deal."

Once Sloane released her grasp, Avery gathered her clothes, some of which landed in the strangest places. "How did that get up there?" Avery stood on her toes to retrieve her bra, which was slung across the flat edge of the free-standing stainless steel hood over the stove.

"I'm not sure, but I think it's proof I got the better end of the deal this time." Sloane leaned against the refrigerator and savored the view of Avery struggling to dress.

When the bra went back on and then the shirt, Sloane pushed herself away from the fridge. "Fun's over."

"I love that about you." Avery kissed Sloane on the lips.

"What about me?" She wrapped her arms around Avery's waist.

"How you always make me feel wanted."

She pulled Avery in tight. "I can't help it. It's as natural as breathing."

That couldn't be truer. As Sloane's first real love, everything about Avery captivated her. From the way she laughed to the way she snored, Avery had Sloane under her spell.

More centered now, Sloane knew what she had to do next. If not for Gus and Fabi, for Avery and Reagan. "Screw orders and screw the DEA. I'm going after Diego."

"I knew you would."

"You did?"

"I know you, Manhattan Sloane." Avery shrugged as if the answer was clear as day. "You always do the right thing."

Whatever doubt Finn had stirred up, those words ousted them. She wouldn't give up on Avery, and she wouldn't give up on finding justice for Shellie.

"I'll build a case for murder that West and the DA can't ignore. Hell, I'll get the media involved if I have to, but I won't give up, not this time."

* * *

A fake smile, firm handshake, and feigned interest came easy to Finn, but tonight, serving as Kadin's plus-one tested her patience. Coming straight from work in the same suit she worked in made it worse. She needed to wash away the stink of releasing Diego Rojas and forget the sting of Sloane's words. *"They are not just people; their names are Michael Wong and Shellie Rodriguez. Say it...Michael and Shellie."* Even now, she couldn't say their names.

The more she thought about it, the more the politics of her new job disgusted her. She had all the responsibility yet made none of the big decisions. Doubt crept in, and she questioned whether the things she had to do as second in command were worth the pay raise.

Tonight, she'd rather take a hot shower and curl up in bed with a trashy book than listen to high-priced lawyers drone on about briefs and settlements. Yet she came. Forever the dutiful daughter and girlfriend, she walked into another of her father's elaborate dinners, on the arm of a woman she'd walked away from almost a month earlier.

After the elevator door opened, Finn took a deep breath. She grabbed Kadin's hand and forced a smile as she stepped out to the forty-eighth floor of the Pyramid Building. The floor's main attraction was its spectacular 360-degree view of San Francisco. On occasions like tonight, the conference room converted into an elegant dining space with dim, romantic lighting.

"Thank you for this," Kadin whispered into her ear while they walked deeper into the room. "It means a lot to me."

Finn stopped and turned to take in Kadin, both beautiful and classy in her black and white sheath dress that hit an inch below the knee. A similar outfit had caught her eye the first time they met at her father's law firm. From that moment, she had to have her.

"I know how important tonight is for you." She pulled Kadin close. "I wouldn't have missed it for the world."

When she pressed her lips against Kadin's, the months of subtle and not-so-subtle pestering for her to find a safer line of work faded into the background. It always did. In bed or simply in her arms, Kadin checked off every box for a perfect partner.

Other times, Kadin reminded her too much of her father, a driven advocate of the law who wished she had followed in his footsteps. But when she pulled back and glimpsed her surroundings, the purpose of tonight's gathering jolted her back to reality. "Let's go find our seats."

Finn settled into an hour of eating, forced smiles, and feigned interest like she'd done a dozen dinners before. Only this time, she did it for Kadin, not her father. Somehow, that took most of the edge off it.

Underneath the round table for ten, her father sneaked his foot to his left and tapped it against Finn's—their signal he needed rescuing from a long, boring conversation. They'd done this for years. Over time, they developed a code to tell each other when they needed rescuing or when the other wanted to go home.

Finn smiled and whispered in Kadin's ear, "Gotta save Daddy." After Kadin acknowledged with a grin, Finn laid a hand atop her father's. "Sorry to interrupt, but I need a word with you, Daddy."

Chandler nodded and turned his focus to his table partner. "Sorry, Harold. We can finish this at the office tomorrow." He then shifted in his seat toward Finn and mouthed, "Thank you."

He looked at her closer. "You look tired, pumpkin."

"Long, hard day at work."

"Riding a desk takes practice." A smile formed on his face when he patted her hand. "You'll get the hang of it." Not the reminder she needed tonight. If she were still a field agent, she would've found a way to get both what she and Sloane wanted. But the chain of command offered her limited options as the Assistant Special Agent in Charge. She loved the DEA, but she hated the political red tape that came with management.

"That's what I'm afraid of." After a pause, she added, "Daddy?"

Her tone prompted a quizzical expression. "Yes, pumpkin?"

"I need your advice on something, but not here. Can we talk later? Maybe tomorrow?"

"Of course." He squeezed her hand. "I better get the formalities over."

Chandler Harper tapped his crystal goblet with a knife, the sharp clanking directing the room to come to a hush. He stood. At well over six feet and with broad shoulders, his still-trim sixty-year-old body alone would catch everyone's eye. However, tonight, his dark blue tailored suit with a gold bar popping off either side of his white collar, highlighting his dark grenadine tie, commanded the room's attention.

"Thank you, everyone, for coming tonight. Per her request, I promise to keep this short. Kadin Hall," he turned toward her, "you've been with the firm for a grueling six years. From your first day, you set the bar high as a dogged advocate for your clients, negotiating more high-value contracts than all of our other associates combined. Tonight, I'm proud to welcome you aboard as HMR's newest junior partner."

When thirty sets of hands offered polite, congratulatory applause, Finn kissed her on the cheek. "I'm so proud of you."

"Thank you." Kadin leaned into the kiss and lingered for several seconds as if savoring Finn's words of encouragement. Finn didn't want to admit it, but deep down, she knew moments like this with Kadin had come to an end.

Finn stepped out of the shower, having washed away the stink of the day or at least most of it. The warm water helped relax her tight muscles but did nothing to ease the bad taste in her mouth. She'd released Diego, a child-killer by anyone's definition, and that gnawed at her conscience. In addition to having let Sloane down, she was having a hard time living with herself.

After slipping on her sleep shorts and tank top, she stared at her empty bed. Not in the mood to share conversation, let alone her body with someone on an emotional high, she'd used a headache as her excuse. Kadin resisted, but she said good night in the parking lot of the Pyramid Building.

After curling beneath the covers, she picked up a book on the nightstand. A trashy romance, she figured, would help her forget what she'd done. As she popped on her reading glasses, the doorbell rang.

"Damn it, Kadin." Finn knew by her body language when they parted ways that Kadin didn't want to call it a night. Kadin's heavy sigh and averted eyes had clawed at her, but she couldn't bring herself to join in her excitement.

Finn could accommodate a quick fuck but nothing more. "You win."

After throwing back the comforter, she headed to the front door. She opened it, expecting to find Kadin still in her sexy black and white sheath dress, an arm hung high on the doorframe, holding a bottle of champagne.

"Hi, pumpkin." Grinning, Chandler waved a bag from her favorite ice cream joint. He'd ditched his suit coat and replaced it with a pullover sweater.

Not what she expected, but not unwelcomed. Now embarrassed by her attire, she covered her chest with an arm. "Daddy? What are you doing here?"

"Thought you could use a pick-me-up tonight." Inviting himself in, he plowed his way past her. "Besides, you said you wanted to talk."

"I guess we're having ice cream." Finn locked the door and joined her father on the couch.

He held up two pints. "Swirls or no swirls?"

"Swirls." Finn snatched the container from his hand before he changed his mind.

"Damn, I knew I should have ordered two swirls."

Finn dug in with her spoon and pulled out a healthy portion. The first cold, sweet bite took the edge off the day. "Much better than a trashy book."

"Or female company?" He raised a single eyebrow.

"Daddy." Unsure who was more embarrassed, Finn ended her reply on an uptick.

"I saw Kadin after you left." He swallowed a good chunk of dessert. "She told me you'd be alone tonight."

"Ah, so you thought you'd come right over."

"Even she could tell you were troubled. We both wanted to make sure you were okay."

Chandler had made it clear that Kadin had signaled that she still wanted their relationship to work, but Finn sensed their time had passed. At the start, sparks flew both in and out of bed, and Kadin had her entertaining the idea of marriage. She thought she'd never do that again after her first love died, but when she did, the insecurities and the nagging for a safer job came. If Finn didn't let her father steer her career, she wouldn't let Kadin either.

Finn only nodded.

"She loves you."

"Love isn't the problem."

"Is that what you wanted to talk about tonight?" Avoiding eye contact, he fumbled with his spoon.

"No, it's about work."

"Phew." Chandler wiped his brow. "I'm a little out of practice in the love department."

"Don't worry, Daddy. I'm not about to discuss my love life with you."

"All right then." He shifted more comfortably in his seat. "What's bothering you?"

"Today, I had to release a confidential informant the SFPD was holding on murder charges."

"Is there a greater good involved?"

"Isn't there always in my line of work? There's always a bigger fish to go after, but no one seems to pay for their crimes."

"You've been through this before, pumpkin. Why did this one get under your skin?"

"You mean other than one of his victims was only sixteen?"

"Sixteen?"

"Yes, and she was a friend of a close friend." Finn closed her eyes and shook her head at the bitterness of the situation. She had a hard time deciphering which felt worse—Shellie's age or that she was someone special to Sloane. If it were the latter, Finn had a bigger problem. Sloane was married, or so she assumed, and that meant she was off-limits. But Finn couldn't deny the growing connection she felt every time she was in Sloane's orbit.

"This is a tough one."

"You're telling me." She speared her ice cream, standing the spoon upright. "I can't live with this one, Daddy."

"Can you up-channel the issue?"

"Wouldn't do any good. US Attorney Quintrell has already signed off on it."

"What else can you do?"

"That's just it. I don't know. If I resign, nothing changes."

Chandler rubbed his clean-shaven chin. "Maginot Line."

"I'm not following."

"If you can't go through it, go around it."

Going around her boss and Quintrell meant going around her oath. She swore to "well and faithfully" discharge the duties of her office, and what her father was proposing flew in the face of that. She had vaguely entertained the idea but needed her father's push to choose the right thing.

"You're right, Daddy."

"I'm always right." He smiled and stabbed at Finn's pint of ice cream with a giant grin on his face. "Now, give me some of those swirls."

"Hey, get your own." She snatched the container to the safety of her chest. "Those are mine."

CHAPTER EIGHT

Moments earlier, the Oakland hills peeked through a thin line of orange in the predawn sky. Slivers of light glowed in the distance, guiding Sloane onto Bryant. The street cleaners had wrapped up overnight rounds of washing away yesterday's remnants as she drove up. By the time she'd parked in the SFPD garage and exited the elevator, a faint yellow glow filled the windows lining the sixth-floor hallway.

Given the fact that the lights were off in the squad room, she assumed Eric had yet to make it in. For the unsanctioned operation they cooked up overnight, she estimated she'd have two hours before prying eyes rolled in. She turned the corner to a surprise. "Do you ever go home?"

"Unlike you," Eric peeked up from his computer terminal, "I don't have a pretty wife to keep me in bed."

Sloane hadn't given it much thought, but Eric led a lonely life. He lived alone in a small apartment and only spoke of attending the occasional ballgame with his father when he was in town. As far as she knew, like her, his only friends were on the job. *What a waste.* Why hadn't he married? A tall, youngish, fit, handsome man, loyal to a fault, he personified husband material.

"Are you in?" She removed her outer coat and slung it over the back of her chair.

"Yeah. I gotta hand it to the gang task force. They keep good notes."

"How do you want to divide this up?" Sloane logged onto her computer terminal.

"I'm almost halfway through GTF. Why don't you start with vice?"

"You got it."

Sloane accessed the case files flagged by vice for the last twelve months. Her goal: to gather the name of every snitch used by every detective in the city for the past year—with no one becoming the wiser. Poaching a snitch was the equivalent of sleeping with another detective's wife. No one did it. If word got out how she accumulated these names, no detective on the force would have her back again.

They searched for names, addresses, hangouts, and affiliations of anyone who provided actionable intelligence on anything drug- or gang-related. Each worked on their own in silence, compiling their lists and making notes until the elevator dinged down the hallway.

Eric tapped on his desk. "Time to pack it up."

Sloane nodded and logged off.

Moments later, Lieutenant West walked in, loaded with her briefcase and travel coffee mug. "You two are in early."

"Just wanted to catch up on some paperwork." Eric stood up from his chair. "We'll be in the field most of the day gathering intel on a new dealer spotted near Mission High School."

"I wish everyone on this floor had your initiative. Keep me posted." West headed into her office.

Junior partner or not, Sloane had enough experience to know going outside official channels meant taking chances and bending the rules. The less Lieutenant West knew, the better.

"Ready for some breakfast?" Eric grabbed and zipped up his warm coat.

"Sure." Sloane retrieved her jacket. "I missed omelets with Avery and Reagan this morning."

While they walked toward the elevator, Eric slung an arm over her shoulder. "Then I think we're going for omelets. How about Sally's?"

"Sounds good." Once in the elevator, Sloane leaned against the far wall. "Nice move back there."

"This is another teaching moment, grasshopper." Eric held up the notes he'd been taking down for the last two hours. "I did *not* lie. The paperwork is right here, and we *are* spending the day in the Mission District, tracking down a drug dealer. I didn't, however, specify which one." He finished his lesson with a full, toothy grin.

"I like your style, Decker."

* * *

Hand-tailored designer suits meant money, but when they were worn by bureaucrats, more times than not, it meant they wanted you to think they came from it. Finn Harper came from money and could spot a poser with ease. Something about AUSA David Quintrell's Brioni wool two-piece suits gave her the impression he worked hard to impress. He had transferred from the Central District to the Northern District of California a year earlier. She would have liked to cut him some slack, but him showing up an hour late for a scheduled meeting pissed her off.

"Sorry to keep you waiting." Quintrell strolled into the eighth-floor conference room in San Francisco's Federal Building sixty-four minutes late, according to Finn's watch. "I only have ten minutes, so let's make this quick, Nate."

Smug and late. "You'd have more than ten minutes if you were on time for once," Finn mumbled under her breath. She predicted this wouldn't go well. A man in his forties should have better manners. In order to preserve his pristine conviction rate, this Assistant US Attorney insisted on dotting every I and crossing every T before he'd agree to pursue prosecution. She expected nothing less from him today.

Prichard shot Finn an annoyed look and then turned to Quintrell, sliding a folder across the conference table. "Did you look at the Rojas file?"

"What do you need from me?" Quintrell unbuttoned his single-breasted suit coat and ran a hand through his short black hair before sitting at the head of the table.

"We're in the early stages of bringing him on as an asset, but he's been skittish since Los Dorados has a history of eliminating weak links. Now we have him on manslaughter, and I want to cut a deal so we can take down the entire enterprise."

Unable to keep her disapproval in check, Finn shifted in her chair and rubbed her lips.

"You disagree, Agent Harper?" Quintrell tapped his caramel-colored finger against the dark cherrywood conference table.

Finn hesitated. Everything about Quintrell and Prichard screamed politics—always out for the big busts and sweeping prosecutions. Sometimes that meant making hard choices for the greater good, but this didn't make the cut in Finn's book. Justice fueled her corner of the world, not politics. She'd never cut a deal with a child killer.

"A sixteen-year-old girl died, as well as a promising college student. He needs to pay for that. I was the one who flipped Rojas, and I'm confident, given time, I can find another asset who can help us take down Los Dorados."

"Damn it, Harper." Prichard popped his head toward her. "We've been through this."

"I'm sorry, sir, but someone needs to speak for those victims and their parents. There has to be another way." Finn expected to take a spear. They'd bickered about this earlier, but once Prichard kicked it to the US Attorney, he rightly expected her support.

"It took us six months to find him, and I'm not starting from scratch." Prichard sucked in his upper lip, shaking his head from side to side. "He's our only way in, and I'm taking it."

Us? I did all the legwork. Finn rolled her eyes.

Quintrell appeared unamused by their squabbling and checked his watch. He turned to Finn. "How did you find Rojas in the first place?"

"A teenager busted in Oakland for possession gave up Rojas as his dealer. I tracked him down, did some digging, and discovered his older brother who raised him recently started a nickel stretch for burglary. I suggested we could get his brother's sentence reduced if he cooperated."

"Has he given you any actionable intel?" Quintrell finally showed a glimmer of interest.

"Not yet. We were working with Contra Costa County to reduce the brother's sentence. Now he wants immunity for himself on top of that arrangement." Everything about this deal gave Finn a chill. She was sure Rojas believed he had the DEA over a barrel, and Prichard played right into his hand.

"Is he still in PD custody?" Quintrell's glimmer waned.

"We couldn't risk Los Dorados thinking he'd been compromised, so I had him released before they knew he was missing. I have a team tailing him." Prichard leaned forward, placing his elbows on the table to emphasize his point. "Look, this is the highest profile case we've had in years. I honestly believe Rojas can provide us with enough information to take down a drug syndicate that stretches over two states. We need to get to the source, and this is our one chance."

Other than being unamused and unimpressed, Quintrell was hard to read. He twisted and cracked his neck before standing and buttoning his jacket. "This sounds like a hot one. Sit on him for a few days so I can bounce it upstairs."

Finn assessed the delay without asking for more evidence as uncharacteristically weak. She didn't know what to think of it.

"A few days?" Prichard's voice ended on a high pitch.

Quintrell reviewed something on his phone. "I need to line up our resources with other ongoing prosecutions in the office. It shouldn't take too long. My secretary will get back to you."

Prichard's expression matched Finn's disappointment. He didn't receive his green light, and Finn didn't convince either of them that Diego Rojas needed to pay for the deaths of Shellie Rodriguez and Michael Wong.

Prichard marched out into the hallway. The veins above his collar popped against his red-splotched skin. "You're pushing it,

Harper." After they entered the empty elevator, he turned to her. "You're good, but don't you ever undercut me like that again. If you do, you'll find yourself in Bakersfield sifting through drop spots in cattle manure."

"Cutting deals with nonviolent offenders is one thing, but a murderer?" Finn squared her shoulders, confidence growing inside her. "It's never right to let someone like this walk."

"You don't think I know that?" Prichard leaned into Finn's face with a clenched jaw. "I'm thinking about the hundreds of victims who might die if we don't get Kiss off the streets and every member of Los Dorados behind bars."

"I understand the concept of the greater good, but it does nothing to serve justice for Shellie and Michael and gives little solace to their parents."

"You're still young and optimistic. We can only do so much with the resources we're given, and I get paid to make the hard choices. Now, if you can't live with that, I suggest you find another line of work. Are we clear?"

"Crystal."

* * *

After talking to five hookers and as many drug addicts, Sloane still had no clue where to find Diego or his lab. On top of several of her own snitches, she and Eric still had another two dozen of San Francisco's lowlifes to track down to have a "friendly" conversation. She'd been camped out next to a run-down, hourly-rate motel in an unmarked sedan for the last two hours with the hope of finding the next one on her list. The result: her back ached and every little thing grated on her nerves.

"Now, this one pisses me off." After reading the next name on the list of snitches they'd compiled earlier that morning, she threw the papers on the seat next to her. "How did vice get their claws into Amber James? She's been on my roster for years."

"She's double-dipping." He shrugged. "Happens more than you think."

"I know." She quivered as if spiders had crawled on her skin. "It's kinda like sloppy seconds."

She gave Eric a hard look when he laughed. She'd become territorial over her snitches and took pride in how dialed into the community she'd become. Why didn't she see this coming?

"You'll get over it." He laughed even harder.

A ding forced her to fish her iPhone out of her pocket. The notification screen lit up, showing an incoming text from Finn. Hadn't she done enough? Sloane thought before unlocking the phone to read the message. *Plz meet me Red's Pub 6pm re Rojas. U won't be sorry.*

"I can't believe her." Grumbling something else, she shoved the phone back in her pocket.

Eric had a puzzled look on his face. "She's only a snitch."

"Not her. Finn Harper. She wants to meet."

"You're playing with fire, Sloane." A disappointed sigh escaped from Eric.

"I told you, she's nothing to worry about. She wants to talk about Rojas."

"If you say so. Do you plan to meet with her?"

"I don't know." Sloane retrieved her phone and reread the message. "She *did* say I won't be sorry."

"Do it." Eric turned his head toward her. "Could be the break we need."

"I have a feeling I'll regret this." After she pulled out her iPhone for the third time and mumbled under her breath, she returned Finn's text with a single word, *okay.*

What are you up to, Finn?

* * *

Sloane was no stranger to Red's, though two years had passed since she last visited. She didn't need to. She had Avery. While not considered a trendy San Francisco hotspot, Red's had served as a cornerstone of the LGBTQ community for decades under the same ownership. When she walked in, nothing had changed. No gimmicks, no fancy furnishings or decorations, just your basic bar that offered a limited selection of greasy finger food.

When Finn suggested meeting here, the hairs on Sloane's neck tingled to a sense of trouble. Questions she had about Finn's sexual orientation disappeared, replaced by new ones about their past.

Dressed in a brown leather jacket that opened to a low-scooped white T-shirt, Finn caught Sloane's attention. Reminiscent of her junior high school style, this soft, casual look made her appear more approachable, a significant departure from the polished outer shell she had sported at their first two meetings.

Finn's choice of a table in the far corner made for an ideal location to hold a conversation away from prying ears—and from prying eyes for those worried about that sort of thing.

"I'm here." Cold and impersonal, Sloane took a seat across the table. "What do you want?"

"Thanks for coming." Finn met Sloane's glare with a soft smile designed to put Sloane at ease. It didn't work. "I hate how we left things the other day."

Sloane checked her phone and scrolled through a few apps. She figured if she hurried, she could make it home in time for dinner. "Can we speed this up? I have better things to do than listen to you gloat over poaching my collar and giving him a pass."

"Gloating is the last thing I want to do. I pushed back on this as best I could, but my boss won't budge."

Sloane kept her eyes trained on her iPhone, sending the message she didn't want to be there. "It seems your best wasn't good enough."

Finn folded her arms and eased back into her chair. It became a game of patience to see who would break the silence first.

Sloane looked up, but Finn remained silent, refusing to break eye contact. *What are you up to?* She placed her phone on the table. "All right...I'm listening."

"Thank you." Finn smiled, acknowledging the break in hostilities. "Looks like the AUSA is cutting a deal with Rojas, and I can't live with that. Shellie and her parents deserve better." Finn pushed a USB stick across the table.

"What's this?"

"Surveillance video from inside the Firepit showing Rojas selling Kiss to Michael Wong, Shellie Rodriguez, and Deni Scott. Should be everything you need to get a conviction."

Sloane raised a confused eyebrow. The responding officers the night of Shellie's death noted security cameras but no active recording system. Who then disposed of the equipment?

"How did you get this?" Sloane inspected the stick.

"We were tailing Rojas. As soon as the first responder showed up at the Firepit, my team removed the recording equipment. We didn't know the extent of things, but we couldn't risk losing Rojas as an asset until we sorted it out."

"What's the catch?" Sloane sensed she could trust Finn, but she had never come across a Fed who offered a suspect on a platter to local cops without strings.

"No catch. Letting Rojas walk is wrong. Two people are dead because of him. I can't change things on my end, but I know this is personal for you. You'll do the right thing."

Sloane cocked her head from side to side. Bloated bureaucracies could be inflexible and uncaring, and it often required the kindness of an individual to secure justice. She sensed Finn could be such an individual, but she'd been wrong before. After all, she bounced Diego Rojas.

"So there's nothing in it for you?" Sloane intended her accusatory tone.

"Not a damn thing." Finn paused as if searching for the right words. "Correction, probably an unemployment check."

"You're willing to lose your job over this?"

"I am." Finn nodded, slow but sure. "I understand if you can't keep my name out of it."

Pulling the USB stick toward herself, Sloane searched Finn's eyes for any sign of deception but found only sincerity. "Tell me one thing."

"Anything."

"Why are you sticking out your neck for me?"

"We were friends once, weren't we?" A faint grin grew on Finn's lips.

"That was a long time ago. Why would you risk so much for someone you barely knew twenty years ago?"

"I knew you, Sloane." Finn's cheeks blushed.

"You never really knew me. How could you?" Sloane's defenses were up, and the words came out too sharp. The second they flew out of her mouth, she regretted them.

"I knew you liked me."

Sloane's memory was fuzzy. She wracked her brain to recall any sign she may have missed all those years ago. As she did, her heart fluttered, and she became that awkward thirteen-year-old who got tongue-tied whenever Finn looked her way.

"You knew?"

Finn's expression changed. *Sorrow or regret?* Sloane couldn't be sure.

"I knew. Why do you think we were always the last ones picked up? I used every excuse I could think of to spend more time with you after practice. I liked you too."

"Wow." Sloane fell back against her chair. *How could I have missed that?*

How different her childhood might have been if she knew Finn liked her. Maybe she wouldn't have spent the rest of her teenage years questioning her sexuality and sanity.

"So, you knew you were gay back then?"

"Hell no. I barely understood my feelings. Not until you left school did I put it together. I've always regretted not telling you. This," Finn pointed at the flash stick, "is my way of making it up to you."

Sloane twirled the USB stick between her fingers and considered everything Finn had said. "Thank you."

Finn slid a folded piece of paper across the table. "This is where he's staying. My guess is he'll remain there until we cut a deal. After that, he may go into witness protection. You have a small window of opportunity here."

"What are you proposing?" Finn had piqued Sloane's curiosity. She wasn't merely handing over evidence, Finn planned to hand over Rojas.

"We have Rojas on a loose leash until we cut the deal. He knows it and has been cautious about where he goes. He's figured out what our teams look like and has given them the slip a few times, but we've always been able to catch up with him."

"You're willing to let him off the leash?"

"I can come up with something and recall the team that's tailing him." Finn nodded. "It might take several hours to get another team on him. So—"

"So, we can wait outside, and once he sees his babysitters are gone, he might lead us right to his lab."

"And if he doesn't, you can still pick him up and make your collar." Finn pointed to the USB stick. "This is a murder one indictment served on a platter. No DA in his or her right mind will give it up without a fight."

"How much time do I have?"

"Twenty-four hours at most."

They stood.

Shaking Finn's hand would have been the prudent thing, but after everything Finn had said and done, it didn't feel like a handshake would suffice. Instead, Sloane wrapped her arms around her, just as she'd fantasized doing for months following the accident. When the full length of their bodies pressed together, her childhood dreams of holding Finn's hand and kissing her cherry lips rushed into her head.

Her pulse slowed, and her breaths became longer and more deliberate. When she was about to melt into Finn's warmth, a voice in her head screamed *Avery!* And she jerked away.

"Thank you, Finn. I'll be in touch." She hurried out the door, cursing herself for being such an idiot. *Damn it, Eric, you're right. I am playing with fire.*

CHAPTER NINE

Sloane couldn't have hoped for anyone better as a partner and mentor than Eric Decker. He treated her no differently because she was a woman or a lesbian unless they needed to use gender or orientation as an advantage. Eric only treated her as a junior detective who had earned her chops as a beat cop in one of the most active, crime-ridden districts in the city. Never strict about going by the book, he taught her to always do the right thing. When she had approached him last night about her and Finn's plan to arrest Diego, Eric didn't surprise her. He had only one question. "When do we go?"

After Eric parked their unmarked vehicle halfway down the block from the address Finn had provided, Sloane field-checked her service weapon, ejecting and reinserting the loaded magazine. "Last chance." Determined more than ever, she predicted he wouldn't back out.

Eric gave her a reassuring grin. "Send the text."

With no other words needed, she nodded and pulled out her iPhone and texted Finn two words: *In place.*

After Finn arrived at work, she sifted through the personnel training files of the agents assigned to the San Francisco Division. She grabbed the records of Agents Shipley and Barnes, the team keeping tabs on Diego Rojas, went straight to her office, and closed the door behind her. When she flipped through the files, she recalled the phone call she received from Sloane late last night.

"I'm in. Can you be ready on your end by noon?" Sloane had asked.

"I'll be ready."

As the division's new Assistant Special Agent in Charge, Finn managed the training and certifications every agent required to perform their duties. The agency kept electronic records, but firearms certification required paper copies with signatures, an archaic method that ensured accountability and one that Finn had determined she could exploit. She pulled out the current certificate for Barnes and left the previous one in place.

Now she waited. With time passing at a snail's pace, she tried busying herself, but the blowout she'd likely face after her boss found out that Sloane had arrested Diego kept her antsy. Should she back out? Not on her life. She'd given her word. Instead, she tapped her foot at a steady rhythm against the carpet while chewing the top of her pen into a mangled mess.

Her cell phone buzzed. An incoming text from Sloane. *In place.*

Without a single hesitation, Finn sent Barnes' firearms certificate through the shredder and then dialed his cell.

"Barnes." He clipped his tone.

"Agent Barnes, this is ASAC Harper. We have a problem."

"What kind of problem, ma'am?"

"Your firearms certification has expired. I have to suspend you from field duty until you recertify."

"What? I qualled two months ago. Check the files."

"I did. The electronic records show you attended training, but your file is missing the signed certification. Regulations require I sit you on a desk until I clear this up or you recertify."

"This is bullshit."

"Are you disobeying an order, Agent Barnes?"

"No, ma'am. When is our relief coming?"

"Let me worry about that. You two report back to the office ASAP."

"Yes, ma'am. We're packing things up and heading in now."

Finn ended the call and then texted Sloane: *Done. You have 2 hrs*

Eager to know whether the risk she took paid off, she tapped her mangled pen a few times on the desk. "Screw this." She grabbed her suit coat and keys and left the building.

Sloane read Finn's text. Within a minute, a black Ford SUV pulled away from the other end of the block. She and Eric didn't need to exchange words when the vehicle turned the corner. Diego's babysitters had left, and now they had to wait to see if he'd take the bait. Not ten minutes later, Diego emerged from the apartment building and headed down the street away from Sloane and Eric.

"Looks like we're on foot," Eric said.

Both unbuckled and followed Diego from a safe distance. For six blocks, she and Eric didn't speak while turning down several streets. Then, in a part of town where neighbors asked no questions and stayed to themselves, Diego entered the upstairs unit of a run-down duplex.

"This could be it." Sloane slid her hand inside her jacket flap and drew her service firearm from her shoulder holster.

Eric did the same, and they approached the front stoop and ascended the stairs.

"Was that a cry for help?" Eric whispered through his grin.

"Yep, a cry for help." A lie, but Sloane played along. They'd have to be on the same page when questioned about probable cause.

She tested the doorknob. Locked.

Eric had the superior leg strength, so he positioned himself on the right side nearest the doorknob.

Sloane took up position on the left and counted down using her fingers, three-two-one-zero.

On zero, Eric raised his right leg and kicked in the door. The wood of the frame splintered in a loud crack, and the door thudded against the wall on the left.

Sloane was first through. Her heart raced, but she remained steady. Having done this many times together, they'd perfected their technique enough to predict the other's moves.

Weapon drawn, she blocked the door from reclosing with her foot and assumed the close-quarters weaver stance with her arms folded in close to her body. The first open space appeared to be the living room. No targets in sight. "Go."

Eric burst through, weapon drawn. The room contained only a single tattered couch in the center and a scratched flat-screen TV on a stand against the wall. At the end of the narrow room, an open doorframe led to the kitchen.

Scuffling noise from the backroom caught Sloane's attention. She moved toward the sound. "Police!"

Eric took a few steps further in with Sloane three feet to his left. Rojas and another perp came into view. A shot rang out. Something whizzed past Eric's ear. He dove to the floor to evade a possible second shot.

Sloane's heart pounded, but her training kicked in. She trained her weapon on one perp, held her breath, and fired before he could get that second shot off. Double tap to the chest. Blood spattered the cabinets as her target fell to the floor.

Eric rolled to his knees and aimed his firearm at the other perp, Diego Rojas. "Hit the floor! Hit the floor!" Unarmed, Rojas raised his hands before falling to the floor in surrender.

Eric moved in, cuffed Rojas, and checked on the downed perp, freeing Sloane to clear the other rooms in the duplex, a single bedroom, bathroom, and closet. With no other spaces to check, she slumped against the wall. Given the amount of blood she'd seen, the man she shot had to be dead. Her hands shook. A volcano boiled in her stomach and crept up her throat. Lunch landed on the floor and her shoe, leaving a burning, bitter taste in her mouth.

She'd shot a man before, but never had she taken a life. After wiping her chin, she told herself, "Get it together, Sloane."

After taking a deep breath, she pushed herself from the wall and holstered her firearm. Squaring her shoulders, she returned to the kitchen. "All clear."

"I called it in." Eric pulled Rojas up to a sitting position against the kitchen wall, hands cuffed behind his back, and pointed at him. "Stay."

Eric placed both hands on Sloane's shoulders and looked her in the eye. "You okay?"

"I'm good." She was still shaky, but the queasy feeling had subsided and her pulse had slowed to normal.

"This was a good shoot. You didn't have a choice." He rubbed her arms in a way partners should, reassuring her she'd done the right thing.

She nodded, convincing herself she'd be okay.

"You did your job, Sloane. You're a damn good cop, and I wouldn't have walked through that door with anyone but you backing me up."

Eric said the words she needed to hear. After another deep breath, she scanned the blood-spattered floor then focused on Rojas. "The Feds can't help you now, you son of a bitch. You'll rot in Quentin for the rest of your life."

Finn cursed under her breath and drove toward the location Sloane had sent her in a vague text saying Rojas had taken the bait, and it didn't end well. *He bit. Shots fired. One down. Ellis & Franklin.*

Who was down? Diego Rojas? Sloane would've said if it was him, wouldn't she? No matter who it was, all hell would soon break out on the DEA end. She resigned herself to two possibilities: she'd either be working in Bakersfield or standing on the unemployment line by the end of the month.

She turned onto Ellis Street. A police cordon had cut off the city block, allowing only emergency vehicles through. After pulling up to the checkpoint, she flashed her badge and credentials to the uniform officer controlling access. He directed her to park in the first available spot, a few feet short of the coroner's van setting up shop. "This isn't good."

She scanned the scene until her gaze fell upon Sloane. *Thank God, she's all right. Her partner too.* After slinging a lanyard and her attached credentials around her neck, she approached the patrol car Sloane leaned against. When Sloane finished her conversation with Eric and Lieutenant West, Finn stepped forward. "Sloane, what happened?"

Sloane turned toward the sound of her name. Finn? What was she doing here? Someone in the DEA could link her to the crime scene. Whatever the reason, she welcomed the comforting face after taking a life.

Sloane explained the events of the last half an hour and pointed to the backseat of the patrol car. "And now Diego Rojas will pay the price for three deaths."

"I'm glad you weren't hurt." Finn stroked Sloane's arm. "I'll do my best to keep the political bears at bay once the news hits our office."

Sloane returned Finn's gentle touch with one of her own on the small of her back. "I appreciate that, Finn. Eric and I have your back too."

Eric raised an eyebrow.

The CSI van crept by. Sloane caught a partial glimpse of Avery in the front passenger seat when it passed. *Is she crying?* Sloane yanked her hand away from Finn's back as if caught doing something wrong. She had done nothing amiss this time, but if she were honest, that hug last night was dead wrong.

The technician parked several yards away. Avery stepped out and went right to work, setting up her command post.

Fuck. The snub stung Sloane like a wasp. Every fiber in her wanted to explain, tell Avery it wasn't what she thought, but her mea culpa would have to wait until they were alone.

Expecting her wife to follow her routine, Sloane waited. Avery should first survey the scene, help set up the equipment her team would need, and then let her technicians start their systematic process of collecting evidence. Lastly, Avery would return to the command post to catalog and organize their findings. She didn't reappear.

She's avoiding me. I need to fix this. She and Eric needed to book and question Diego, but first, she needed to make sure Avery's imagination didn't fixate too much on her and Finn.

Sloane turned to Eric. "Hey, before we go back to the squad room, I should tell Avery's team about losing my lunch earlier."

"Sure, but make it quick."

As soon as Sloane stepped inside the duplex, her chest tightened. Nothing could shake the sense of finality that she'd taken a life here. When she took a few more steps inside, the coroner and his assistant maneuvered past her, wheeling a gurney between them. On top stretched a black plastic shroud encasing the body, but there was no covering up what she had done. She killed him. When the plastic brushed against her hand, her gut twisted like a bowtie, making her unsure if she'd ever have the stomach for it. *Killing is an awful thing.*

Focusing, she shook off the unnerving sensation and continued into the kitchen. One of Avery's techs had snapped a few photographs of a section of blood spatter on the kitchen wall. She cocked her head to make sense of the pattern. Parts of it almost resembled a floating butterfly. It confused her that something so violent could produce something so beautiful.

She pulled her attention away from the wall. "Santos?"

The tech raised his head. "Bedroom."

"Thanks. By the way, that vomit in the hallway is mine."

"Good to know. I'll make a note."

When Sloane turned down the short corridor, she struggled to make out Avery's faint voice and settled on, "I can't deal with this right now."

So, she did see something outside.

Sloane stopped and gulped. After a year of marriage, she preferred one of Avery's tongue lashings over her silent treatment, which meant among other things days or weeks without sex or watching her sensual dressing routine. At least when they argued, their emotions ran hot, and more times than not, ended in equally hot sex. Straightening her back and shoulders, she turned the corner and entered the bedroom.

Following her usual procedure, Avery was working the perimeter first, as evidenced by the yellow hard plastic number tents along the walls. Busy marking boxes full of various powders, most likely the ingredients used to press the Ecstasy into Kiss, she had yet to inspect and tag the mechanical pill press resting on a wooden platform in the room's center.

Sloane leaned against the doorframe. She watched Avery write something on her clipboard and then reach up and push back a few strands of hair behind her ear. Sloane took in a sharp breath at Avery's exposed long, smooth neck. It was only last night, she nuzzled into that patch of skin before falling asleep.

"Hey." Sloane's voice was soft as a whisper.

Avery popped her head up from the clipboard. "You shouldn't be in here. Homicide has the scene now."

"You didn't come back outside." Sloane slid her hands in her front pockets to mask her nerves. "You're avoiding me."

"No, I wasn't avoiding you." Avery stood from her kneeling position and gave her a curious look. The redness around the rims of Avery's eyes told Sloane she'd been crying. *I need to fix this.*

"I've kept my promise." At least today she had.

Sloane disappointed herself. The night before her wedding and the Michelle debacle, she promised to never touch another woman like that again. Yet without thinking, she had. But were last night and today completely mindless? Deep down, if she were honest with herself, she felt a pull toward Finn. Though she was positive she wouldn't act on it on her worst day, it still bothered her.

"What?" Avery squinted her eyes and went about the room, inspecting this and that and scribbling on her clipboard. "I can't think straight right now. I'm shorthanded today and have a lot to do. Can we talk when I get home tonight?"

"We can and we will." Sloane reached out for Avery's arm when she maneuvered toward the pill press. "I love you, Avery."

"I love you too." Avery reached around the press and released a lever. Something clicked. A rapid electronic beeping pierced the air. She took a second to recognize the sound, turned her head in one sharp motion with panic set in her eyes. "Bomb!"

Sloane grabbed Avery's hand, yanking her toward the door. They had only seconds before the booby trap exploded.

"Bomb! Run!" Avery yelled loud enough to alert her team.

Sloane's pulse raced, but her focus sharpened. She had to get Avery out of there. With a tight grip on her hand, she extended her stride out the bedroom door. If she let go, she feared she'd lose her forever. With the end of the hallway in sight and the exit steps beyond, she pulled harder and stretched her legs to their maximum.

Then, a loud, fiery blast. The concussion knocked out portions of the roof and bedroom wall connected to the living room. Shrapnel flew in every direction.

The world around Sloane slowed, just as it did in the accident with her parents. A hot gust of air blew her off her feet and catapulted her in the air. She floated and flailed her arms. A sharp pain radiated up from her ankle, but she couldn't scream. The blast had forced all the air from her lungs.

A sudden stop.

Her body thudded against a wall, forcing a sudden inhale of smoke and dust. More pain. Everything hurt. As rafters, beams, and debris rained down, she fell to the floor, and everything went black.

Seconds later, Sloane's ears rang, something low-pitched. Her head pounded, and her whole body ached. Thoughts slowly coming into focus, she moved her arms. Explosion. Fire. She opened her eyes, but the smoky dust cloud made it hard to see. "Avery!"

When Sloane didn't hear a response, panic set in. "God, no. Avery."

Nearby, Avery's technicians lay dazed and injured. Groans and the crackling sounds of settling rubble filled the room. Smoke and dust choked out much of the oxygen. As they came to, the injured coughed. One voice cried out, "Help me. Please help me." Another screamed, "Oh, God! Where's my leg?"

Sloane tried to push herself up, but a sharp pain shot through her lower leg and forced her back to the debris-littered floor. Her foot had twisted to an odd angle, and a bone protruded from her ankle. "Fuck!"

Only getting to her wife mattered. Sloane dragged herself back toward the bedroom. Her stomach knotted and her breathing was labored as she clawed her way over drywall and wood fragments. Adrenaline masked the pain from her ankle. She called out again, "Avery! Avery!"

A pile of debris, several massive beams crisscrossed like fire kindling, stopped her advance. She spotted a bloody arm. "Oh, God. No!"

From the other room, voices yelled out. "Help them. Sloane? Sloane?" She recognized one voice as Eric's.

"Over here!" she shouted. "In the hallway." Moving forward, she reached out and grabbed the hand peeking out from the pile of heavy wood. Avery answered her silent prayer when her hand twitched, followed by a faint groan. "Thank God. Avery, can you move?"

Eric turned the corner and stopped short of the debris. "God." He bent to help Sloane.

"No!" She shoved away his hand as if it burned. "Help Avery." Another moan. "We have to help her."

In a desperate rush, Sloane pushed herself up on an elbow and pulled at the drywall atop the pile while Eric shifted a large beam to expose Avery from the chest up. Several oozing, deep gashes had blood covering most of her face.

"I got you, baby." She grabbed and squeezed Avery's hand. "We'll get you out."

Avery shifted her head toward Sloane's voice and opened her eyes. "Babe." Her weak voice cracked. A slight, cold squeeze of Sloane's hand signaled she didn't have much time.

Eric tried moving more beams, but they'd wedged atop one another, each at an odd angle. Impossible to lift, he'd have to cut them. He pulled and strained so hard the veins in his neck popped.

"They won't budge. Can you move, Avery?" He tried again.

More alert, Avery tried but couldn't move her legs, nor her other arm. "I can't, I'm pinned in."

Desperation fueled Sloane. She dropped Avery's bloodied hand and pushed while Eric pulled, but nothing moved enough to free her. Images of her mother pinned in the wreckage of their family car flashed in her head.

A slight smell of gas wafted into the hallway. Sloane's eyes grew wide and locked with Avery's. "Not again. Not again." At a feverish pace, Sloane pushed and pulled on anything in sight. Her heart and breaths whipped into a frenzy. She couldn't give up like she did before. "Not again."

Finn burst in from the living room. "Gas. Fire. We have to go."

Eric tried again to lift the beams while Sloane clawed at the debris faster and faster. She ignored her own pain, enough to double over a horse. "We have to save her."

Finn rushed to Sloane and grabbed her by the arm. "There's no time. We have to go!"

Desperate, Sloane clutched onto Avery's arm. "Not without her."

Avery blinked her eyes and took a deep breath. She pulled on Sloane's sleeve. "It's no use. Go, Sloane. Save yourself."

Not those words again. Sloane stopped and fixed her stare on Avery. "I can't leave you."

Avery turned to Eric. "Save her."

Eric gave her a reluctant nod and lifted Sloane up by her arm.

She grabbed Avery's hand like a vise and thrashed to break Eric's grip. "Nooooo."

Sloane fought to keep her gaze on her wife. She memorized the color and shape of her eyes and the love she drew from them. Then her grip ripped away. "Nooooo! Let me die with her."

In one violent tug, Eric struggled to move Sloane toward the exit. Tears rolled down Avery's cheeks. She reached out for one last touch, "Go, baby. Reagan…She needs you. I love you, Sloane. I love you."

Eric's feet slipped several times when he pulled Sloane to her feet, still squirming to break his grasp. Finn grabbed her other arm to help.

Tears streamed down Sloane's cheeks, making her screams indecipherable. They made her give up, and soon she'd have no reason to live. Soon an explosion or fire would consume the woman she loved and confirm her greatest fear.

Within seconds, Eric and Finn buddy-carried her limp body out of the living room and the duplex to the exterior stairs. As they reached the bottom step, the duplex exploded in a loud, bright flash of fire, blowing them to the ground. Debris flew in every direction, and pieces of walls and cabinets rained down on them.

No one could have survived that explosion. Sloane lay there frozen in the knowledge Avery had died. The horror of witnessing her mother burn to death flooded back, and her body drowned in the terror and agony of her truth—*Everyone I let in dies.*

By the time a half-dozen fire trucks arrived on scene, it had hit her. Reagan had lost her mother like she had lost hers. The dam broke. Sloane wailed and clutched her stomach, unable to loosen the wrench of reality. She called Avery's name until a paramedic held her down and gave her a shot of something to calm her. Before she faded out of consciousness, she mumbled, "I'm cursed."

CHAPTER TEN

Standing amidst the debris, Finn stood helpless as paramedics splinted Sloane's ankle before strapping her to a backboard and onto a gurney. One arm guarding her queasy abdomen, the other bent at the elbow with a balled-up hand covering her mouth, Finn could do nothing but watch. She hardly knew Sloane, she reminded herself, yet her heart was ripping in two. None of this would have happened if she hadn't broken protocol, citing righteousness to assuage her conscience. Her motivation, though, was more personal—it was for Sloane. Now, Sloane had paid a steep price for her breaking the rules.

Sloane remained unconscious, but Eric held her hand all the way to the ambulance. When he stepped up to board, a paramedic raised his hand and warned, "No room, you need to follow."

Eric didn't put up an argument, but he pointed at the medic. Anger dripped from his voice. "She's a cop, a damn good cop. You take care of her, you hear me?"

"Don't worry, I got her." The paramedic used a reassuring tone and gave Eric a nod. "We're taking her to Bayside."

After securing the back doors, Eric pounded twice on them, signaling the ambulance could take off.

Once the other ambulances left, carrying away Avery's injured techs, Eric looked left and right. He located the correct patrol car and locked stares with Diego Rojas. With each step he took, his face grew redder in a fast and furious march. Ripping the rear door open, he snatched Diego by the shirt collar out of the backseat and hurled him against the fender. "You son of a bitch."

"Decker!" West shouted.

Smaller and not as strong as Eric, Finn flew up behind him, her training and instincts kicking in. Simultaneously, she pulled the back of Eric's shirt collar and pressed her foot down hard on the back of his knee. Forced to loosen his grip on Diego, he fell to his knees.

"Eric, don't. He's not worth it."

While Eric remained on the ground and nursed his knee, Finn returned Diego to the backseat and slammed the door. Hands on her hips, elbows locked, she lowered and shook her head to shed the self-blame. If not for her act of kindness, Sloane and others wouldn't have been hurt, and that woman wouldn't have died. She couldn't let Eric ruin his career over something she caused.

Finn helped him up. "We already lost one good member of your department today, let's not make it two."

"He has to pay." He lunged toward the patrol car, but Finn positioned her body between him and Diego.

West placed a hand on Eric's shoulder. "If I have to get the governor involved, there's no way he's walking." She waved over a uniformed officer and pointed toward Diego. "Johnson, book him into county." Once Johnson acknowledged, West looked at Eric. "He can wait. You go check on Sloane and go back to the squad room after you're calm."

"What about Reagan?" Eric clenched both fists, his face still red as the fire trucks clogging the street.

"I'll send a patrol to her school and have them take her to the hospital."

"I should be the one to tell her."

"You're right, but after we know more about Sloane. Are you okay to drive?" West placed a palm on his heaving chest.

"I'll drive." Finn pulled Eric along before West could object. "Come on, Decker. Let's go."

Once on the road, Finn called into her office to advise Prichard about Diego Rojas and the explosion. His shortsighted directive that they take jurisdiction and still use Rojas as an asset set her patience on edge. "This thing is already headline news," she told him. "There's no way Rojas can give us any more than he already knows."

"We've invested too much time and money to just hand him over to the locals."

"Yes, sir, I know that. But a CSI agent was killed, and I doubt the locals, as you call them, will give him up without a fight."

"Quintrell is breathing down my neck. Find out where they're holding him and consult with the district attorney. Then get back with me."

After finishing her call, she slipped her phone into her pocket, mumbling, "Asshole."

"I can't believe he still wants to make his case using Rojas." The muscles in Eric's jaw rippled as he ground his teeth.

"Yeah, well, that will never happen. Not if I can help it." Weaving her way through heavy traffic, she tried to wrap her head around why this case had become so crucial to Prichard and Quintrell. She didn't understand what had them all hot and bothered to return Rojas to federal jurisdiction.

Eric studied Finn for several beats. "Sloane told me what you did. You got guts, Harper."

"Maybe, but I probably won't have a job after this."

After several more twists and turns in traffic, she worked up the nerve to ask about her assumption. "Was Avery her wife?"

Eric nodded and cleared his throat when his voice cracked. "I was her best man."

"And Reagan?"

"Avery's teenage daughter. This is an awful mess."

So much loss. Sloane without her wife and Reagan without her mother. Finn was familiar with the pain of loss, but at least she had her father to get her through it. "Does Reagan have a father?"

"Dead."

Finn glanced at Eric as he scraped a shaking hand against his stubbled chin. He appeared heartbroken. It all began to sink in. Sloane and Reagan would be alone in their grief.

She parked her car in Bayside Hospital's lot for official vehicles and turned off the engine. The silence in the car thickened while guilt mounted. She twisted the vinyl on the steering wheel. "I feel responsible for all of this."

"So do I." His face had turned pale.

After a few more silent moments, Finn shifted in her seat to face Eric. "When you question Rojas, I want to be there. He was my asset, and I want to see him go down."

Eric studied her again as if debating whether he could trust her. He paused after opening his door. "Under one condition."

"What's that?"

"You give us everything on him."

"Happy to."

Once inside, the emergency room head nurse pulled them aside. "Sergeant Sloane is still unconscious and being prepped for surgery. A compound ankle fracture is tricky. It'll be at least four hours before you can see her." She handed Eric a business card. "This is my personal cell. Call me, and I'll update you."

Eric thanked her and turned to Finn. "You ready to get answers?"

"Most definitely." With four deaths to lay at his feet now, she jumped at the chance to extract every bit of information out of Diego Rojas. More than ever, she wanted to put Los Dorados and their Kiss operation out of business.

Diego Rojas repeated the same phrase throughout the booking process. "I want a lawyer." He made his one phone call to the public defender's office, the last critical piece of procedure needed before Eric and Finn questioned him. Finn guessed he realized whatever leverage he may have had with the DEA to stay out of prison had burned up in that duplex.

In the rank interrogation room, sitting across from Diego and his public defender, Eric pointed to ADA Kyler Harris to his right. In her forties, she looked the part of a hard-nosed prosecutor. She was professional and poised with her crisp skirted suits and perfectly bobbed black hair.

"She is your only hope of keeping a needle out of your arm. You've racked up four bodies."

One at a time, he slammed four pictures on the table. "Michael Wong. Shellie Rodriguez. One of your fellow dirtbags. And Avery Santos." Eric slapped down an official SFPD photograph. "She was a friend of mine."

The public defender, clad in his department store dark suit and clearance sale Oxfords, examined the photographs. "Is there a question here, Sergeant?"

Leaning against the door, Finn had many questions, but the first answer she wanted was who ordered and rigged the lab to blow.

"Two innocent people are dead because of the crap you peddle. Now, a damn good CSI is dead because you rigged your lab with a bomb. My question is, was it worth it?"

Diego squirmed in his chair and blurted, "A bomb? I had nothing to do with that. You can't pin that on me."

Eric jumped up, and his chair flew out from under him. He slammed his fist on the metal table, causing Diego to gulp at the small dent left behind. "That was your damn lab, your damn drugs. Her death is on you!"

When he cocked his clenched fist back, Finn rushed forward and blocked it with her arm. "He's not worth it." Finn's eyes pleaded with him to choose another path. Like in the car ride from the explosion scene, she recognized the strain in his jaw. She figured he'd reached his breaking point.

Lieutenant West burst through the door. "Take a break, Decker."

"I got this, Eric." West placed a hand on his shoulder. "Get some air."

After giving Diego a death stare, he stormed out to the observation room and joined Prichard and AUSA Quintrell.

Lieutenant West motioned for Finn to join her at the table with ADA Harris to continue the questioning. Finn could cut through Diego's bullshit and get the information they wanted.

She pulled up a chair and leaned back, confident she had the upper hand. "You've stepped in it, Rojas. If you had nothing to do with rigging your lab, then you should ask yourself who did and why?"

Diego squirmed in his chair.

"It's obvious Los Dorados knows you're a snitch. The deal I offered you is off the table, including your brother. Now, let's make this quick. You're looking at a death sentence in San Quentin, either by the state or by Los Dorados. And your brother, he still has four and a half years left at Solano."

Diego's eyes widened, assuring Finn she'd hit his soft spot.

"But you know how prison life goes when they don't follow the rules. He could end up in solitary at Pelican Bay. If you give us everything you know about Los Dorados, the DA will take the death penalty off the table and offer you twenty-five to life."

Diego and his lawyer whispered back and forth and nodded in agreement.

"He wants two things." The lawyer's Adam's apple bobbed once, giving Finn the impression he was in over his head. "First, to serve his time at Solano with his brother. Second, my client contends he had nothing to do with the explosive device. He fears for his life and wants you to place him in the protective wing with weekly visits with his brother. You make those things happen, and you have a deal."

The offer posed a simple concession. Diego would avoid the death chamber, which wouldn't please Sloane or Eric, but they would have actionable intel to take down Los Dorados. Finn could live with that.

"Give us something we can go on, and you have a deal." ADA Harris leaned back and folded her arms over her chest, waiting for the return volley.

Finn leaned forward, elbows on the table; she'd been after this information for months. Her grin faded when she tallied up the heavy price Sloane's family had paid for her to get to this point.

Diego tapped his fingers on the table at a rapid pace and then rubbed the back of his neck.

Finn didn't care about his nerves nor that the information could put a bounty on his head. "Enough of this stalling crap. You told me before that Los Dorados was behind the manufacturing and distribution of Kiss. Let's start at the beginning. How did you first get involved?"

"You already know my brother, Miguel, brought me into Los Dorados to sell X and crack in Oakland. After a while, he introduced me to Caco."

"Caco?" After months of legwork, Finn had a name of someone up the chain, despite Los Dorados running such a tight ship. Her instincts were right. Diego was the key.

"He's the only one I took orders from. He provided everything to set up my own operation..." Diego recounted his first meeting with the mysterious Caco.

* * *

Oakland, California, six months ago

Diego and Miguel turned up the sidewalk toward a dilapidated pre-WWII home in the Lower Bottoms, a gang-controlled area on the west side of Oakland. After the appropriate three rapid knocks, the door opened, and a trusted Los Dorados lieutenant greeted them with only a nod.

Without a word, the man escorted them to an unfurnished back room. Specks of dust floated in the scant streaks of light cast between the wood slats covering two broken windows. Several other members of Los Dorados stood in a semicircle, silent, giving the impression any one of them would slice Diego's throat if he spoke out of turn.

In the middle stood Caco, polished in his imported silk suit and $200 haircut and taller than the rest. Not in street clothes, not clad in layers of chained bling, nor inked in tattoos like the others.

Caco broke the silence. "Miguel tells me you are quite the soldier and have sold more product than anyone else. You have my respect."

"Thank you, Caco." Diego held his head low, hands clasped in front of him. He dared not make eye contact until asked.

"I'm told you are ready for more responsibility. Is that correct?"

Diego kept his head bowed. "Yes, sir. I am."

"Then look me in the eye and tell me so."

Diego lifted his chin and stared at Caco. "I'm ready for any task."

Caco cocked his head left and right. He inspected him, rubbing his chin with his left hand, on which half of his pinky was missing.

"All right then, we shall see if you are ready. I am extending our market to San Francisco. You will set up production." Caco snapped his fingers, and another man came forward. "Rafael will teach you. He will provide you with the ingredients each month. You will produce and sell the product as you see fit. Rafael will also collect. If you are one penny short, you will pay the price. If you do well, I will pay you beyond your dreams. If you disappoint me…"

"That won't happen, Caco. I will make you a rich man."

"I am already rich. The only question is, are you capable of making yourself rich also?"

"Yes." Diego puffed up his chest.

Finn considered Diego's story. Why would Caco have Diego produce his own supply of Kiss and not provide the finished product himself? In a moment, she realized that she'd stumbled across a brilliant decentralized manufacturing operation, one that ensured if law enforcement compromised one site, others in the region would still be viable.

"Ingenious. How many production sites does Caco oversee?"

"I know of five. Mine, Oakland, Richmond, Vallejo, and one in San Jose. But I'm not sure where. Caco told us to move our labs each month to avoid detection."

With the operation more extensive and sophisticated than Finn had suspected, she hated that she'd proved Prichard right. They needed to find the money source to take down the entire operation.

"Where does Caco get his materials?"

Diego shook his head. "He never told me, and I never asked. I overheard Rafael mention one time, though, that Caco had dealings in Mazatlán."

Diego confirmed Finn's suspicion about the cartel. Even if they took down Los Dorados in northern California, the cartel had an enormous reach with tentacles in every border state and then some. In the middle of a drug war, Finn had to concentrate on winning this battle. She, along with Eric in the other room, had her sights on Caco from Mazatlán.

* * *

The door leading into Reagan's last class of the day, her least favorite, Algebra II, swung open. The trim teacher, dressed in khakis and a light blue button-down, stopped scribbling numbers on the whiteboard stretched across the wall at the front of the classroom. When he turned toward the motion, he pushed up wire-rimmed glasses held together by a Sesame Street Band-Aid. Reagan giggled. He broke those glasses a month ago and still hadn't replaced them.

"Can I help you?"

All eyes in the classroom turned toward the door, including Reagan's, who welcomed the disruption from the mind-boggling lesson on polynomials.

The school vice principal stepped in, accompanied by a uniformed SFPD officer. In mid-sway, she caught the lanyard strung around her neck that dangled a half-dozen keys and a faculty badge. "I need Reagan Tenney."

Reagan knitted her brow at the sound of her name. She recognized the officer as the one who had taken her statement at the Firepit the night Shellie died. Did this have something to do with her death? Was she in trouble because of it? Her chest tightened at the prospect.

The teacher turned toward the rows of student desks, his eyes zeroing in on the back of the room. Before he called out her name, Reagan closed her book and stuffed it into her backpack. A queasiness bubbled in her stomach while she slipped on her jacket and grabbed her belongings. As she walked toward the officer, she glanced at the empty seat in front of her, the grim reminder her best friend would never finish high school.

In the privacy of the empty hallway, the officer's radio squelched some codes about a robbery in progress, prompting him to turn the volume down. "Miss Tenney, there's been an accident, and I'm here to take you to the hospital."

Reagan thought the worst and tightened all her muscles, causing her stomach to turn rock hard. "Is it my mom? Is it Sloane?"

"All I can tell you, miss, is that Sergeant Sloane was injured and is in surgery." He extended an arm toward the school exit. "I'm here to escort you."

As she walked down the hallway, chills crawled up her spine when repeated calls to her mother's cell phone went unanswered. *Mom must be really upset if she's not picking up.*

She sat in the surgical waiting room, an ache forming in the back of her throat as her questions to the officer standing watch went unanswered. She looked down at her hands. She was clutching her silent cell phone so hard her light brown fingers had turned white.

With nothing to do but wait, she ran countless possibilities through her head, her worries focused on her mother and what would happen if Sloane didn't make it. As a single parent, Avery had spent her days either working or taking care of Reagan, not dating much and not with time-consuming hobbies. The few times she had dated, Reagan had done her best to tank the relationships before they took root. She now regretted her adolescent tactics.

Reagan never considered her mother unhappy or lonely until Sloane came along, but once they dated, Avery came alive. Her joy and giddiness spilled over at home and made Reagan want the elation of being in love for herself.

Soon Eric appeared. She'd seen him at the Tap and the house enough times to know Sloane considered him not only her partner but a family friend. Trembling, she darted toward him and wrapped her arms around his waist. "I'm so scared. No one will tell me anything."

"Let's sit down, Reagan." Eric squeezed his arms around her extra tight.

Once they found two seats in an area far enough away to provide privacy, Eric placed his hands over hers. "I have bad news, honey."

"Is it Sloane? The officer said she was hurt." A queasiness in her stomach persisted, knowing how this would devastate her mother.

"There was an accident at work today, and Sloane was hurt. She's in surgery right now and should be okay. Your mother was also in the accident." Eric swallowed hard. "But she didn't make it. I'm sorry, honey. Your mother is dead."

Reagan sat pale and slackjawed. Sloane was the one who had a dangerous job, not her mother. Her body shook slowly at first. Then faster and faster. Processing his words was unbearable. Dead. He said she died. That couldn't be right. It had to be a mistake, but the tears in his eyes told her it wasn't. Deep gasps for air replaced her silence.

Eric wrapped an arm around her and leaned her back in her chair. His tears mixed with hers, soaking his shirt. Except for the shock and pain, her mind was blank. The only constant in her life was gone.

Soon, a doctor in surgical scrubs with slumped shoulders and a lumbering gait entered the waiting area. The uniformed officer directed him toward Reagan and Eric, who he acknowledged with a nod.

"Reagan, I have to talk to the doctor," Eric whispered to her. "Will you be okay for a few minutes?"

Reagan raised her head. Her sobs had slowed, but her mind remained blank. She barely registered what he had said. Eric eased his arm away and pushed her back into her chair when he stood. "You wait right here." He pointed toward the tall, stubble-faced doctor. "I have to talk to him for a minute, okay? I'll be right back."

Eric pulled the doctor a few feet away. "How is Sergeant Sloane?"

"She's in recovery and doing well." The doctor removed his surgical cap patterned with rainbow-colored lightning strikes. *Mom would've liked it*, Reagan thought. "We repaired a compound fracture of the left fibula with a plate and screws and stitched up several deep cuts. She'll be in a cast for a while, and she'll need physical therapy, but she should make a full recovery."

"Thanks, Doc. When can we see her? I have her stepdaughter with me."

"Give her about another twenty minutes, and we'll have her in a patient room. Someone will get you." When the doctor placed a hand on Eric's shoulder, his tone changed from clinical to comforting. "Word has it the CSI killed in the explosion was Sergeant Sloane's wife. I'm very sorry for your loss."

"Thank you." Eric pressed his lips together, his Adam's apple bobbing in another hard swallow. "I don't know how we'll get past this one."

At a sensation on her arm, Sloane stirred, rustling her clothing. The confusion still had a grip on her. Her mind hazy, she didn't have the strength yet to open her eyes. *Where am I? What happened? Avery?* Bits and pieces of the day flashed through her head. A car. A house. Squad cars. Avery. A loud noise. They jumbled and overlapped. She tried to make sense of the pieces before she opened her eyes, but she fought waking up, fearing once she did, her life would never be the same.

A voice. Did someone say her name?

The sound pulled her further from her haze, ending the battle between life as she knew it and the one that would exist after she woke. She opened her eyes. At first, her surroundings were a blur, and then shadows came into focus one at a time. Avery came into view, but younger. Mid-length caramel blond hair against light brown skin surprised Sloane; she expected it to be longer. Her hazel eyes drooped with emptiness, unlike the soft warmth that had filled them this morning.

"What are we going to do, Sloane?" Tears dropped on Reagan's cheeks.

Sloane focused on the woman inches from her arm. The voice wasn't Avery's, but Reagan's. She reached up to wipe the teardrops from Reagan's cheeks.

Her mind had yet to come into full focus. "What's wrong, Reagan?"

"What are we going to do?"

She shifted her focus. The bed, machines, and curtains in the room's middle told her she might be in a hospital. She looked down to find her leg in a cast. The words "I love you" sprang into her head. Then a sense of panic washed through her. A flash of memory knotted her gut and swelled her throat.

Avery was trapped. Had been. Tears fell from her eyes. Avery was dead. Reality choked the air from her lungs. She grabbed the hand of her stepdaughter, the only living reminder of the woman she loved. Her voice cracked between the tears. "I don't know."

CHAPTER ELEVEN

One week later

Why do we have funerals? Why can't everyone say goodbye to Avery on their own time, not mine?

Sloane would sooner curl up on her couch with a bottle of Johnnie Walker than sit in the front pew of the chapel she associated with death. She'd been here twice to honor other fallen brothers in blue. The services were the same with full departmental honors. Local and state VIPs, along with off-duty officers representing agencies from hundreds of miles away, packed the chapel, while throngs of citizens paid their respects. Sloane wanted none of it, preferring to mourn her wife in her own way.

"Avery was part of the SFPD family. She deserves this," Eric had told her days ago. "I'll take care of everything."

"Then you do it the way she would've wanted, not her parents."

Sloane shifted on the cold, hard pew, adjusting her leg atop the stupid knee walker her surgeon convinced her she needed. The basket attached below the handlebar made her look like an oversized kid on a trike.

Damn, my leg is killing me. Where's my Norco? She forced her hand into her front pants pocket and struggled to fish out the container of pain pills. The hard back of the pew refused to give way, making her task more manageable. Soon her efforts morphed into a challenge: pull out the small container before tipping her leg off the fucking knee walker.

The department chaplain didn't pause in his speech but raised his eyes from the papers atop the podium when Sloane won her battle, booming the words, "Fuck yeah" loud enough for the front two or three rows to hear.

She didn't even like the meds, making this episode more pathetic. They made her nauseous, and she hadn't taken a decent shit in days, which made the hard pew even more uncomfortable. But she needed the little pills. Her ankle throbbed, and knives shot through it whenever she moved. At home, she alternated between Norco and scotch, but when she left the house today, her head was a mess and she forgot her flask. She wished she hadn't and had the added liquid courage to get through the endless speeches reminding her of how much she'd lost in the explosion. *Just as well*, she thought. Being high and drunk wouldn't help her keep the peace today with her in-laws.

Across the aisle on the pew to her right, Avery's rarely seen homophobic parents looked as uncomfortable as Sloane. They'd never accepted Avery as a late-bloomer nor their marriage and sitting in a chapel next to other gays and lesbians appeared to be making their skin crawl.

Besides a strong showing from their fellow men and women in blue, many neighbors, friends, and staff members from the Tap filled the large chapel. Sloane pictured Avery alive and taking charge, directing foot traffic and ordering around the staff to bring in extra chairs for those standing.

After swallowing a Norco, she snickered at the vision of the poor staff members scurrying around, following Avery's orders. Her ill-timed laugh caught Reagan's attention and earned the ire of her now former in-laws, Luiz and Maria Santos. Thankfully, the aisle separating them placed Sloane outside spitting distance from Luiz. If the Santoses had had their way, some priest Avery had never met would be standing up now and granting Avery absolution for her sins. Loving and marrying Sloane would be at the top of that list.

"What?" Reagan, seated to the left, scowled at Sloane as if scolding an unruly kindergartner. If not for the opioid buzz from the previous pill, Sloane would've complimented Reagan on her choice of the knee-length black dress that covered her cleavage and arms down to her elbows. Then again, like herself, everyone was wearing black, so Reagan simply blended into the crowd. Even the SFPD dress uniforms were black.

"Nothing," Sloane whispered. The comfort she had drawn from imagining Avery alive faded when the SFPD choir broke into another hymn. Their melodic voices rattled the rafters and reminded her why Eric had brought her there—to celebrate Avery's life and service.

Sloane only half-concentrated on the ceremony, willing herself to not have another breakdown. Over the past week, she'd had too many of those, almost one every waking hour since she came out of the anesthesia in the hospital. For insurance, she popped a second Norco on the way to the gravesite to make it through the burial.

Though Avery was not a sworn officer deserving of full-departmental honors, Eric ensured uniformed pallbearers carried her casket. The ceremony ended with a six-person team folding the American flag with reverence and presenting it to Sloane. The morbid souvenir did little to soothe her pain.

The nasal sound of bagpipes playing "Amazing Grace" accompanied Avery's casket into the ground. Clutching the three-point folded flag against her chest, Sloane couldn't watch her wife disappear into the earth for eternity. Instead, she closed her eyes and imagined Avery next to her, holding her hand and whispering, "At least it didn't rain today, babe. You know how much I hate the rain."

The pills still had Sloane on an opioid buzz when she arrived at the Tap for the reception. Dylan had set aside a comfy chair along with a padded stool to prop up her leg. He'd offered to place it at her and Avery's usual table, but she refused. If she couldn't sleep in her own bed, how could she bring herself to sit at the table where she and Avery shared their first kiss? How could she look at the table where she proposed and where they dined on their wedding night?

Dylan brought over a glass of her favorite scotch. "I thought you could use this." He placed it down after she offered a weak nod. "Hope everything is to your liking because I plan to pamper you and Reagan today."

She craned her neck and pushed herself up a few inches off the chair and scanned the buffet table. "Everything looks great. I really appreciate it. Did you put out the empanadas Reagan likes?"

"I sure did." He looked at Reagan, who had sat next to her. "I'll have someone bring you a plate right over."

"Thanks, Dylan." Reagan didn't smile and only nodded.

When Sloane glanced at Reagan, guilt crept up on her. Since Eric brought her home from the hospital, Reagan had yet to spend more than an hour away from her. She tended to Sloane's bandages, fetched her food and drink, and helped her to the bathroom until she got the hang of the crutches. *Staying busy must be her way of coping*, she thought.

"Can I get you anything?" Reagan repositioned Sloane's cast to the center of the footstool. Sloane was ashamed to admit she enjoyed having Reagan as her nursemaid. She craved the sound of Reagan's voice while she fussed. Reagan possessed the same mannerisms and her voice had the same lilt as her mother's. And when Sloane closed her eyes and listened, she could hear Avery giving her words of advice.

"You take a break; you've earned it." Sloane patted Reagan's hand. "There're plenty of people around here who can treat me like a queen."

As if on cue, Eric stepped up to their table. "Can I get you two anything?"

Sloane waved her hand at Eric and turned to Reagan. "See, we're royalty today. We don't lift a finger." She returned her attention to Eric. "No, I'm fine."

Eric frowned and raised an eyebrow. "I know you haven't eaten since this morning, and that was only toast. I'm fixing you a plate." He shifted his attention to Reagan. "Help me watch her and make sure she doesn't just move it around the plate like she does at home."

With no fight in her today, Sloane didn't put up an argument. Her stomach queasy from the Norco, she nibbled here and there from the plate Eric fixed her. Several guests had dropped by her table to pass along their sympathies and offer support in the coming weeks. After each awkward departure, she took a swig of her scotch. With Dylan refreshing her drink without prompting, she'd lost track of how many shots she'd put away. She figured it must have been several since she no longer felt her broken ankle and was more lightheaded than she could remember being in years.

She turned her attention to Reagan. "You have two sets of grandparents here. You should spend more time with them."

"I don't like Mom's parents. They hated that Mom was gay, and they hate you."

Sloane had met them only once before, following her and Avery's engagement. Though that meeting didn't go well, Sloane learned how Avery acquired her unique physical appearance. She got her father's dusky skin and height and her mother's dark blond hair and hazel eyes.

"I know, honey." She patted Reagan's hand. "But they're leaving tomorrow. At least sit and talk with them for a few minutes before we leave, okay?" She scanned the room and found the Santoses seated at the same table as the Tenneys.

"Now's your chance. They're all together." When Reagan rolled her eyes, Sloane slurred, "I'll send Eric over to rescue you in about fifteen minutes. Would that help?"

Reagan sighed but agreed. After she joined her grandparents at the other table, Sloane finished her scotch and waved at Dylan for a refill.

"I think you've had enough for now." Eric raised an eyebrow, concern etched on his face. "How about some coffee?"

"When your wife is killed, you tell me when enough is enough." She shot Eric a cold stare.

Eric had no clue what was swirling in her head. Why would he? She never told him she shouldn't have let her guard down and fallen in love. Deep down, she knew better. Every time she let someone in, they died—her parents, officer Bernie, and now her wife. They all died because of her.

Dylan scurried over and delivered another round.

"Thanks, D." Only the alcohol coated her tone. She was too tired for much else, and it would take a lot more than an unwelcome concern to rile her up.

Eric gave Dylan a furtive headshake and a hand signal to cut Sloane off for the day.

Too drunk, too high, and too clouded by her own sorrow, Sloane ignored the pain in Eric's eyes. *Cut me off? Screw you.*

Not five minutes later, Reagan stormed back and slumped down in her chair next to Sloane. "I can't believe them."

"You can't believe who?"

"Grandpa and Grandma Santos. They want me to live with them and said they'd take me to LA tonight. They don't care what I want."

Sloane turned her stare to the Santoses. They came from meager means, running a neighborhood bakery in a low-income area of Los Angeles, and she'd cut them slack. Too much, she realized.

"If they think they can get their claws into you now that Avery is dead…" She snatched up her crutches. "…they have another think coming."

Not too familiar with California guardian laws, Sloane recalled Reagan's grandparents had some rights, but they had crossed a line. She wobbled when she stood, but Eric steadied her.

"Let it go, Sloane." Eric's calm voice didn't persuade her.

"You have shitty advice today. Reagan is my daughter, not theirs. I need to make that fact crystal clear." She turned to Reagan. "Stay here."

Sloane placed the crutches under her arms and hobbled over to the grandparents' table with Eric steps behind her. With every step she took, her anger boiled a little hotter. Avery had talked about how she loved her parents, but that until they accepted her sexuality and Sloane as her wife, she didn't want them in Reagan's life. Sloane intended to remind them of that.

She stopped a foot short of Luiz and Maria and blurted out, "What the hell were you thinking, asking Reagan to live with you? Did you ever think of talking to me first?"

All eyes focused on her. Caleb stood and offered his chair, but Sloane raised one of her hands from a crutch. "I'm fine, Caleb, thank you." She turned back to the Santoses. "Well?"

Luiz glared, the lines along his face telling of a hard life working twelve-hour days at the bakery. He wiped his mouth with a napkin. "I wasn't aware we needed your permission to speak to our own granddaughter. She's our flesh and blood, not yours."

So, this is how it's going to be. "Well, you do. She's my stepdaughter, and Avery appointed me as her guardian after our wedding." So far, so good. Sloane managed to not blow up the beach while drawing her line in the sand.

"She is not your daughter, but she *is* our granddaughter." Maria turned to look Sloane in the eye. She had no other children or grandchildren, and her gaze suggested desperation to hold onto family.

Sloane clenched her jaw to cap the volcano steaming within. A heat formed from her neck and rose to the tips of her ears, sobering her enough to hold her temper for the moment. "The law says I decide what's best for her."

"You corrupted our daughter." Luiz refused to look her straight in the eye, but he made his contempt clear. "You're sorely mistaken if you think we'll let you corrupt our granddaughter too."

Pressure built with those words. Like Mount St. Helens, she erupted. "For God's sake, I buried my wife today!" A crutch fell to the floor. She pointed a finger an inch from Luiz's face. "You couldn't wait a single damn day to start this fight?"

Caleb retrieved the crutch.

"Let's table this for another day." Eric steadied her by the elbow. "Mr. and Mrs. Santos, I have to ask you to leave."

"You're the reason our daughter is dead." Luiz shot up from his chair and grabbed his coat while Maria did the same. "This isn't over."

"You son of a bitch." Sloane dropped her other crutch and lunged toward Luiz on one leg.

Before she reached him, Eric pulled her back. "That's it. You two need to leave now, or I'll have you escorted out." After the Santoses stormed out, Eric helped her into Caleb's chair.

"Is there anything we can do to help, dear?" Janet rubbed Sloane's arm.

"Short of bringing Avery back, I don't think so." The Santoses were right, and the truth of Avery's death ran over Sloane like a box truck, leaving her dizzier from breathing hard. On the verge of another breakdown, she tried to focus on anything else, but her jumbled mess of a mind wouldn't let her.

"We want you to know as far as Caleb and I are concerned, you are and will always be Reagan's second mother." Janet's voice floated softly like a feather. "Avery was a daughter to us, and since the day you married her, we've considered you a daughter too. That will never change."

Tears pooled in Sloane's eyes right before the dam broke. She'd lost her wife, and now this kind woman was offering to substitute for the mother she'd lost twenty years ago. Her body shook at her kindness, forcing her to cover her face with her hands. She whimpered, "Thank you."

"My dear, dear Sloane." Janet wrapped an arm around her and pulled her in tight. "You're not alone in this."

Eric kneeled beside Sloane. "Do you want to go home?"

Several guests still milled about. She shook her head and wiped the tears from her face. "No, not yet. Let me say goodbye to a few people first." Her ankle throbbed and her toes were swelling like balloons, but she needed to get through it. "I would like to go back to my chair, though, so I can elevate this damn thing."

"Your wish is my command." Eric helped her stand, and then to her surprise, he swooped and cradled her in his sturdy arms. "Let's go, Princess."

She rested her head against his strong, broad shoulder, his arms cradling her like a father would hold a newborn, gentle and loving. Not since the morning Avery died had she received anything more than a hug. She missed the comfort of being held. In those few steps across the room, she closed her eyes and imagined Avery's arms around her, warming and soothing the ache in her. Then he placed her in the chair, and Avery's arms vanished.

She discovered Dylan had changed out her scotch for coffee and water. *Damn it.* After that dustup, she didn't want to feel anything. Stuffing her hand in her pocket, she fished out her Norco bottle and popped her third pill of the day.

One by one, she thanked her guests, Finn at the end.

"Hey." Finn's voice bordered on shy.

"Hey." Sloane tried to flatten her tone. The full effect of the Norco had numbed her, but not so much she'd forgotten the last time she'd seen Finn.

Finn sat on Reagan's empty chair. "Your daughter looks so much like her mother."

How does she know what Avery looks like? The pain pill and last bit of scotch slowed her thinking. "Huh?"

"The photo display at the funeral home."

"Ah." Sloane nodded at a slow, medicated pace before inspecting her glass of water, wishing it was scotch. "She sounds a lot like her too."

"That must be both comforting and cruel at the same time."

It was. At night, when Reagan tucked her in the makeshift bed in the living room, Sloane would close her eyes, ask a question, and listen to Reagan's voice. When she called her name with the same familiar lilt, she swore Avery had walked into the room. Then, she'd open her eyes to Reagan sitting beside her, and the cycle of tears would start all over again.

Sloane locked her gaze on Finn. "You should've let me die with her." Her lips quivered.

Her stomach tightened when a hot burning sensation bubbled in the back of her throat. What little food she had in her stomach, along with a mixture of scotch and water, came up. The burst of foul liquid missed her propped-up leg and landed on the floor. She coughed and gagged, but she couldn't get the nasty acid taste out of her mouth.

"Here, sip on this." Finn handed Sloane a glass of water from the table and rubbed her back until she composed herself. "Avery was only half right. Reagan needs you, but you also need her."

Focusing, Sloane shook her head. "Avery's father was right. She's dead because of me."

Finn shook her head with disgust. "He's a piece of work."

"You saw that, huh?"

"It was kinda hard to miss, but I think you handled it the best you could. If you need any legal advice, Daddy runs an incredible law firm and has a stable of lawyers who would love to help you." Finn fished through her purse and pulled out a business card and handed it to her without reading it.

"Thank you." Sloane tucked the card in her coat pocket. "But Luiz is all bark, no bite."

"He's wrong, you know." Finn's eyes welled up as she placed her hands atop Sloane's. She welcomed the touch. "I'm to blame. If I hadn't—"

"No, you did a good thing." While she shifted her hands to cup Finn's, Sloane shook her head hard to fling the guilt out of her. "I'm the reason she was in there. I'm the reason—"

"Don't blame yourself—"

"You don't understand. It was my fault."

"What was your fault?" Finn's sad eyes turned confused.

Sloane shook her head again, unable to say the words. She couldn't say she'd made Avery angry and distracted her like she had done with her father. They all died because of her.

"Look at me, Sloane." Finn raised Sloane's chin with her hand. "You didn't place that explosive device. Someone else did. I promise you I'll find who did and make him pay for taking Avery away from you."

Sob after sob, Sloane's body quaked. Only she knew what happened inside that room in the duplex. One thought ran through her mind: she was meant to be alone. Maybe the Santoses were right—Reagan would be better off with them.

Across the room, Reagan emerged from the restroom and ran to Sloane's side. She glared at Finn. "What did you say to her?"

"We were just talking about your mother." Finn's eyebrows arched.

Reagan's nose and face wrinkled when the pungent smell of Sloane's mess wafted upward. She stepped out of the curdled puddle. "Oh, God. Not again." She waved to get Dylan's attention.

He dashed over. "I'll get someone to clean this up." He took off in a rush.

"Let's go home." Reagan took on a mothering tone, something Sloane regretted but was helpless to do anything about. "I'll get your walker."

"I don't think she'll be able to use that thing or her crutches." Finn looked left and right. "Where's Eric?"

"He went to help my other grandparents." Reagan glanced toward the main door.

"How about I call her a cab or Uber?"

"We live only a block away."

"I can make it." Sloane slowed her sobs and tried to stand but wobbled.

"Whoa." Finn grabbed her by the elbow and sat her back in the chair.

Eric walked through the front door. Reagan called him over and explained about Sloane's condition. Eric placed a reassuring hand on Reagan's shoulder. "Get her things. Finn and I can carry her home."

Weak but somewhat alert, Sloane didn't fight when Finn and Eric each slung one of her arms over a shoulder. She surrendered when they walked her up the street toward the townhouse. With each step they took, Sloane stepped with her right leg, the motion stirring unpleasant memories. Every step toward her house equated to a step out of the duplex where she left her wife to die. Her loud, gut-wrenching wails pierced the damp, night air all the way home, not the giggles and laughter she shared with Avery a few weeks ago on their anniversary.

Once inside, Reagan took charge. She had the Tenneys fix sheets and blankets on the couch for Sloane's bed. Janet and

Finn offered to get her ready for bed, but Reagan stopped them. "I got this."

She'd done this every night since Sloane's return from the hospital. After the first challenging evening, she developed a routine that worked. She'd change Sloane's clothes, position an ottoman at the edge of the couch to give her more room to prop up her casted foot, and then pull her covers up and kiss her on the cheek. Sloane closed her eyes and fell asleep.

"She'll be fine for a few hours." Reagan padded to the kitchen. After filling a glass with water, she placed it along with aspirin and Sloane's pain pills on a couch-side table.

"You do this every night for her?" Janet's mouth was agape.

"Sure." Reagan nodded and shrugged.

"You sweet, dear." Janet pulled Reagan in for a tight hug. "You shouldn't have to do this on your own."

"We're fine." Reagan pried herself from Janet's arms. "Eric helps when he's not working."

"But he goes home at night, right?" Janet received a nod from Reagan. "That's it. I'm moving in with you until Sloane is back on her feet."

Reagan wrestled with her grandmother's offer. She could use the extra help when she returned to school. Then again, staying busy is what was helping her cope with her own grief. She had a routine, and if she kept to it, she wouldn't have time to think about how much she missed her mother. "But—"

"No buts, young lady. You need time to grieve too. I'm staying."

CHAPTER TWELVE

Leg in a cast, unable to drive, and restricted to a couch day and night, Sloane came to consider her townhouse a prison. In a dark funk, she wore the same shorts and tank top for days and smelled bad too. She'd opted for only one sponge bath since the funeral, citing the clunky cast as her primary excuse.

Every corner of the townhouse evoked a heart-wrenching memory. When the kitchen light flicked on, the morning ritual of cooking breakfast and sliding against each other as she and Avery danced to music floated in the air. When sunlight shined through the dining room glass door, the bay beckoned her to relive the evenings they spent in the deck chairs watching tankers float by.

Numbing herself any way she could proved the only way Sloane got through the day. Janet, though, had eyes in the back of her head and made for a strict babysitter, a talent that must've been honed during her years as an elementary school teacher. She kept track of when Sloane had last taken a pain pill and when she could take the next, but Sloane outsmarted her. Janet had yet to discover her secret stash of Johnnie Walker in the space between the couch cushions.

"You're not due for another pain pill for an hour, so I brought you another icepack, dear." Janet applied a large, frozen blue therapeutic bag over Sloane's cast. "Any preferences for dinner tonight?"

Sloane forced herself to a more upright position on the couch without tipping over the fresh ice pack. Nothing these days sounded good to eat. She simply wasn't hungry. Maybe the Norco had her too constipated or the scotch had her nauseous, but her appetite had bottomed out. The only thing she could think of was Avery's favorite. "Migas would be nice."

"Well then, that means I have extra time on my hands before dinner. How about we get you into the shower and a fresh set of clothes?"

"I don't know, Janet." Personal hygiene had taken a backseat as had everything other than nursing her ankle and wallowing in grief. "I don't have the energy today."

"A quick shower will do you wonders. I'll set everything up and then come back and help you wrap your cast." Before Sloane could object, Janet bounced out of the room.

Sloane slid her hand between the cushions and pulled out a half-empty bottle of scotch. She took one large swig. Then a second. The liquid warmed her throat but did little to warm her mood. Instead, the alcohol relaxed her body, and she sank further into the cushions, focusing on the cold emptiness around her.

Once Sloane's eyes closed, the liquor's warmth masqueraded as Avery's warm body pressed against hers. She imagined herself in Avery's arms with her head resting on her chest and let the memory of Avery's rhythmic breathing take her to a time before the explosion. These escapes never helped, but she couldn't end the cycle. She didn't know how. She was stuck with no relief in sight.

A tug on her shoulder brought her back to reality. When she opened her eyes, Reagan was standing over her, saying she needed to take a shower.

"Come on, Sloane." Reagan pulled her up and threw one of Sloane's arms over her shoulder. "I got you."

When they reached her bedroom door, the room she and Avery had shared, Sloane froze. "Please, not here."

"We don't have a choice. It's the only walk-in shower on this floor. No more sponge baths for you. Janet's orders." Reagan readjusted her grip. "Besides, everything is ready."

Unconvinced, Sloane remained nailed to the floorboards.

"Mom would hate to see you like this. You always dressed so cool around her."

A memory tugged at Sloane. Avery once told her that her modern tomboy look of jeans, T-shirts, and wool sweaters "oozed cool and sexy at the same time." Sloane didn't pattern her style after anyone in particular, rather she developed it over time. Reagan was right. Besides missing the way Avery's eyes devoured her when she rocked her favorite jean jacket, she missed the way she felt in it.

"Maybe it's about time." Sloane took a deep breath and pushed forward past the guest room and into the master bathroom, where Janet waited.

"You made it. Sit." Janet offered her a seat atop the toilet lid. "Everything is ready, including the plastic stool in the shower." She wrapped Sloane's cast with a special plastic bag and secured it with a rubber band. "I can stay."

"I'll be fine. If I need help, I'll give you a shout."

Sloane could easily maneuver in and out of this shower, even with her casted leg. After her grandmother had her first stroke, she had equipped the stall with handicap rails to accommodate her frail body. Never did she think she'd use them while grieving Avery.

"I'll pull out clothes and have them ready for you when you finish up." Janet's puffy-cheeked smile never failed to put Sloane at ease.

With some effort, Sloane undressed and hopped the few feet to the shower and turned on the water. After it warmed up, she grabbed the handicap rail and sat on the plastic stool buttressed against the far wall. Using the hose and wand, she let the water beat down on her shoulders and back.

Soon images of her slinging Avery's leg over her shoulder the morning of their anniversary while the water pounded her muscles flooded back. When their insides had finished pulsating, she remembered pulling their wet bodies together and savoring the feeling of touching skin to skin. Avery's breasts pressed an inch below her own, she had stroked the length of her cheek with her fingertips before kissing her. She whispered, "I love you, Avery Santos."

"*Pick yourself up, baby.*"

"I can't."

"*Reagan needs you more than you know.*"

"I know she does, but I can't do it without you."

"*You can.*"

"Where do I start?"

"*By getting dressed.*"

Simple yet true. Avery always gave her sound advice. Taking the first step meant getting back into a routine.

While the soap and water refreshed her body, it also diluted her grief. She hoped its effects would last longer than her scotch. Once she toweled off and put on clean underwear, she grabbed the crutches Reagan had left inside the bathroom door. She hobbled into the bedroom, where she found Janet and Reagan sitting on the bed.

"You look so much better." Janet drew one hand to her chest and pointed to the bed with the other. "I pulled out this purple sweater and a pair of sweatpants. I didn't think you could get a pair of jeans over that cast."

"Thank you, Janet. These will do." Sloane ran her hand over the sweater laid atop the foot of the bed and remembered the first time she wore it for Avery. Her eyes watered. "I wore this on our first date."

"It's quite fetching." Janet rubbed a section of purple wool between her fingertips.

"Avery thought so." She ran a hand across the sweater one more time. "It was the first time I saw her checking me out."

"Mom was checking *you* out?" Reagan jerked her head back. "I would've thought it was the other way around."

"Oh, I did my share, but your mom surprised me that night. I didn't think when she asked me out for a drink, it would turn into a date."

"Wait." Janet did a double take. "She asked *you* out for the first date?"

Her disastrous first encounter with Avery played in her head and almost brought a smile to her face. "She wanted to apologize for biting my head off when we first met. The next thing I know, she's kissing me on the cheek."

"That's sweet." Janet's rosy cheeks glowed through a wide smile. "So, you kissed on the first date."

"Oh, no. Avery made me wait weeks for that, but it was so worth it." Sloane dressed. For the first time in days, it felt good to remember.

* * *

A month after Sloane woke up in the hospital with a cast on her leg and no wife, Janet returned to Reno, taking her daily encouragement with her. The townhouse took on an oppressive atmosphere, not unlike how she felt when she first moved in after the accident. When Reagan went to school and the house emptied, her couch reminded her of solitary confinement. It became clear why inmates who transferred back to the general population after months in isolation were worse off than when they went in. Like Sloane, they had only their regrets to keep them company while in there, and she had plenty.

From the singing that had caused her parents' accident to the insecurities that had cost her Avery, she had a lot to regret. But mostly she regretted ever believing that she wasn't meant to be alone. She was a death magnet; it was only a matter of time before fate took everyone around her.

Now that the Norco and booze had run out and the nearest liquor store was too far for her to get to with her walker, she developed a new way to cope. Every day at precisely 10:55 a.m., five minutes before the Tap opened, she hobbled to the front door of her townhouse. She exchanged crutches for the knee walker and pushed out the door and down the street. Before she settled into the comfy chair Dylan kept out for her at the Tap, she told him to send over a scotch.

"You're getting along pretty good on that walker." Dylan set the drink down in front of her.

"It gets me where I want to go." Sloane shrugged, swirling the liquid in her glass and musing she had nowhere else to be but here and home. Sipping long and slow, she welcomed the warm feeling it provided like an old friend. Scotch never got too close, never passed judgment; it always made her feel better.

"Can't do much else until I get this cast off." She didn't want to do much either. She especially didn't want the company. When Dylan made no effort to retreat behind the bar, she peeked up from her glass. "If you don't mind, I'd like to be alone."

With a sigh, he returned to his perch but kept an eye on her from behind the bar. His periodic surveillance kept Sloane uneasy.

When a few regulars stopped by her table, she politely brushed them off, preferring solitude over companionship. With the server, she managed a weak "thank you" when he delivered a second round. After checking her watch, she calculated Reagan would be home from school in an hour.

"Sloane?"

She turned. "Finn?"

"Mind if I join you?" Finn had on the leather jacket that reminded Sloane of their younger days. Sympathy, however, had replaced the glint of attraction that had been in her eyes when they reunited almost two months ago.

"I don't need your pity."

"You don't have it." Finn pulled out a chair and sat next to Sloane.

"Then why are you here?"

"Because we're not so different." Finn's lips pursed.

Sloane studied her for several beats, unsure what she meant. Her fleeting curiosity failed to chip away her apathy, so she swigged the last few drops of her old friend and waved at Dylan for a refill.

Finn eased Sloane's hand down, but Sloane jerked it back. "You're where I was ten years ago."

"And where was that?" She thumped the glass on the table.

"At the bottom of a scotch bottle, blaming myself for killing the woman I loved." Finn pointed at the empty tumbler, still ringing from Sloane's fit of temper. "You drink to forget."

"Sometimes forgetting is easier than remembering." Her eyes inched up. Finn had struck a chord, but Avery was the latest in a trail of death she'd caused, starting with her parents.

"I know how overwhelming survivor's guilt can be, Sloane. When I was in law school, I fell in love with a woman." Finn's eyes brightened to what must have been a warm memory. "She looked a lot like you. We had two wonderful years together until another car hit us head-on. I was unhurt, but Isabell died."

Moisture pooled in Sloane's eyes. *She understands.*

"I was behind the wheel and blamed myself for the accident. Second-guessed everything I did that night. What if I had left the restaurant five minutes earlier? Five minutes later? Stayed in the right lane instead of the left? Would she still be alive? There was a time when I wished I'd died with her."

Tears trailed down Sloane's cheeks. "How do you get past it?"

"Time. I didn't heal until I looked at things the other way around. What if she had survived and I was the one who died? I would've wanted her to be happy and find love again."

"I can't forget Avery." Sloane buried her face in her hands.

"You'll never forget a love like that. Just like I've never forgotten Isabell."

"What about the rest?" She searched Finn's eyes again.

"The rest?"

"Have you found love again?"

"I've loved a few women, but none were *the one*. I haven't given up hope, though."

* * *

For a week, Sloane ruminated on Finn's words, every syllable of them soaking into her bones. While they didn't completely pull her from her funk, they made her feel less alone. Others had said the right things, but no one had made a dent in her grief like Finn had. She told herself their history likely made the difference and that it was, at the very least, only a beginning.

Sloane made her daily run to the Tap, and soon Dylan held up a serving tray with her requested glass of scotch. Only this time, he included two plates of fries and BLT sandwiches she didn't order. "It's break time. How about you join me? I made enough for both of us." Before she could object, he laid out the plates and Sloane's drink on the table.

"I'm not hungry." As it did most days, her appetite had left her today.

"Eat." He held out a rolled-up napkin along with a stern look and refused to drop his hand until she took it. "Good. Ketchup?"

She nibbled, he prodded. She used a spoon to scratch the skin under the top edge of her cast, and he laughed. This game went on until she ate half the food on her plate.

"I can't wait to get this damn thing off."

"When will that be?"

"Next week. Then I go into a walking boot." Sloane rolled her eyes. "Joy, another contraption to get used to."

His expression turned serious. "Do you remember the night I met you?"

"I remember you were skinnier back then."

"Too much of my good cooking." He laughed and rubbed his belly. "I remember you looked sad and lonely, and then your grandmother explained what had happened. You coped by coming in here almost every day after school, filling up ketchup bottles and salt and pepper shakers in exchange for free fries. Remember?"

Sloane nodded as the memory of those lonesome months during which the only bright spot came from this ex-hippie's kindness bubbled to the surface.

"You never grew out of your sadness until Avery came along. Any fool could see she made you happy. Now she's gone, and I see that sad, lonely girl again. You're coming here again to cope, only this time instead of filling shakers, you're filling yourself with scotch."

"My wife is dead. I'm nursing a broken ankle. What do you expect? Little Miss Sunshine?" Drinking too much too often beat a sobering reality. She downed the rest of her drink to counter its bitterness.

"Of course not. I know you're hurting, and I hate seeing you like this."

She threw her chin toward a particular table on the other side of the room. "I proposed to her right over there."

"I knew she would say yes. Come to think of it, that was the only time you ever bought the house a round." He nudged her on the shoulder. "Cheapskate."

The corners of her mouth turned upward. "Cop's salary."

"Is that a smile?"

A male voice called out from the main entrance, "I thought we'd find you here."

She looked toward the voice. "Fucking great."

Concern etched Dylan's face. "Do you want me to throw them out?"

"Hold that thought." She waited for Luiz and Maria Santos to walk up to her table. "What do you want, Luiz?"

"If you had answered one of our calls or returned one of our messages, you would know we're here to visit with our granddaughter," Luiz boomed, his voice as loud as a foghorn.

"My nonresponse should've told you something." The scotch in Sloane's belly fueled her anger. "Visiting her isn't up to you." She lowered her leg from the stool Dylan had set up for her and then reached for her crutches but slipped.

"Whoa." Dylan caught her by the elbow.

Maria took out her cell phone and started video recording Sloane.

"Why am I not surprised you're drunk again?" Luiz shook his head. "The PI we hired was right. You're in here drinking every day."

"You're having me followed?" Her sharp words helped her to steady herself on the crutches. "Who the hell do you think you are?"

"I'm Reagan's grandfather; that's who I am." Luiz's face reddened as he waved his arms in the air. "And based on what the PI told me and what I see today, I don't think Reagan is in a safe, healthy environment."

"You're one to talk." Luiz's words were a little too rehearsed for Sloane's liking. She suspected his visit coincided with a greater agenda. "Safe environment? You think having Reagan come live with you in a gang-controlled part of East LA is a safe environment for her?"

"At least she'd have someone sober to come home to after school." Luiz stepped up to Sloane, face-to-face, the onions he had for lunch curling Sloane's nose.

Dylan stepped in and eased Luiz back with his hand. "It's time for you to leave."

"And who are you?" Luiz shot Dylan daggers with his eyes.

"I own this place. If you don't leave, I'll call the police and have them throw you out. You and I both know how that would turn out."

Luiz harrumphed.

His smugness snapped Sloane's self-control like a twig. Death magnet or not, she wouldn't let Luiz run roughshod over her.

"If you think I'll let you see Reagan after this, you're delusional. You'll never see her before she turns eighteen. After that, it's up to her. You can turn your judgmental, homophobic ass around and go back to your little bakery in Los Angeles. And if you try to contact her without my permission, I'll file a restraining order against both of you."

"We'll see how much longer you can keep her from us." Luiz stabbed her chest with a finger. "You'll hear from our lawyer." He grabbed his wife by the arm and stormed out.

Dylan steadied Sloane on her crutches and helped her back to her chair. "Assholes."

"I'm such an idiot." She threw a crutch on the hardwood floor.

"I would've done the same thing." He raised an eyebrow.

"You don't get it." She may be grieving, but she knew the Santoses had set her up and she'd walked right into it. "I just gave them everything they need to win a custody fight."

"What do you do now?"

"I clean up my act."

CHAPTER THIRTEEN

Diego Rojas had never enjoyed wearing red. He complained it made him stand out from the monotone dingy fashion worn by much of the Bay Area streetwise. These days he didn't have a choice. His entire wardrobe composed of red inmate clothing provided by the San Francisco County Jail at 850 Bryant. But that would change in twenty-four hours. Tomorrow, he would trade in his red pull-up pants and sweatshirt for Solano Prison blues and start weekly visits with his brother.

He had a signed agreement with ADA Harris to reveal the final crucial piece of intelligence on Los Dorados after she put him on a transport bus bound for Solano Prison. The last piece of information consisted of the number to his burner phone, which had been destroyed in the explosion. With the crime scene technicians unable to find enough remnants, Eric needed that number to lead him to Caco.

For the past six weeks, solitary confinement served as Diego's home, the price for snitching on Los Dorados. He spent twenty-two hours a day in a six-by-eight-foot cell, mixing only with a small section of the general population when he traveled to and from the showers.

A guard appeared at the battleship gray bars separating Diego from the rest of the prisoners. "Shower time."

Dressed in a fresh set of reds and flimsy black rubber flip-flops, Diego threw a thin white bath towel over his left shoulder. He readied himself for the ultimate reminder of his incarceration and placed both hands through the center hole in the bars, one hand holding a well-worn bar of soap.

After the guard handcuffed him, he took the same route to the showers he'd taken at the same time every day for the past forty days. Today he had an extra pep in his step because this would be his last trip to the stench-filled inmate shower stalls. He would, though, miss having the shower all to himself.

With other cells on his right and dirty windows on his left, he followed the guard down the linoleum-tiled corridor. Once through the entrapment area, he made a left turn.

Like every day before, he leaned against the wall and waited while the last round of inmates exited the shower and passed him. When the final two inmates pulled up even with him, a scuffle broke out. Within seconds, the fight grew into a strangely quiet melee that involved half a dozen. Three inmates pummeled the single escort guard and pulled him to the ground while another two pulled Diego into the fight. Once he was on the floor, a third inmate pounced on him.

A sharp blade sliced his abdomen, impaling him once, twice, three times. In acute pain, he rolled to his side as a second guard entered his line of sight at the end of the corridor. The guard's voice echoed off the tiled walls when he talked into the radio microphone tethered to his shoulder. "Four eighteen in progress, corridor bravo six. All hands. Need all hands."

A piercing alarm blared throughout the jail, placing the facility on lockdown. Seconds later, his eyes fluttered open as dozens of booted feet, likely guards, swarmed the hall. In a blur of wheeling action, metal batons cracked body parts over and over until the fight quelled.

Something had dampened Diego's cheek. Teetering on the edge of consciousness, he rolled to his back, drew a hand to his face, and inspected his fingertips. Blood. He'd been lying in a pool of his own blood.

A guard squawked on his radio. "Inmate down. We need a stretcher."

After what seemed like hours later, two sets of hands loaded Diego onto a stretcher and weaved him down a twisting maze of corridors. One rectangle box of ceiling-mounted fluorescent lights after another flashed in and out of his vision. The pain had subsided, but he felt weaker with each passing minute. When they burst through two double swing doors, he sensed his chances of survival weren't good.

"Wheel him over there," a voice yelled out. Then the well-weathered, stubble-faced doctor leaned over him. His Adam's apple raced up and down. *Not him,* Diego thought. This one had a reputation of caring more for the vodka bottle in his lower desk drawer than his patients.

"On three," the doctor ordered. Diego hoped he had yet to crack open that bottle.

The stack of case files on Eric's desk had multiplied like bacteria cells on a Petri dish since Sloane went on medical leave. He had refused a temporary partner to help him work through the mounting caseload, rationalizing that Sloane would be back soon enough. Instead, he prioritized the cases and worked on ones he could handle by himself, holding back ones Sloane would want to tackle when she returned. With Lieutenant West's permission, he shifted the rest to other teams in the narcotics unit.

After thumbing through several folders, he found yesterday's report of a random locker check at a high school. In a field interview, the school resource officer reported discovering a handful of small drug stashes. One contained a heart-shaped pink pill. After he read the summary report, Eric's interest lay in where and from whom the high schooler got the pill. "A cousin?

Rohnert Park?" He was making a mental note to follow up when his desk phone rang.

"Narcotics. Decker."

"Sergeant Decker, this is Simpson from holding. You have an inmate in protective custody, Diego Rojas."

"Yeah? What about him?" The hairs on the back of Eric's neck tingled.

"He was involved in a prisoner altercation. They rushed him to the infirmary. It doesn't look good."

"No, no, no, no." Eric threw the phone down. The handset dangled over the edge of his desk, swinging like a pendulum.

His only link to Caco, his single lead to who planted the bomb that killed Avery, lay dying on a stretcher. He stormed out of the squad room and flew down three flights of stairs to the jail. Winded, he slammed his badge against the bulletproof window protecting the desk sergeant.

"Decker. My collar's in the infirmary."

The sergeant who spent more time in fast-food lines than the gym picked up his desk phone. "Let me check."

"He could be dying." Eric ground his teeth and expelled a sharp breath.

"I have to clear you."

"Open the fucking door!" Eric's voice traveled and rattled the barrier.

A uniformed lieutenant appeared behind the desk sergeant. He eyed Eric. "Open the door, Sam."

The door buzzed. Eric shoved it open and darted through without as much as a nod to the lieutenant. Running into the infirmary, he barked, "What the hell happened?"

The doctor and his assistant were working at a feverish pace to stem the blood loss. Wires dangled from monitors, and steady beeps showed Diego had a heartbeat.

"Shank to the abdomen." The doctor wiped sweat from his brow with a forearm, his latex gloves covered in blood.

Eric rushed toward Diego and took a position beside the medical staff. He leaned down, only a few inches from Diego's face.

"What's the phone number, damn it? What's the phone number?"

Diego coughed and spat up blood. A groan.

With his hands, Eric grabbed Diego's face to force him to focus. He then modulated his tone to make his message clear. "Damn it, Diego. Do the right thing here, and I'll make sure your brother gets out early. What's the phone number?"

Diego coughed through a slow, thready voice. "Two... eight...five...four...four...two... one."

The beeps stopped, replaced by one long single deafening sound. On the monitor, a flat line indicated that his heart stopped.

The doctor started chest compressions. He yelled out commands for injections, but the monitor didn't change. After twenty minutes, the doctor stopped, removed his latex gloves, and checked the clock on the wall. "Time of death ten forty-two."

In that instant, the game changed. Los Dorados' reach had weaved its way into the city's jail. Eric alone had the critical piece of information that could break their hold on California's drug market. Diego's death and a conversation he had with Finn a few weeks ago left him with one question: who had leaked Diego's whereabouts?

Eric left the jail. Instead of heading up to his squad room, he went toward the front door. He now suspected everyone in the building, leaving him with only his instinct to trust. After walking two blocks and out of earshot of anyone from 850 Bryant, he dialed his cell phone.

"We need to talk."

A heavy breeze swirled in from the bay, discouraging tourists from exploring the walkway in front of the Willie McCovey statue, Eric's chosen meeting place. On non-game days, the sparsely populated paths on the outer edges of China Basin Park outside the Giants baseball stadium offered an ideal meeting place. Their wide-open access made it easy to spot anyone approaching in either direction for hundreds of feet.

The chilly air prompted Eric to flip his collar up and stuff his hands in his coat pockets. His gaze settled on the flashes of sunlight dancing off the cars on the top level of the Bay Bridge as they zoomed into San Francisco. How many vehicles packed with bags of illegal drugs like Kiss would make it into his city today? Too many to count. Years of fighting this shadow war convinced him he couldn't stem the tide.

While he waited, he tried but couldn't recall in his twelve years on the force ever feeling unsure about whom he could trust in an investigation. In the past, he could always tell the good guys from the bad, but not this time. His instincts told him that someone on the good side had turned dirty.

He turned to the sound of his name.

"Decker." Finn paused when he turned. "Interesting choice of meeting places."

Her shoulder-length hair fluttered in the stiff breeze, while, like his, her hands sought shelter from the cold in the pockets of her jacket.

"You didn't have to help Sloane like you did, giving her the video from the Firepit." He scrutinized her face, settling on the fact he had no choice but to trust her. "You risked your life to save her at that duplex. That all tells me I should trust you."

She arched an eyebrow. "Is there a reason you shouldn't?"

He checked his surroundings to confirm no one could overhear. "Diego Rojas is dead. Shanked. I'm sure the incident report will read as a jailhouse fight spun out of control, but you and I both know this was a hit."

"Shit." She shifted several times, rubbing her forehead.

Unwilling to tip his hand yet about Diego's last moments, he needed to know what Finn knew. "A few weeks ago, you mentioned your office was slow-rolling on Los Dorados. Do you know why?"

"I've been pressing Prichard for weeks." She shook her head. "He refuses to budge on any of the leads Rojas gave us. He only said Justice was still coordinating across different regions and that our piece of it was on hold."

"Did he say who at Justice was pulling strings?"

"No, but Quintrell has been hot and cold on this case, so he must be under pressure too."

"First, someone was on to Rojas and tried to kill him at his lab. Now, someone got to him while in the secure wing of county jail." Eric rubbed the back of his neck to relieve the strain resulting from the facts underlying his next words. "We have a leak."

Finn nodded. "Only a few people knew about Rojas. The question is, what are we going to do about it?"

Eric reminded himself of the agony he witnessed in the remnants of Diego's lab. A piece of Sloane died along with her wife that day. For her sake, he needed to make everyone who had a hand in her pain pay dearly, starting with Caco. "We find the leak. We find Caco."

* * *

The doctor should have warned Sloane before he removed the cast earlier this morning. She expected her ankle to be stiff and for the hair underneath the plaster to be long, but she didn't expect this. "Dear God. It smells like a dead rat."

The doctor laughed. "It's all the dead skin that's collected for the last six weeks. A few hot showers should do the trick."

She'd lost the knee walker and crutches and, in their place, gained a walking boot. Her stride lumbered in the new contraption, a clumsy but welcomed freedom. Left with no other choice, she'd have to adapt for the next few weeks, but after that she'd be back in sneakers.

Choosing the short walk to the mailbox as the first real test, she hobbled down her driveway and up the street to collect her mail. The doctor warned Sloane her leg muscles would ache from months of nonuse. He was right. "Damn, I'm out of shape." The months of physical therapy the doctor recommended now sounded like a good idea.

On her way back to the townhouse, she flipped through the mail, discounting the mass mailings and local ads. She focused on the letters, stopping on one envelope from Avery's bank. Her lips quivered.

"I should've handled this weeks ago." Unable to accept the hard truth, she'd let her wife's unfinished business pile up. Now with the Santoses nipping at her heels, she needed to return to adulting and take care of it.

A car rolled up to the front of her house. A young, sloppy twenty-something stepped out while she plodded up her driveway. "Are you Manhattan Sloane?"

"Yeah, why?" She turned around. "Who's asking?"

The young man handed her a large, sealed envelope. "You've been served." He then turned tail, heading to the safety of his Prius and speeding off down the street.

Sloane stared at the envelope and read the label on the center: Jerry Heller, Attorney at Law, Los Angeles, California. "Fucking great." She ripped it open and scanned the legal documents inside. Blah, blah, blah. "Guardianship of the minor grandchild Reagan LeAnn Tenney."

"Son of a bitch. They'll never get their hands on her." She crumpled the papers in her fist, the good feeling she had a moment ago breaking down along with them. Just when she had made an inch of progress out of her grief, the Santoses' long reach pushed her back. *One step forward, two steps back.*

After slamming the mail on the kitchen counter, she pulled out a fifth of the scotch she'd sworn off but had discovered last night hidden between bottles of cooking oil in the back of the cabinet. She needed to forget. If she swallowed, she'd forget that the Santoses were fighting her because Avery couldn't. Forget that she had no idea how to be a mother without Avery to guide her. Wise choice or not, scotch posed a smoother road than the rocky one she found herself on, so she raised the bottle.

"You can do this without me."

"What if I can't?"

"You've already proven you can. She trusts you."

"I'm going to lose her."

"You won't."

She believed Avery's advice, like she always did, and told herself traveling the wrong road would only give the Santoses more ammunition. For the first time, she wanted to fill the shoes Avery had laid out for her.

As she returned the bottle to the counter, the doorbell rang. "What now?" Grumbling, she hobbled to the front door and opened it.

"Eric?" The look on his face worried her. "What's wrong?"

"We need to talk." He pushed his way through the front door and into the living room.

"Okay?" Annoyed, she followed him inside.

In the kitchen, his stare went to the open bottle of scotch on the counter. He grabbed the bottle. "I thought—"

"I am. It's just—"

Her cheeks grew warm. They must have been a bright shade of red, she thought. Not a week ago, she sat in this room and told him that she knew if she didn't stop drinking, it could cost her Reagan. She meant it and was determined more than ever to turn the corner.

"The important thing is that I didn't go back there."

"You know I'm only a phone call away, Sloane. Always." He put the bottle down. "You don't have to do this alone."

After retrieving the legal papers, she handed them to Eric. "The Santoses are trying to get guardianship of Reagan." She pointed at a particular paragraph. "They claim they're concerned about Reagan's wellbeing because I suffer from severe depression and substance abuse."

"This is a load of crap, and we both know this will never float in court." Eric's eyes trailed over the papers. "You just lost your wife, for God's sake. It's normal to drink more after what you've been through."

"You and I both know it was becoming more than that."

"You'll fight this, won't you?"

"You bet your ass I will. I love Reagan. She's my daughter." Whether it was having a clear head or the idea of sticking it to the Santoses, she was sure now Reagan belonged with her.

She sat on the couch to ease her throbbing foot. Eric sat next to her. "Enough about this. What has you all fired up?"

"Diego Rojas is dead. Shanked."

She took in a long, deliberate breath. Shanked meant it took time to bleed out and he saw death coming. He deserved whatever he got, and his fate proved the law and justice often weren't the same thing. "Good. Someone saved the state a lot of money."

"Finn and I think it was a hit."

"Finn? You've been coordinating with the DEA?"

"Not the DEA, just Finn Harper. Prichard placed her on modified duty pending an inquiry into the explosion, so she's not overseeing the case anymore. She told me, despite the good leads Rojas provided, they're sitting on the intel, and she can't figure out why."

"At least Avery's killer is dead. That's all I care about." Sloane's antenna went up when he pursed his lips. "What aren't you telling me?"

"You weren't ready to hear this right after the explosion, and then you went into a tailspin afterward. I didn't want to upset you more."

"I'm stronger than you think, Eric. Just spit it out."

"Diego swore he didn't place the explosive. Which, if true, means the cartel was on to him. Someone else placed that device, likely to silence Rojas before he could tell us what he knew."

Her mind raced with her eyes darting back and forth. If Diego didn't plant the bomb, that meant Avery's killer was still out there. "Do you have a suspect?"

"Diego gave us a name: Caco. He runs Los Dorados. We think he ordered the hit on Diego and ordered the lab rigged."

"The DEA is going after him, right?"

"No." Eric shook his head. "They're sitting on it."

Sloane jumped off the couch. She landed on her booted foot, and pain radiated up her leg. She winced, clenching her jaw and fists. "They know this Caco guy killed Avery and they're sitting on their damn hands? How deep does this go?"

"I don't know, but Finn volunteered to help us find out. To help us get everyone responsible for Avery's death."

Sloane dropped to the couch and buried her face in her hands. Caco may have planted the explosive, but if not for her, Avery would've spotted it.

Eric scooted over and placed an arm around Sloane's shoulder. "We'll get him, Sloane."

"You don't understand. It's my fault Avery's dead." She pounded her fist on the couch.

"It wasn't your fault." He rubbed her back.

The guilt all but consuming her, she rocked back and forth when the words came out. "I'm the reason Avery was upset and didn't spot the explosive. She's dead because of me, just like my parents."

Silence.

"This is the grief talking." Eric's voice sounded different, softer. "None of it was your fault."

She needed to tell him, make him understand that grief didn't grip her, guilt did. "You don't get it. When Avery pulled up to the scene, she saw me touching Finn in almost the same way I'd touched Michelle the night before our wedding."

"Shit." Eric rested his elbows on his knees, shaking his head twice.

"Avery looked upset, so I went inside to clear things up with her. Then she pulled the lever on the pill press, and..." She leaned back against the couch. Her wails pierced her to her core. "It's my fault. I killed her. I killed Avery."

Eric pulled her into a hug. Once her tears stopped, he withdrew his arm and turned her with his hand to face him. "No one could have spotted that explosive device."

"It's my fault." She shook her head and embraced her guilt.

"Listen to me. I've seen Avery's crime scene photos. They automatically uploaded to the secure cloud. She took several photographs of the pill press, and none of them showed an explosive device. It was not your fault."

"But she said she couldn't think straight."

"Did she say it was because of you?"

"No, but—"

"Even if she was upset and distracted, there was no reason to suspect someone rigged the pill press. It's not your fault."

"I can never be sure. How do I live with this? Where do I start?"

"You start by doing first things first, Sloane."

"And what is that?"

"I can think of two things you can do to heal. First, you get yourself a good lawyer, and you fight the Santoses. You're a great mother and are exactly what Reagan needs. Second, since you've been cleared by the shooting board, you get back to work and keep yourself busy. And when you're ready, we'll go after Caco on our own."

Eric's advice supplied fresh air to her lungs. Avery's voice had given her similar advice… *Start by getting dressed.* Focusing on Reagan and keeping busy seemed easy enough, though she sensed peace wouldn't come until she put Caco in a pine box.

"You're right." Sloane slapped both her knees, shot up, and hobbled toward her front door. She sifted through dozens of business cards in a bowl on top of the entry table and pulled out the one she needed. After retrieving her phone, she dialed the number on the card. "Hello, my name is Manhattan Sloane. Is this Kadin Hall? I got your name from Finn Harper. She said you'd help."

CHAPTER FOURTEEN

Ready for change, Sloane reminded herself. After that twenty-something process server blindsided her with the Santoses' custody suit, she wanted it more than ever. If not for herself, for Reagan. First things first, Eric had told her, and being a mother to Reagan topped her list.

Every evening after the explosion, if Reagan didn't cook, they either scoured the freezer for something to microwave, ordered delivery, or trekked down to the Tap for dinner. That would change tonight.

Nothing too complicated. She prepared grilled chicken, rice, carrots, and a salad, but Sloane took pride in it nonetheless. She hobbled to the top of the stairs leading to the lower level and Reagan's bedroom. "Reagan! Deni! Dinner!"

"Be right up," Reagan yelled back.

Minutes later, Reagan turned the corner to the kitchen as Sloane put the final touches on the three plates she'd prepared. "Wow. You cooked." Her voice contained more than a hint of surprise, which under any other circumstances, Sloane would consider a jibe.

At the counter, Sloane looked over her shoulder. "Good. You made it up. You're staying, aren't you, Deni? We have plenty."

The girls exchanged glances and arched eyebrows. Deni turned to Sloane. "Sure, Mrs. Sloane. It looks good. I'll text my mom and let her know I'm staying for dinner."

It wasn't fancy, but the food served as a good start. During dinner, the conversation remained light and had an upbeat tone, convincing Sloane she'd swerved back onto the right track. After the girls cleaned up the dishes and Deni left for home, Reagan and Sloane retreated to the couch, each with a bowl of ice cream.

Ashamed of how she'd checked out as a mother, Sloane turned her expression serious. "Honey," Sloane lifted her eyes to meet her failings head on, "I need to talk to you about something."

Reagan put her bowl down and shifted on the cushion to face her like Avery used to do. "Sure, what's up?"

"I was served with some legal papers today. Your grandparents are taking me to court so they can become your guardians."

Reagan's eyes narrowed and her jaw clenched. *So much like her mother*, Sloane thought. When Reagan drew in a deep breath, Sloane knew she was sucking in her anger.

"I won't go." Reagan's spine straightened in a perfect line.

Sloane softened her expression to diffuse the tension. "When your mom married me, her parents refused to have anything to do with her. She told me—and them—that they'd never get to see their only grandchild grow up until they accepted me and our marriage. I intend to honor her wishes."

Sloane dreaded the conversations the Santoses would have with Reagan if they succeeded in becoming her guardians. Without her there to draw the line, they'd insist her and Avery's wasn't a real marriage. "You're better off with someone normal," they'd say.

Reagan's posture relaxed after she released a long breath. "Good. After the things they said about you at Mom's funeral, I want nothing to do with them."

Sloane searched her memory, but that day remained a blur. She remembered confronting the Santoses about asking Reagan to come live with them, but the details escaped her. "What did they say?"

"They called you a pervert. Said you perverted Mom, and they should raise me." Reagan's voice thickened. "They blame you for Mom's death. I hate them." Tears rolled down her cheeks.

The insults didn't hurt Sloane as much as the truth. *It doesn't matter what Eric said. You'd never forgive me if you knew I killed your mom. Where would you go if you knew?* She slumped into the couch, the truth pummeling her like a prizefighter. *She can never find out.*

Sloane pushed her guilt aside. She rested a hand on each of Reagan's arms. "I don't think your mother would want you to hate them. Despite how they treat me, they're still your flesh and blood. Hate what they do, hate what they say, but don't hate them. There may come a day when they'll accept your mother's choices and me as your mother. Until then, I'll do everything in my power to fight this."

"I'll try." When Reagan wiped her tears and straightened her shoulders, she had steeled her voice. "But I still want nothing to do with them."

"Fair enough." Sloane saw the best parts of Avery—her compassion and tenacity—reflected in Reagan. Those drew out a faint smile. "Now that I'm out of that cast, I plan on helping a lot more around the house. I'm going back to work tomorrow. How about we start the day off right with a hot breakfast like we used to?" The tiny grin on Reagan's face appeared genuine, not forced. "I sure could use someone to help me just like your mother used to do."

"I'd like that." Reagan's grin grew wider and blushed her cheeks.

"Okay then, I'll meet you in the kitchen at seven a.m."

After they put their dessert bowls in the dishwasher, Sloane returned to the couch. She bundled up the sheets and blankets that had served as her makeshift bed for the last two months.

"I'm sleeping in my bedroom tonight." Sloane paused when Reagan's jaw slacked. "Can you grab my pillow and PJs?"

After dashing around and picking up Sloane's things, Reagan followed her trail to the master bedroom. "Must feel good to have that cast off."

"You have no idea." When the doctor removed that plaster from her ankle, Sloane equated it to shedding chains. It took the rest of the day to appreciate the freedom it offered and the renewed sense of self-reliance it gave her. Reassured her wounds could heal, Sloane was certain the time had arrived for her to sleep in the bed she had shared with Avery—another "first things first" to healing her wounded heart.

While Reagan helped Sloane put a fresh set of sheets on the bed, they chatted about school and boys. When they fluffed the pillows, Sloane recognized her wheedling tone.

"Sooooo, can I go to the movies with Emeryn Friday night?"

"Is this dinner and a movie with a friend or is this a date?" Sloane squinted when she folded her arms over one another, tucking her hands under her armpits.

Reagan shifted on her feet and slipped a few strands of long hair behind her ear. Her mother had a similar habit when she tensed or couldn't concentrate.

"Ummm…more like a date."

A lump formed in Sloane's throat. One night lying in bed, Avery had talked about Reagan dating someday. "Do you think she'll be interested in boys or girls?" she'd asked before saying it didn't matter. "I'll help her pick out just the right outfit and fix up her hair and makeup."

That day had arrived, but Avery wouldn't be there to witness Reagan make the slow transition into womanhood. Reagan would experience a slew of things her mother wouldn't be there to share. Sloane had to step up but doubted if she could do it as well as Avery.

"So this will be your first real date." Sloane sat on the edge of the bed and patted the fresh covers beside her, inviting Reagan to sit. "Are you nervous?"

"I guess so." Reagan was more interested in inspecting her shoes than looking Sloane in the eyes.

Definitely nervous.

"I remember my first date. She was cute, blond, and uber smart."

"She sounds like Mom."

"What can I say? I have a type." Sloane shrugged. "She was my trig tutor. I surprised myself when I paid attention long enough to pass my final."

Reagan laughed.

"After the test, I asked her out for dinner and a movie. I was so nervous at the restaurant. When I got up to use the restroom, I popped up so fast, I knocked down the server delivering our meals. I ended up with linguini and sauce all over me."

Reagan fell back on the bed, holding her stomach from a side-splitting belly laugh. She laughed more when Sloane joined her.

"I can laugh about it now, but I was so embarrassed back then. She was great about it, and we ended up dating for a month before she went off to college."

Reagan rolled over on her side and propped her head up with a palm, arm bent at the elbow. "So what's your advice?"

Sloane rolled over and matched Reagan's posture. "Understand Emeryn may have been brave enough to ask you out, but odds are he's just as nervous as you are. Be upfront about it when he picks you up. It should put you both more at ease, and hopefully, neither of you will wear your dinners."

On the surface, Reagan appeared grateful for the pep talk, but disappointment tinged her voice. "Thanks, Sloane." She pushed herself off the bed and walked toward the door.

Reagan's slumped shoulder told Sloane something troubled her. She sat up. "Hey, Reagan."

She imagined what Avery would have offered at the moment. She'd want to help her pick out the perfect outfit or do her makeup, but those two shared similar styles—a far cry from Sloane's boyish qualities.

"I know I'm not your real mom and that we didn't talk too much about important things like this before your mom died." Sloane paused to find the right words. "But I want you to know that you can talk to me about anything."

Reagan retraced her steps to the edge of the bed and kissed Sloane on the forehead. "You became my real mom the day you married Mom. I know we agreed that I should call you Sloane, but if it's okay with you, I'd like to call you Mom."

"I'd like that." The corners of Sloane's mouth turned upward, exposing her first genuine smile since Avery died. "I'd like that a lot."

"Okay, Mom it is." Reagan matched her smile. "I'm heading off to bed. See you in the morning. Good night, Mom. Love you."

"Good night, honey. I love you too." By the time Reagan disappeared out the door, Sloane had a sense they'd be all right without Avery.

Reagan calling her Mom for the first time was bittersweet. From the day she married Avery, she hoped a day would come that Reagan considered her more than her mother's wife. She never guessed Avery would have to die for that day to materialize.

Once Reagan retreated downstairs to her bedroom, Sloane readied herself for bed. She changed, washed up, and brushed her teeth. After removing her walking boot, she stood at the edge of the bed, gathering the courage to get in.

Putting weight on her ankle felt odd, but not as strange as staring at the bed she had shared with Avery. The last time she slept there, Avery had wrapped her arms around her with the lavender scent of her just-washed hair tickling her nose. She remembered how the rest of the world had faded away as the warmth of Avery's body lulled her into a gentle slumber.

She flipped up the covers and adjusted the pillows several times, still unsure if she had rushed this. Her throbbing ankle didn't give her a choice, though. As she sat on the bed, she ran a hand across the sheet on Avery's side. The slight sag in the mattress reminded her of what she had lost.

"I miss you so much, baby." Her lips quivered.

Moments later, she swung her legs up and under the covers. She hesitated a few times, and then, the second her head hit the pillow, she sobbed. Reality suffocated her. Never again would she hold Avery in her arms and nuzzle up next to her in the dark.

She wouldn't wake up next to her in the morning and watch the gentle rise of her breasts as she slept until the irritating alarm woke her. Tears rolled down the sides of her face, past her ears, and soaked the clean pillowcase.

"How do I do this, Avery?"

"*One day at a time, babe.*"

Her wife's words echoed in her head.

Though it was painful, she stayed in their bed. She turned on her side, grabbed Avery's pillow, and gripped it against her chest. Tears fell onto it until exhaustion took her into a deep sleep. She dreamed of her early childhood, of days when she and her mother sang the afternoon away. She dreamed of nights with Avery when they laughed and made love until the sun came up. She wanted to stay in that dream world forever, but she knew somehow that it would only last until the alarm clock brayed and pulled her back to a sharp reality.

CHAPTER FIFTEEN

Today marked Sloane's first drive into work without her wife by her side, one more in a series of firsts for the last two months. The first breakfast...the first visit to the Tap...the first holiday...the first sleep in their bed...all without Avery.

Chatter or laughter had filled most of their rides into work together. The thick silence in the car today reminded her of times when they'd been quarreling and quiet would line the trip. She and Avery had a rule: arguing or not, they kissed before walking into the building. That wouldn't happen today...or ever again.

Pulling onto Bryant Street, she glanced at the front passenger seat. An empty space had replaced Avery there like it had done in her bed last night. The fragrance of her lavender perfume had faded, and two stray hairpins mixed with spare change in the center console were the only evidence she'd once occupied their car.

When will this stop? Not until she'd exhausted the list of firsts they shared, she feared.

After driving into the secure parking garage, she pulled into the same spot as she had on the morning of their anniversary. She lingered in the memory of them fogging every window in the car that day—until her iPhone alerted her to an incoming call. "Damn it." Without looking at the caller ID, she snatched up her phone.

"Yeah, Sloane."

"This is Kadin Hall. If this is a bad time, I can call back."

She exhaled and closed her eyes, imagining the taste of Avery's lips one more time. "No, Kadin, it's fine. I gather you looked at the documents I emailed you."

"I did, and you won't like what I found out."

"My life can't get much worse at this point." Sloane braced herself for more bad news. "Hit me with it."

"In the court petition, the way the plaintiffs referenced your alleged depression and substance abuse issues got me thinking, so I did a little digging. The Santoses also filed a complaint with Child Protective Services, alleging you were an unfit guardian."

Fucking figured. The Santoses treated Avery like dirt. It was only logical they'd fight dirty too. "So now I have to defend myself against CPS too?"

"No, you don't. When CPS learned the complaint came on the heels of your injury and your wife's death, they considered Reagan's age and the source of the complaint. They declined to investigate."

"Finally." Sloane waved her free hand in the air. "Some common sense."

"Sloane…" Kadin paused, hesitant. "I know this is an emotional time for you, and I don't want to overstep. But as your lawyer, I can't stress enough the need for you to stay focused on Reagan's wellbeing. Which means not using alcohol or other substances as a regular escape. If this is an issue, have you considered seeing a therapist to get you over the hump?"

Great. Just fucking great. Now I have to explain myself to a lawyer I barely know. "I'm sure you mean well, Kadin, but no, this is not an issue. At least not anymore. The only therapy I need is for this ankle to heal and to get back to work, which I start today."

"Good, consider the topic closed."

"So what's next?"

"It appears the Santoses have moved on to Plan B, which is to contest guardianship. They're also asking for an immediate visit."

"They're a piece of work." Sloane bit her lip. "They blamed me for turning Avery gay. They shut their own daughter out of their lives because she married me. When they stopped visiting altogether, Avery decided she didn't want them in Reagan's life until they accepted her sexuality and me as her wife."

"This is all good information we can present in court. They've requested an expedited hearing, citing their concerns about Reagan's safety. I can stall for time."

"No, the sooner, the better. A protracted legal battle is the last thing I need now that Reagan and I are on the right track. How fast can we get in front of a judge?"

"I'll call in a favor and see if I can get an emergency hearing."

"That's all I can ask. You don't know how much your help means to me."

"I'm glad Finn referred you. I'm making your case my number one priority, so you call me day or night if anything comes up."

After wrapping up the call, Sloane remained in the car to mentally prepare herself for another series of firsts without Avery. Minutes later, in the elevator, she was numb. She and Avery had regularly used that time to figure out what to cook for dinner or make last-minute lunch plans if their schedules allowed.

After stepping onto the sixth floor, she turned her eyes left down the hallway toward the CSI lab and stopped in her tracks. For two years, she had looked in that direction and known Avery was safe behind those doors, but that ended today.

Eric appeared from the squad room and placed a comforting hand on her shoulder for a moment. "It'll get easier, I promise."

Sloane continued to stare at the lab entrance. "I hope so." How long would it take to walk past that door and not feel the emptiness? She couldn't imagine it ever happening.

"Come on. Let's get to work." Eric nudged her toward the squad room. "You're lucky. You missed the pipe burst a few weeks ago. Took days to get the stench out. The good news is, they replaced all the pipes above our desks."

The wheels in her head churned. "Did they fix the ones over the interrogation room?"

"Nope." Eric grinned so hard his dimples must have hurt.

"Sweet." A smile crept onto her face. *Did I just joke around? Huh. Another first.* A tinge of guilt hit her, but she squared her shoulders. *Avery would say it was about time.*

"It's good to see you smile." Eric jabbed her side with an elbow. "I've missed it."

"I have too."

Sloane nearly turned an emotional corner, but the moment she breezed through the squad room doors, an onslaught of welcomes and condolences flew at her from every direction. She tucked away the lump in her throat and fielded each greeting with an unemotional, short one- or two-word response. Once she managed to limp through the gauntlet, she retreated to the safety of her desk.

As she draped her jean jacket over the back of her chair, a pile of case files, each folder stacked with care, caught her eye. "Looks like I have some catching up to do."

"Modified duty is still duty." Eric grinned. "I need a second pair of eyes on these cases. Tell me what I missed."

Since her foot still swelled, sometimes at the drop of a hat, elevation supplied her only remedy at work. She flipped over a small metal trash can, settled into her chair, and propped her walking boot on top of it.

One by one, she reviewed each of the cases she had missed during her two-month absence. Most were straightforward, involving tweakers, dealers, and isolated, small-time manufacturers. Then she came across the case where a resource officer had found a single heart-shaped pink pill during a random locker check at a city high school.

"Did you ever follow up on the locker raid?" Sloane cocked her head up from the file. "One pill they found sounds like it could be Kiss."

Eric tore his concentration from his own paperwork and glanced up to his left. "Shit. It slipped my mind. That was the day when Diego bought it."

She read more of the high school safety officer's notes. "Says he got the pill from a cousin in Rohnert Park. I didn't realize Kiss had made it into Sonoma County."

"Might not be worth the trip. Nothing else has popped up there or here in the city."

"Do you think Los Dorados packed up and moved on?"

"Don't think so. I've been keeping tabs on every city Diego identified as Kiss lab sites, and Kiss is still circulating around the East Bay. It may have disappeared from San Francisco, but not the Bay Area."

She stared at Eric for several beats until she piqued his curiosity.

"What?" He narrowed a single eye.

"Where is it?"

"Where's what?"

"The Rojas file." She couldn't blame Eric for holding it back. After the explosion, she had avoided anything having to do with the case. She knew everything that was important: Avery was dead, two of her techs were injured, and the man responsible was under arrest. Anything beyond that would've been torture. Now that she had learned Diego wasn't the end of it, she needed to get back in the game. She was feeling stronger but this would likely test her.

"You sure?" Eric had that protective look of his.

"No, but just give me the damn file." She reached out a hand, palm up.

Eric pulled the top file from his desk drawer but hesitated to let go of it. A slight nod of her chin showed she'd prepared herself, or so she hoped.

In a morbid exercise, she soaked in every detail from the day of the explosion, categorizing each word as either pre- or post-Avery's death. *Just get the damn facts*, she told herself. By the time she finished the report, she was numb. She needed to get out of there before she lost it.

After pushing the file across Eric's desk, she excused herself and hobbled with her walking boot down the corridor to the ladies' restroom. Sidling up to the bank of sinks, she splashed water on her face to wash away the sting of reliving Avery's last day.

She rested both hands on the countertop, eyes focused on the water flowing through the chrome drain in the sink. Everything from that day swirled through her head like a tornado. *Followed Rojas to the duplex. Who shot first? Double tap to the chest. I took a life. I made Avery cry. Why did I distract her? Explosion. I did this. I killed her.*

Sweat ran down her face while her heart hammered so hard the room spun. The freight train in Sloane's ears drowned out everything around her. She didn't hear her name until a hand pressed against her shoulder.

"Sloane, are you okay?" Concern etched Lieutenant West's face.

She turned off the water and raised her gaze. "I'm sorry. What?"

"Are you okay? Are you in pain?" Lieutenant West repositioned herself to look Sloane in the eyes. "If you're not ready, I can put you back on disability for another month."

Another month in solitary was the last thing Sloane needed. She grabbed a handful of paper towels and wiped her face dry. "I appreciate your concern, but getting back to work is what the doctor ordered. Today's a bit emotional, but I'll get through it."

"Don't push yourself." West's expression remained soft. "I want you riding a desk for the first week, okay?"

"Sure, L-T." She'd say anything West wanted to hear to convince her she was ready, but pushing herself was exactly what she needed to do.

West glanced toward the floor. "How much longer in that boot?"

"Another two weeks, and then I can wear sneakers. I should get back to my desk. Have a lot of catching up to do." She crumpled the damp paper towels and threw them in the trash can before walking out.

Eric pushed himself off the wall when Sloane emerged from the restroom. "You worried me." He examined the pale complexion and damp brow she noticed in the mirror moments ago. "Let's get coffee. I'm buying."

"In that case, you're on."

Around the corner from 850 Bryant sat one of the few coffee shops in town where no thief with a brain would dare to attempt to pull off a robbery. Anytime, day or night, at least a half-dozen cops sat inside guzzling down copious amounts of caffeine and chowing down on sugary pastries.

When they arrived, Sloane inhaled the potent mix of coffee aromas. She snagged a table nestled between two uniforms on one side and two other detectives on the other while Eric picked up their orders.

While she waited, she reviewed the Rojas file in her head. In his statement, he mentioned other mobile labs in Oakland, Richmond, Vallejo, and San Jose. He pointed out one location in Oakland without specifying the address where he met Caco for the first time. Not much to justify a transfer to Solano and not Quentin. She added things up—Eric had left something out.

When Eric arrived with their orders, she didn't wait for him to sit down before belting out the first question. "So what's not in the Rojas file?"

"Not much gets past you." He sat and organized the food and drinks. "The explosion destroyed his burner phone. We couldn't get anything off of it, and he was holding back its number until we secured his transfer to Solano."

"And now that he's dead, we have nothing else to go on?"

He reached into his front pants pocket and handed her a small piece of paper.

After unfolding it, she read the scribbled seven-digit number. "But…" She raised her eyes to meet his. "How?"

"I made it to the infirmary before he died. I promised to help his brother if he gave me the number."

Sloane darted her eyes back and forth as she sorted through the possibilities in her head. If Eric was doing his job by the book, Lieutenant West would've been his first stop, and she would've handed it over to the Feds. But he'd taught her going by the book didn't always equate to doing the right thing.

"No one else knows?"

"No one." He shook his head at a slow pace. "You decide what we do with it."

"I don't want the Feds near this."

"Neither do I."

"We go off-book." In her head, she finished her sentence. *Caco is mine.*

"I think we'll need help on this one." Eric leaned back in his chair and ran a hand over his stubble. "We'll need to know what the Feds are up to. You may not like this, but I think—"

"We bring in Finn."

She never liked wild cards, but something told her Finn wasn't one. She had already broken protocol to help her, and her gut told her she'd do it again.

"I'll call her." He pulled out his cell phone.

"I'll do it." She owed Finn that much.

* * *

When Finn suggested meeting near her office the following day, Sloane hesitated. Besides the parking issue, the meeting had to be off-book, and she couldn't chance anyone from the Federal Building recognizing them. Finn's condo made for a more private meeting place.

The address Finn passed along piqued Sloane's interest. Neither parking nor prying eyes would be an issue because condo buildings along that part of Market Street provided a valet for guests. That meant money, with every unit well into the low- to mid-seven figures. If she didn't inherit the property like Sloane did, how could a government slug afford to live in the heart of the Embarcadero? She needed that question answered before she tipped her hand.

After tossing her keys to the valet, she located the elevators. *Dear Lord, Barry Manilow?* The moment she stepped in, "I Write the Songs" droned at an agonizing pace. The floor numbers on the display screen ticked up even slower. When the bell chimed at Finn's floor, she felt like a seventh-grader again. She couldn't escape to recess fast enough when the door opened. *Thank God!*

She lumbered down the ornate hallway in her walking boot. The fragrant mix of orange and yellow sunflowers and bear grass atop two narrow tables, one on each side of the corridor, confirmed her suspicion—money.

After Sloane rang the bell, the apartment door opened, and Finn's smile lit the hall. "Good to see you out of that cast. Come on in."

The last time she saw Finn at the Tap, an intoxicating amount of scotch had marred the encounter—something she now regretted. That small spark between them when they first met in Lieutenant West's office had disappeared, replaced by a heavy melancholy that she found oddly relieving. The fact she found herself attracted to Finn that first day while married to Avery made her stomach turn. Its absence meant Sloane had one less thing to worry about.

"Thanks for meeting with me." Sloane hobbled past. On her way into the main living area, she took in the elegant contemporary architecture and furnishings that presented an upscale, yet cozy feel to the room. When she stopped at the wall of windows framing the dining area, her breath hitched. She offered a low whistle at the magnificent view of the city and the Bay Bridge.

"Nice digs for a government salary." Her comment had an accusatory tone. Maybe a little too much. "You've come a long way since El Sobrante."

"Trust fund." Finn joined her at the window, her eyes following the mounting traffic as it flowed across the bridge. "Right after you moved away, Daddy's law firm took off, and we moved to Atherton."

Relieved to have Finn prove her suspicion wrong, she turned her gaze to her. "You didn't want to follow in your father's footsteps?"

"Let's just say he wasn't thrilled when I went into the DEA right out of law school."

The more she learned about Finn, the more she liked her. After she moved away and lost touch, she imagined for months how Finn's life would turn out. Using her own childhood expectations as a model, she thought Finn would marry a man she met in college and have one or two kids and an office job that barely paid the bills. She didn't imagine all this.

Another thing Sloane didn't account for was that tragic events would define both their paths.

"Tell me about Isabell."

"I called her Izzy." Finn's lungs overfilled with air, and then she exhaled. "The first time I saw her, I knew she was trouble. She wouldn't take no for an answer from the professor and weaseled her way past the waitlist into a seat on the first day of class."

"Sounds like a woman who knew how to get what she wanted."

"Oh, she did. She was relentless when she needed to be, yet was compassionate to a fault."

"Fiery and gentle, just like Avery."

"She was both those things, which made for an exciting romance."

"They do make a spicy combination." Sloane shifted her weight to relieve the pressure on her booted foot. "Mind if I sit down? The foot still swells."

"Oh, I'm so sorry." Finn pointed toward the small sectional. "Take the inside corner so you can prop up your leg. Can I get you something to drink?"

Sloane plopped down on the couch and positioned her boot on the cushion, dangling it over the edge to make sure she didn't dirty the spotless white fabric. "Water would be great."

Finn poured a glass of water from a pitcher in the refrigerator in her small, sleek kitchen.

"Thank you." Sloane took a sip. The surprising taste prompted her to inspect the glass. "Delicious. What's in it?"

"Just some lime and mint. When we moved to Atherton, the cook always had it on hand." Finn joined Sloane on the couch. "She spoiled me, and now I can't seem to break the habit. I always keep a container in the fridge."

"Cook, huh?" Sloane snickered while sneaking a look at Finn.

Finn shrugged. "Daddy did well."

"So why the DEA?"

"Izzy. The other driver was high. Drugs took her from me, so I wanted to put drug dealers behind bars. How about you?"

"Bernie, the officer who rescued me after my parents' accident, later died. I wanted to honor him." Sloane locked her gaze with Finn. "He was helping me find you when it happened."

For a moment, Finn laid a hand on Sloane's. "I wish we would've found each other back then."

"Me too, but it sounds like our paths were chosen for us." With similar paths and lovers, their lives were bound to cross again. Sloane figured if Finn could get past losing someone she loved, she could too.

"I think you're right." Finn shifted on the couch, marking her intent to change the subject. "So, on the phone, you said we needed to talk. I'm assuming this is about Diego."

"Eric said he met with you right after Diego was killed and that you both think it was a hit."

"I don't believe in coincidences involving lowlifes, so yes, it had to be a hit."

"It had to be Caco."

Finn nodded. "I see you've caught up."

"He had to be the one behind the bomb at Diego's lab." Sloane was more determined than ever to go after everyone involved in Avery's death. "I'm going after him."

"I wish I could help, Sloane. Ever since the lab explosion, Prichard has suspected I was the one who tipped you off. And now that Diego is dead, he's limited my access to the case. I was trying to find another source, but he shut me down. The strange thing is that I think he and the US Attorney are slow-rolling the case, but I can't figure out why."

"What if we already had another lead? Would you be willing to help me off-book?"

Finn's head tilted. "What do you mean?"

"What if we had the number to Diego's burner phone?"

Finn studied Sloane for several beats. "I'm in. We have a leak somewhere, and I don't know who I can trust at the federal level. I know I can trust you, Sloane."

"Feeling's mutual, Finn." Unsure where this case would lead, Sloane had the sense that with Finn on her side she'd find answers.

CHAPTER SIXTEEN

Sloane braced herself for the tedious process of working this case off-book. It would take a considerable amount of time and resources and require access to restricted law enforcement files and data systems. To pull this off, she'd have to go about her daily business working her official caseload and still collect every piece of information on Diego Rojas, Kiss, and Los Dorados with no one finding out.

Sloane waited in her car until Eric pulled into his usual section of the SFPD parking garage. She called him on his cell. "I'm in my car a few rows over. Let's talk."

Moments later, he opened her passenger door and slid into the front seat. "Are we ready to do this?"

"I am, but I don't want your fingerprints on this." As much as she appreciated everything he'd done and would do for her, she needed to cut him out. If anyone risked their job to track down Diego's burner phone, it would be her. "You've done enough by holding back Diego's number. Many more rules need breaking, and I'll be the one to do it. Finn and I can take it from here."

Eric didn't appear happy about her decision, but his sigh signaled he understood it. "Promise you'll bring me in when you get close. I know Finn is good, but you know I'll always have your back."

Considering Eric's history and his reluctance to take a backseat, she respected him more for doing so. She stared him square in the eye. "I promise."

The SFPD law enforcement data system required a secure login and a criminal case number to conduct an information search, logging and tracking each one. Sloane had to be cautious and make sure nothing linked back to Eric. She waited until he went into the field.

After picking a case file from her desk at random, she logged on and entered the case number. Keying in a few words, she started a reverse phone search for the different local area codes with the phone ending in 285-4421. She first tried area codes 415, 408, 510, and 650, the general locations of suspected Los Dorados labs.

When those didn't pan out, she remembered the lone Kiss pill discovered in a Rohnert Park high school. She entered the area code 707, the one that covered the county north of the Golden Gate Bridge. That number came back to a prepaid phone registered to no specific name. Bingo! Burner phone.

Once Sloane had the number and phone carrier, a single phone call to the manufacturer had them searching for the cell phone records. She learned they shipped the phone from their distributor to a big box store in Rohnert Park, about an hour north of San Francisco. The same city where the high schooler said he bought Kiss from his cousin. On the right track, she had to dig deeper. If Caco or someone in his organization bought the phone there, along with checking the purchase records, she could access the store's surveillance tapes. The prospect of putting a face to a name meant a road trip.

* * *

Finn had run up against a wall. Years ago, the DEA digitized their case files. It controlled access to them via computer login through an encrypted access card issued to every employee. Each time she accessed a case, the system recorded her name. To complicate matters, Prichard had classified the Los Dorados case and limited access to a specific list, excluding her. Her antenna went up because nothing about the case involved national security. She'd have to figure out another way to access those files.

She decided to start with Carol, the secretary she shared with Prichard. In her early forties with a large brood at home, Carol often cut corners with security protocols. Overworked, underpaid, and underappreciated, she often had no other choice but to do so. Finn's shared experience in this regard was something she thought she could use to her advantage. For her plan to work, she needed Carol's attention along with her sympathies. *Sorry, Carol, but I need those files.*

Finn flicked her index finger and knocked over her paper cup, spilling cold coffee across her desk and onto her pants. "Damn it! Carol? I spilled. Do you have any napkins or towels?"

Carol rushed in from her nearby desk with a handful of fast-food restaurant napkins. "Here, Agent Harper." She handed Finn half the stack while she wiped the desktop with the other half.

While both women dabbed at the spreading liquid, Finn mumbled under her breath loud enough for Carol to hear. "How the hell does he expect me to do my job if the IT guys can't figure out access controls."

"What's wrong, Agent Harper?"

"Monthly reports are due tomorrow, and I'm having problems accessing two case files. As usual, Agent Prichard is nowhere to be found."

Carol snorted. "He does have a knack of disappearing at the worst times."

"Tell me about it." Finn pulled the case management system up on her computer screen and entered a case number. A message flashed. "See. Access denied. I had no problem last week. What the hell?"

"I can stay and help you," Carol offered.

Finn had caught Carol's attention and had her on the hook. Now she banked on the trust that had developed between them to garner more than her sympathies.

"I'll be hours. You have a long commute ahead of you and four kids at home. I can't ask you to stay."

"But—"

"No buts, Carol. I'll just have to take the heat tomorrow."

"And have Agent Prichard be a holy terror all morning? No, thank you." She removed the lanyard from around her neck and offered it to Finn. "I have access to all files. Here, take my ID card overnight."

Finn feigned concern over the breach in security protocol. "I can't ask you—"

"You're not asking, I'm offering."

Finn slumped her shoulders and did her best to sound reluctant. "Thank you, but I think it's best we don't tell Agent Prichard about this."

"Not on your life." Carol walked around Finn's desk, inserted her ID into the card reader, and logged on. "Now you can get your reports done, and we'll all work in peace tomorrow. I'll get my ID card from you in the lobby in the morning."

"I can't thank you enough, Carol. You're a lifesaver."

Carol packed up her things, leaving Finn logged into her account and giving her full access to every case file. A handful of agents still milled about the floor, so Finn didn't have much time. After checking her surroundings, she entered a case number and brought up the records on Kiss, Los Dorados, and Diego Rojas. She worked at a feverish pace to export every bit of information to a flash drive, and within fifteen minutes, she had everything she needed. Now she had to get it to Sloane.

Now familiar with the routine at Finn's building, Sloane surrendered her car keys to the valet and pushed the "up" button on the wall. She hoped for a change, but the second she stepped into the elevator, Barry Manilow instrumental music again wormed its way into her head. Without realizing, she hummed while her head bounced back and forth to "Copacabana." Then the door opened to silence. Sloane shrugged. She'd survived another dose of Barry.

After a few knocks, the door to Finn's condo swung open. Sloane's breath caught. Tight leggings and a sports bra, layered with a formfitting tank top, highlighted Finn's toned body. Every curve had just the right slope. *Why didn't I notice this before?*

She soaked in this sexy version of Finn, starting at the exposed skin below the trailing edge of her black-cropped leggings. The outer lines of her legs bowed right above the knees, hinting that strong legs capable of sustained physical performance lay beneath the nylon spandex. A startling image of those leg muscles thrusting against her center made her chest flutter. A gray U-neck tank top outlined the outer swells of her breasts, sending Sloane's breathing into rapid, shallow intakes. Her gaze followed the black trim of the sports bra, teasing the pleasures encased underneath. *God, they're perfect.*

Finn's slender, yet well-defined bare arms and shoulders spoke to the hours of attention paid to them. An alluring image of those arms pulling her in close until their breasts pressed together left Sloane speechless and, to her surprise, throbbing.

Her body came alive more than it had in months. She should've enjoyed the sensation, but it reeked of betrayal. Despite what her body was telling her, in her heart, she felt married.

"Uh…hi."

"You're early. Come on in." Finn moved to the side so Sloane could pass. "Sorry about the funky smell. I just finished my workout downstairs and haven't had time to shower yet."

"You're fine." When she squeezed by, she noticed Finn's wet, tangled hair. The way the damp strands stuck to her head reminded Sloane of how she used to wear her hair as a teenager, cut short around the ears. She liked it…a lot.

"I was about to grab some water." Finn glanced toward the kitchen. "Would you like something to drink?"

"Sure, mint water would be great."

Desperate for a distraction, Sloane went further inside. The orange glow coming through the wall of windows past the dining area drew her in. Thousands of warm radiant lights outlined the Bay Bridge and presented a unique and romantic tone against the darkening evening sky.

When Finn joined her at the windows, she handed her the glass. "The view never gets old, does it?"

"Thanks. No, it doesn't." Sloane accepted the glass of water before returning her gaze out the window. "I'm a little further south in Hunter's Point. The view from there is amazing too."

"I know."

Sloane glanced at Finn. Confusion forced a pause.

"The night of the funeral, Eric and I got you home."

Most of that night was still a blur, but the flashes of her throwing up on the floor in front of Finn stuck out. Her cheeks and the tips of her ears warmed to a blush. "I was pretty messed up then. Sorry about getting sick like I did."

"You have nothing to apologize for. You were grieving." Finn rested a hand on Sloane's forearm. "From what I could tell, between your injuries and your in-laws, you had a lot more on your plate than anyone should have to have at a time like that."

"That's right. You saw that." Still uncomfortable about the topic, Sloane dipped her head.

"How about I set you up so you can read the case files while I take a quick shower?"

Sloane agreed and followed Finn to a smaller area off the living room, a secondary bedroom converted into an office. The clutter, stacks of moving boxes, and a well-worn couch didn't at all match the image she had of Finn.

"Don't mind the mess. I'm still moving in. The other rooms came furnished, so I keep them sparse for visitors. I spend most of my time in here. Reminds me of the El Sobrante house I grew up in—cramped and clutter everywhere." Finn moved a small ottoman in front of the couch and patted it. "Here, put your foot up."

"Thanks." Sloane ran her hand across the worn dark blue fabric, surmising it to be the site of many hours of studying and reading. "I've gotten pretty good with this walking boot, but I always welcome elevation."

When Finn handed her a tablet with dozens of files open, Sloane inspected the screen. "Dare I ask how you got your hands on those case files?"

"Nope. Make yourself at home. There's popcorn on the counter in the kitchen if you get hungry."

Sloane's eyes followed her as she left the room. Finn's backside fascinated her with all the right curves below the waist and all the right muscle definition above.

"What am I doing?" She closed her eyes and rubbed her face with her left hand, scraping her wedding ring against her nose and lips. After turning her hand, she kissed the white gold band, leaving her lips pressed against it. *This is so right and so wrong at the same time.* How could it not be when she still felt married? And as long as she did, that ring would remain on her finger.

She rolled her neck to shake off her thoughts of curves, muscles, and wedding rings and went to work reviewing the dozens of documents and photographs Finn had uploaded for her. When she tore her gaze from the iPad, she didn't know how long she'd been reading nor how long Finn had been leaning against the doorway.

Sloane prided herself on her ability to read people, but she couldn't quite read Finn's expression. Concern? Maybe. Sympathy? Probably. Attraction? She had before. Then Finn's lips parted but closed again. There. Reluctance. Whatever weighed on Finn's mind, it made her hesitant. Oddly, the silence between them lingered with no sense of awkwardness.

Sloane smiled at the seed they'd planted.

Fresh from her shower and dressed in jeans, a T-shirt, and a light cardigan, Finn pushed herself off the doorframe when Sloane smiled at her. "All done?"

"Almost." Sloane forced her gaze back to the tablet. "Just a few more to go."

"While you finish, I'll grab us that popcorn and more water."

Before she could answer, Finn zoomed out the door. Sloane leaned back on the couch and stared up at the ceiling, blowing out a long breath. "So wrong, yet so right," she whispered.

Sloane closed her eyes and concentrated on an image of her and Avery on their deck, holding hands, watching tankers float by and airplanes climb off the tarmac from Oakland Airport. Avery's voice floated as if she were sitting next to her. "Don't force it, baby. You'll know when it's right."

A hand pressing against her leg shook Sloane out of her daydream.

"Feeling all right?" The lines on Finn's face, along with her narrowed eyes, reflected concern.

"What?" Sloane pushed herself up to clear her head. "I'm fine. Just resting my eyes."

Finn sat on the couch beside her and placed the popcorn and drinks on the nearby coffee table. "All right then, hit me with your questions."

Sloane thumbed through a few open documents. "So, the DEA had been tracking Los Dorados for almost ten years in SoCal and Vegas. Do you know what precipitated their move to NorCal last year?"

"That's a good question. Los Dorados had a well-run operation and, from what we could tell, a quite profitable one. Any time our agents got close to penetrating their organization, they plugged the leak and kept the coroners down there busy."

"Then it looks like we need to find out what changed to make it more profitable to do business up here." After working narcotics for the past two years, Sloane learned money was king, and more often than not, profit dictated a kingpin's reasoning. "Knowing that might break their hold in this state."

"I've been saying the same thing for months but have gotten nowhere with Prichard and Quintrell." The corners of Finn's mouth turned up, but her lips sank inward. She offered a full nod before tossing up her hands in exasperation. "They're more interested in putting out fires when they pop up and snatching up Kiss when it shows up in new cities."

"A reactionary approach gets you nowhere. We need to go after the source." Sloane hadn't worked in narcotics enforcement as long as Finn, but she had seen enough to know that tactic never worked.

Finn nodded. "It's like playing Whack-A-Mole. Something new is always popping up. I wish you were in a position over me and—" Her cheeks turned a bright pink after Sloane raised an eyebrow. "Oh…um…I didn't mean…I mean I wish—"

"I know what you meant, Finn." Sloane's expression likely amplified her amusement. "We all wish we had bosses who kept the big picture in mind. I'm lucky Eric and Lieutenant West do."

"You trust them?"

"I trust Eric with my life. Lieutenant West? I have no reason not to trust her. What are you getting at?"

"We have a leak in this case. Someone must have tipped off Caco that Diego cooperated with us. That would explain the lab explosion and how someone got to Diego in county jail. Who else on your end knew about him?"

Sloane searched her fuzzy memory of the days leading up to Avery's death. "I think just me, Eric, and West in the PD and Kyler Harris from the DA's office."

"We kept information about Diego tight on our end too. I had two teams who tailed Diego before the explosion. Though only me, Prichard, his secretary, and David Quintrell from the US Attorney's office knew about his plea agreement and accessed the case file before Diego was killed."

"That narrows down the suspect pool." Sloane checked off in her head who she could trust. Eric and Finn topped the list. She liked Lieutenant West and ADA Harris, but not knowing them outside of work limited her assessment. "We can eliminate Eric. Can you eliminate anyone on your end?"

"The secretary seems harmless, but one never knows. The others? Wouldn't put it past either of them being the leak."

Sloane placed the tablet down on the coffee table. "First, we need to do a little more legwork on Diego's burner phone."

"Agreed."

"The carrier should email me the phone records tomorrow. In the meantime, we need to take a road trip. I tracked the number to a prepaid bought in Rohnert Park."

"I'll clear the decks tomorrow."

Before Sloane could reply, her cell phone rang. She leaned back to fish it from her front jeans pocket and caught a glimpse at the caller ID. "I gotta take this. Do you mind?"

"No. Want me to leave?"

"No, stay," she mouthed when she swiped the screen to answer the call. Her expression turned serious. "Kadin, please tell me you have good news."

Finn's attention focused like a laser on Sloane's end of the conversation.

"I do," Kadin said. "I called in a few favors, and we have an emergency hearing in San Francisco probate court tomorrow morning at ten. The judge is prepared to hear the Santoses' petition."

Sloane considered the distance the Santoses would have to travel from Los Angeles on a moment's notice, along with having a bakery to run. "What if they don't show?"

"Then the judge will throw the petition out."

A smile grew on Sloane's face. "I like the way you work, Kadin." After Kadin passed along details of when and where to meet, Sloane hung up the call and turned her attention back to Finn. "Our road trip will have to wait a day. I have to be in court tomorrow."

"Was that Kadin Hall?"

"Yes, you gave me her card after the funeral," Sloane explained but kept the details vague. She'd already made herself uncomfortable leering at Finn's...well...perfect body and needed to reel in making herself feel even more vulnerable.

"I'm glad she's representing you." Finn picked randomly at a section of frayed fabric on the armrest. "She's the best."

Sloane noticed Finn's uncharacteristic fidgeting and the sigh when she said "best." *Do those two have a history?* She didn't know why, but the idea made her uneasy.

They wrapped up their work for the evening, and Finn walked her to the door. "We'll get him," Finn reassured Sloane as she shook her hand, holding her grip a few moments longer than necessary. "And Caco will spend the rest of his life behind bars."

One question crossed Sloane's mind before she let go of Finn's hand. When she confronted the man she blamed for Avery's death, would she pull the trigger? The answer was clear.

"Not if I get to him first."

* * *

Ten o'clock at night. Not too late for Finn to thank Kadin for helping Sloane, and going by last week's clock, right on time for her and Kadin's regular booty call. She was thankful their separation still had Kadin knocking on her door once a week; she needed the physical distraction from this evening. She sensed the pull between her and Sloane, but the midst of grief was no time to rekindle their childhood crush.

Four months had passed since Finn last walked down the dull, carpeted hallway to the apartment she and Kadin once shared. Nothing about it had changed, yet everything seemed different. Tonight she wouldn't walk through the door, toss her keys on the entry table, and fall into the arms of the woman who loved her. She wasn't coming home. She came to visit and thank Kadin for helping Sloane and leave physically satisfied. Instead of using a key, she knocked.

If things hadn't changed, Kadin would be in bed, dressed in long flannels and a tank top, a legal pad on her right, and a laptop on her left. She'd have at least another hour of reviewing briefs and poring over strategy for next week's cases.

Finn counted down the time it should've taken Kadin to clear away her work, put on her slippers, and make her way to the living room. She waited for several extra beats, but the door didn't open.

Debating whether to knock again, she raised a hand toward the door and lowered it twice. *Maybe things have changed. I should've called.* As she turned to walk away, the door cracked open, prompting her to pivot back.

"Finn?" Kadin opened the door further, revealing tousled hair. She closed her thigh-length silk robe to cover the bare breasts underneath.

Sexy as ever. "I'm sorry. Were you getting ready to shower?"

"Did we have a date tonight?"

"No. I just thought—"

"You should have called, Finn." Her voice remained quiet but firm.

Finn's throat swelled when she put it together. "You're not alone."

"No, I'm not."

Kadin's expression reflected the pain in Finn's chest. They hadn't discussed dating other women, or men on Kadin's part, but their recent visits had dwindled from multiple nights a week to just once. And what they did, neither of them considered it dating. Their visits had evolved into extended booty calls that included takeout or delivery. Rarely did Kadin stay the entire night, often citing an early court appearance as her excuse. They were both pulling away, but Finn hadn't had the courage to end it.

"Oh." Finn lowered her head, unable to look at Kadin while she ripped the Band-Aid off.

Kadin reached out and lifted Finn's chin with a finger. "We both knew this was coming."

"Doesn't make it hurt any less." Finn strained to hold back the tears threatening to fall. She wasn't any good at breakups even if they were long overdue. And this one was.

"You made it clear you can't live with me when you moved out, and I need more than a part-time girlfriend."

"I can't give you more than that." If it weren't for Kadin continuing to pressure her to be something she wasn't, Finn would move back in tomorrow. Not that that would solve anything. Things might be better for a month or two, maybe three, but Finn knew herself. She would resent any new job she took and Kadin for maneuvering her into it. Once the thrill of being back together had worn off, things would fall apart again.

"I know you can't, which is why I need to move on while I still love you." Kadin's eyes begged for understanding.

"I love you too." Being let down gently eased the pain of letting go. "Take care of yourself."

It *was* time, Finn thought. Time to let go and time to pull the trigger on the buy option for her condo. And when the door closed, so did the book on Kadin Hall.

CHAPTER SEVENTEEN

Rapid staccato clicks of ladies' heels against the tiled floor of San Francisco's courthouse echoed throughout its otherwise hushed hallways. Someone was apparently in a hurry. Sloane was too, but with a sneaker on one foot and a walking boot on the other, she quietly limped through the halls at a pace only a fraction slower than before she broke her ankle.

Despite her long legs, Reagan had a hard time keeping up. "Can you slow down, Mom?"

"We don't want to be late, honey."

Taking full strides and pumping her arms like a power walker, Reagan replied more with a question than a statement. "You said the hearing wasn't until ten."

Sloane glanced at Reagan, now trailing one step behind. "There are two things you never want to be late for, court and your wedding. Either way, you'll regret it for a long time."

"Mom was so pissed," Reagan snickered.

"Trust me. I was pissed too." Sloane shook her head, unable to forget the fiasco she encountered the morning of her and

Avery's wedding day. A seven-car wreck had snarled traffic to a standstill on her way back from picking up a wedding present. By the time she rushed home to change and made it to the Tap for the ceremony, she was only five minutes late, but those minutes had Avery's fears on fire.

"Then your mom was called into work during our reception. It made for a frustrating wedding, but we made up for it on our honeymoon."

"That I didn't need to know." Reagan cringed, jiggling her shoulders and arms down to her fingertips as if shaking off cooties.

Sloane smirked. *She'll get over it.*

Moments later, they turned down another branch of the fifth-floor corridor. A single cherrywood bench placed opposite each courtroom door, also milled from the same rich wood, broke up its stark white walls and never-ending shiny white tiles. On a bench in front of Room 506, Sloane spotted a woman dressed in a tasteful dark pinstriped jacket and pencil skirt, reviewing pages of handwritten notes.

"Good morning. Are you Kadin?"

The woman tore her gaze away from her notes and smiled. "You must be Sloane."

When she stood and shook hands, Sloane noted they had similar heights, the same slim, athletic build, and brunette hair.

"Pleased to meet you." Sloane pointed to her right. "This is Reagan."

"Hi, Reagan, I'm Kadin. Nice to meet you both."

Kadin turned her attention to Sloane. "The Santoses aren't here yet. Can I speak with you in private for a minute?"

Reagan took the hint. "I'm gonna use the restroom before the hearing. Be right back."

After she took off down the hallway, Kadin turned back to Sloane. "Did you get my text this morning about Reagan? She doesn't have to attend today. If the judge thinks differently, she'll hold a second hearing."

"I did, but she told me she was old enough to make up her own mind and insisted on coming. I couldn't have talked her out of it even if I wanted to."

A look of concern formed on Kadin's face. "You know the Santoses will bring up your drinking and opioid use in the weeks following your wife's death."

Sloane was ready for this. If the Santoses had had her followed by a private detective, she assumed they would pull out all the stops to get what they wanted. Last night she had prepared Reagan.

"They'll say I'm a drunk and an unfit parent."

"But you're not a drunk. You're a great mom."

"I checked out on you for a while, but I'm better now."

"I knew you were when you cooked again."

"It could get ugly."

"I don't care. They need to know I want nothing to do with them."

"Let them," Sloane told Kadin. "Reagan and I have already discussed the issue, and she knows I'm past that."

The doors to the small probate courtroom swung open, and litigants from an earlier hearing filed out. No one appeared happy.

"That's our cue." Kadin angled her chin toward the doors.

Sloane glanced down the corridor. "I'll wait for Reagan."

A minute later, Reagan reappeared and fast-walked toward Sloane. Behind her, the Santoses and another man Sloane assumed was their lawyer approached, only slower. Sloane's gaze studied Reagan's cold expression until she reached the courtroom door. "Did they say anything to you?"

"No." Reagan rolled her eyes. "I was too fast for them."

"It's nice to see you, Reagan." Maria used a sweet tone when she reached the door.

Reagan turned around. "I can't say the same, Grandma."

"I see you've been poisoning her against us." Luiz knitted his brow at Sloane.

"You've done that all by yourself, Grandpa." Reagan huffed into the courtroom, leaving two stunned grandparents in her wake.

Sloane thrust her chin at the Santoses in indignation, and without a single word, turned on her boot into the bright courtroom, where white walls and ceiling contrasted with cherrywood accents around the judge's bench and jury box. She made a straight line past the gallery benches to the litigants' tables, all made of the same wood.

"They're here." Irritation dripped from her voice when she joined Reagan and Kadin at their table.

Not long after the Santoses and their lawyer took their seats, the court clerk entered. "All rise…" and read the case number and litigants' names for the court record.

Moments later, Judge Gonzalez, a small Latina woman in her mid-fifties, entered wearing her traditional long, black robe. She took a seat behind the bench.

"Good morning. Please, take your seats. In hearings like this, I like things a little less formal. Both sides will present their case, but I'd like it to be more of a discussion than the presentation of legal briefs." She scanned the papers in front of her and turned her attention to Sloane's table. "I see Sergeant Sloane requested this hearing. What brings you here today?"

Before Kadin could stand, Judge Gonzalez motioned for her to keep her seat. "Remember, let's keep this informal."

"Yes, Your Honor. Kadin Hall for Manhattan Sloane." Despite the laidback atmosphere, she followed underlying courtroom protocol. "The petitioners, Mr. and Mrs. Santos, have asked the court to remove Sergeant Sloane as guardian of their granddaughter, Reagan Tenney. In her stead, they've asked you to appoint them. Reagan's father was killed in a military training accident when she was a toddler. Her mother, Avery Santos, the daughter of Mr. and Mrs. Santos, married Sergeant Manhattan Sloane of the San Francisco Police Department a little over a year ago. In her will, Avery Santos appointed Sergeant Sloane as Reagan's guardian in the event of her death. Tragically, Avery Santos was killed a few months ago in an explosion while serving the city of San Francisco as a crime scene investigator."

"I remember that incident." Judge Gonzalez pursed her lips. "All of you have my deepest sympathies."

Kadin nodded. "Thank you, Your Honor. When Avery married Sergeant Sloane, her parents never accepted her sexuality nor Sergeant Sloane as her wife, purportedly on religious grounds. The tension between them grew, and all contact eventually stopped. Sergeant Sloane contends that her wife did not want the Santoses to have contact with Reagan until such time they accepted her sexuality and her marriage. That situation has not changed. Sergeant Sloane requests you deny the petition for change in guardianship."

Judge Gonzalez sifted through her papers again. "Thank you. And the petitioners?"

The Santoses' lawyer remained seated. "Jerry Heller for the petitioners, Your Honor. The Santoses concede that their daughter's sexuality and marriage to Miss Sloane were in direct conflict with their religious beliefs. However, they contend that the three of them were working through those differences." The lawyer presented the judge with a document. "As their phone records show, you will note their last contact with their daughter was on the day of her death."

"What?" Sloane whirled her head toward Luiz. As far as Sloane knew, Avery hadn't talked to either of her parents for months before she died. The smug look on his face telegraphed that their claim had some truth to it. Sloane turned for confirmation to Kadin, who had just received a copy of the Santoses' phone records from the court clerk.

After Kadin showed her the document, Sloane inspected it and whispered into Kadin's ear. "They may have talked, but there's no way she would've agreed to anything after a few calls. Something isn't right."

"I get that, but this provides doubt," Kadin whispered.

Underneath the table, Sloane pounded her fist against her leg to drown the anger and uncertainty boiling below the surface. *Why didn't you tell me, Avery?*

Jerry Heller pulled at the shirt cuffs protruding from his jacket sleeves. His smugness grated on Sloane. "More importantly, Your Honor, the Santoses are concerned for Reagan's safety and wellbeing. In the aftermath of their daughter's death, the Santoses contend Miss Sloane fell into an alcohol- and opioid-fueled depression." He handed the Judge and then Kadin several documents. "As evidenced by these photographs."

Kadin inspected the pictures. "Your Honor, the fact my client was in her neighborhood tavern is no indicator of alcohol abuse. She has frequented that business regularly since she was thirteen with her grandmother for meals."

"I tend to agree, Miss Hall." Judge Gonzalez appeared unmoved by the multiple pictures of Sloane sipping on a cocktail at the Tap.

"Which is why we also offer this video to support the plaintiff's claim." After Jerry handed the judge an iPad with a video queued up, he turned over flash drives with a copy of the video to the judge's clerk and Kadin.

The video and what it depicted didn't surprise Sloane. Not proud Luiz had succeeded in baiting her, she had prepared Kadin for the possibility of it surfacing.

The judge reviewed the footage Maria recorded, reliving the ugly conversation between Sloane and Luiz when the Santoses confronted her at the Tap about visiting Reagan. Unfazed, she returned the iPad to Jerry, who then gave it to Kadin for a quick review.

"Sergeant Sloane." Judge Gonzalez peered below the table at Sloane's legs. "In the video, you had a cast. Were you also injured in the explosion that killed your wife?"

Sloane's jaw tightened, forcing her to swallow hard. "Yes, Your Honor. A broken ankle was the worst of my injuries."

"It must have been painful."

"Yes, it was."

"Let's talk about that."

Kadin stood. "Your Honor, I don't think—"

"It's okay," Sloane urged Kadin to sit. "I want to be honest about everything."

"I don't think this is a good idea." Kadin shook her head at Sloane, her voice above a whisper.

She gave Kadin a confident look and whispered back, "I need to do this."

Sloane turned her attention back to Judge Gonzalez. "Your Honor. I was at the scene when my wife was killed. We were in the same room when she realized she'd triggered an explosive device. Before we could escape, it went off. I was injured and thrown across the room while my wife was…" Her voice trailed off at the image of smoke and dust clearing to reveal the carnage that left her wife trapped in sure death.

When tears fell from Sloane's eyes, Judge Gonzalez asked, "Would you like to take a break, Sergeant Sloane?"

"No, ma'am." Sloane wiped her tears and cleared her throat. "I'd like to continue."

"Please, take your time."

"My wife was trapped under mounds of beams and debris. I tried to free her, but…" Her throat thickened again at the helpless feeling that had overwhelmed her that day. Her voice became croaky. "But I couldn't. Even with the help of my partner, we couldn't get her out. There was fire everywhere, and the gas main was about to blow. My partner and another agent dragged me out before I could save her. Then the building exploded, and…and Avery was dead."

Despite Reagan's prodding, Sloane hadn't the courage before today to recount the details of Avery's death. Her lips quivered at the first retelling and the guilt of what she'd caused.

Beneath the table, Reagan's hand slid underneath Sloane's where it rested atop her leg. After interlacing their fingers, trembling, and squeezing tight, Sloane turned to Reagan. "I'm so sorry I couldn't save her."

"I miss her so much, Mom." Reagan buried her head against Sloane's shoulder and let more tears flow.

"I miss her too." Sloane briefly covered Reagan's cheek with her other hand before turning back toward Judge Gonzalez. "I won't sugarcoat this, Your Honor. Yes, in the weeks that followed, grief overwhelmed me. I leaned on the pain pills doctors gave me after surgery to numb the pain of losing my wife, but only until that prescription ran out. That was over a month ago. After that, I drank more than I should have, and I know I neglected my responsibilities as a mother."

"You must be Reagan." The judge looked to Sloane's right. "What do you think about all of this?"

"Yes, ma'am, I'm Reagan, and I don't like it at all. Judge, it's been hard on both of us since Mom died. With her ankle, it's been especially hard on Mom Sloane. But every day she talked about my mom, and every night she made sure I did my homework. Sure, I did most of the cooking and cleaning, but that was because she was in a cast, not because she was drunk or anything like that."

"And what about your grandparents?" Judge Gonzalez used a soothing voice.

"I never understood why they stopped visiting until I saw them at Mom's funeral."

"How's that?"

"When I went to say hi, they asked me to live with them. Then they called Mom Sloane a pervert, said she perverted my mom, and that they wanted to raise me right. They hate her."

Reagan turned to Sloane. "Now I understand why Mom didn't want me to see them."

She returned her attention to the judge. "And you know what Mom Sloane said when I told her what they said? She told me not to hate my grandparents. That it's okay for me to hate what they said or did, but it wasn't okay to hate *them*."

Reagan glanced again at Sloane. "She's a great mom, Judge, and she's doing exactly what my mom wanted and what I want now. I don't want to live with them." Reagan glanced at her grandparents. "I don't even want to see them until they accept Sloane as my mom."

"Thank you, young lady. You've shown tremendous courage today."

Sloane stared at Reagan, amazed by the woman she'd become. *You'd be so proud, Avery.* She turned her attention to the judge. "Your Honor."

"Yes, Sergeant?"

"It has been a struggle, but we're getting through it together. Now that I'm walking again and back to work, I feel like we're over the worst. I want nothing more than to get back to raising Reagan in a way that honors her mother."

"I'm getting the picture." Judge Gonzalez consulted her clerk about a few matters. "I have a lot to consider here, but I'm not inclined to believe Reagan's safety and wellbeing are in question."

"Your Honor," Jerry raised his hand, "if you decide against a change of guardianship, the Santoses request immediate visitation."

"Reagan has shown her desire to the contrary, and since she's sixteen, I'm not inclined to force a visitation until I render a decision." Judge Gonzalez shook her head. "I must consider the telephone exchanges between Avery and her parents in the days leading up to her death. They give me doubt whether Avery wished to continue isolating her daughter from her grandparents. I sense no urgency to make a ruling and will take some time to consider all the evidence and arguments presented today. Unless either of you has anything more, we'll reconvene next week." She paused for either lawyer to make a motion, but neither did. "Then, we're adjourned."

"All rise," the clerk announced.

After everyone filed out of the courtroom and the Santoses left in a huff, Kadin stopped Sloane in the corridor by placing a hand on her arm. "You were right to be upfront in there. Your and Reagan's stories were compelling. I think we've done everything we could."

Sloane turned to Reagan. "I hope so."

Reagan smiled. "I know so."

CHAPTER EIGHTEEN

"I got you, baby," Sloane cried as she squeezed Avery's hand. "I got you."

"I can't move." Avery became more alert.

"Gas, fire… We have to go now!" someone yelled.

"We have to save her." Sloane clawed at the debris faster and faster as panic set in.

"There's no time. We have to go now!"

"Not without her." Sloane desperately clutched onto Avery's arm.

"Go, Sloane. Go. Save yourself." Avery pulled on Sloane's sleeve.

Avery's face morphed into her mother's.

"Go, Sloane. Go. Save yourself." Her mother's lips trembled.

"I can't…I won't." Tears streamed down Sloane's cheeks as she faced the inevitable.

Avery's face returned.

"Save her. Save Sloane." Avery pleaded with the person yelling.

Something lifted Sloane up by her arm. With all her might, she struggled to break its grip and hold on to Avery for as long as she could. "Nooooo, let me die with her!"

Tears rolled down Avery's cheeks as she reached out for one last touch. "Go, baby. Reagan… She needs you. I love you, Sloane. I love you." Avery's face morphed one more time into Sloane's mother. "I love you, Sloane."

Sloane opened her eyes, still damp from the tears shed during the nightmare she'd had almost every night for months. Aching from not saving her dear sweet wife and her mother, she reached for the pillow on the empty side of the bed.

Reagan… She needs you. Avery's last words echoed in her head.

Guilt wrapped around her throat like a vise grip. "I'm so sorry, Reagan. I don't know how to be the mother Avery was." Sloane buried her face into the pillow, regretting she'd pretended to be asleep when Reagan returned home from her first date. Avery should've been the one waiting up for Reagan to come home and the one to talk to her for hours over ice cream, not her. Avery would've known what to say, what advice to give.

Her dream reminded her it was all up to her. Words and courage may have escaped her all night, but not now.

After rolling herself up on the bed, she sat on its edge with her feet planted on the floor. "I was such an idiot." Squaring her shoulders, she wiped her eyes dry and started her day.

With no school or work to rush off to since it was a Saturday and only the agreement to meet Finn in a few hours, Sloane and Reagan had planned a leisurely breakfast. While Reagan made pancakes, Sloane prepared the bacon and eggs.

"Would you like some orange juice, Mom?" Reagan carefully stacked the pancakes, placing two on each plate.

The moniker "Mom" lifted Sloane's heart. While every child in the world called their mother that, for Sloane, it meant much more than a name. It meant family. Sloane still had her doubts if she could live up to Avery's legacy, but she decided to trust her instincts as a parent.

"Sure." Sloane slid portions of the scrambled eggs onto each dish and grabbed the plate of bacon before joining Reagan at the dining table. Each of them took her regular seat, leaving what used to be Avery's chair empty.

"Sorry I fell asleep early last night. Tell me about your date with Emeryn."

Reagan dug into her pancakes. "It was…awkward and nice."

Sloane grinned.

"My palms were so sweaty when we walked into the diner, I hoped he wouldn't try to hold my hand. Thankfully, he didn't. I took your advice. About halfway through dinner, I told him I was nervous. He actually spat out his food all over me."

Sloane chuckled.

"Once he helped me scrape the french fry mush off my blouse, he admitted he was so nervous he thought he would throw up."

"Well, he almost did." Sloane wished Avery were there. She'd know what to ask. What to say.

"It got better after that. The movie was good and he…he…umm…kissed me good night." Reagan blushed, the kind Avery would've stayed up all night to see.

"A kiss, huh?" Sloane raised an eyebrow. "Was it a peck or a real kiss?"

Reagan's cheeks turned rosier. "A real kiss. I like him, Mom. Really like him."

The excitement of Reagan's first date and first real kiss would've been ten times better if Avery were here to share in it. She'd want to talk about it for hours later in bed, bemoaning the reality that her baby girl had grown up when she wasn't looking.

"Then I want to meet him, maybe have him over for pizza."

"Not frozen, I hope." Reagan rolled her eyes.

"We can do delivery."

"Is everything all right, Sloane?" Finn's tone left little doubt of her concern as she steered across the Golden Gate Bridge on their way toward Rohnert Park.

Finn's hand slid onto Sloane's thigh, inviting her to shift her gaze toward her. Sloane had been quiet since she fell into the passenger seat after offering a less than warm greeting when she arrived at Finn's condo. Instead of talking, she escaped inside her head, staring out the side window, rerunning last night's events, including the ones she didn't tell Reagan this morning.

"I'm sorry. I'm just a little distracted." Sloane returned her gaze toward the passing trees.

"I don't mean to pry." Finn's soft tone matched the touch of her hand when she moved it atop Sloane's. "I understand you had a custody hearing. Did something go wrong?"

"That's not it. Kadin thinks the hearing went well." She turned her gaze toward the comforting touch that required a genuine response. "I had a bittersweet moment with my stepdaughter last night."

"I guess you've had several of those lately."

"More than you can imagine. I just wish…" Sloane paused to form her thoughts.

"Wish what?"

"I wish Avery could tell me how to be a mother." She hesitated. "I feel like I'm letting her down."

Finn glanced at her and returned her eyes to the road. "How so?"

"Last night, Reagan had her first date and first real kiss."

"Aah…that's wonderful. But?"

"But…" Sloane sighed, agonizing over her overnight cowardice. "She had no one to share it with last night."

"What do you mean, she had no one?"

"It means that when Reagan came home, I faked being asleep, and she went to bed. I waited until morning to ask her how it went. She deserved better."

"Oh." Finn's drawn-out response hinted her sympathies.

"I didn't even tell her I stayed up and wore a trench on the bedroom floor with all the pacing I did in my walking boot. But when I heard a key in the front door, unsure what to say, I doused the light and flew under the covers."

The smirk on Finn's face made her uncomfortable. Mothering alone was still foreign to Sloane, and eliciting Finn's amusement wasn't helping. She turned her head away again and remained silent.

"I'm sorry. Did I do something wrong?"

"It's just that I'm a little sensitive after failing her like I did."

"Did she say she wanted to talk last night?"

"No, but I know that's what she would have done if her mother were still alive. Reagan's father died when she was a toddler, and it was just the two of them until I came along."

Finn's pause made Sloane think she was weighing her next words. "Tell me, what kind of relationship did you have with Reagan before her mother died?"

"Difficult at the start, but then she warmed up, and we became friends. We'd just gotten close when…"

"Then you didn't let her down. You were the mother you've always been and the one she expected."

Sloane turned toward Finn and shook her head. "But that's not the mother she needs." Her voice cracked.

"From everything I've seen, you're exactly what she needs." Finn steered through traffic, passing several slower cars. "Maybe you shouldn't try to do things the way Avery did them. It might feel forced. It'll take time, but you'll come up with your own way of filling in for Avery and being there for Reagan. I'm sure you'll find new traditions and new ways of doing things."

Odd, Sloane thought. Being vulnerable with someone she didn't know well had made her uncomfortable in the past, but Finn put her at ease. Maybe their history played into it, or the way she and Finn were in sync with work. Perhaps it was because they'd both lost someone they loved. Whatever the reason, Finn had a way of saying the right thing at the right moment, helping Sloane navigate her troubles. They'd become friends, of that she was sure.

"Thank you, Finn. What you said helps."

"I'm glad." Finn glanced at her again and gave her a warm smile.

Half an hour later, after Finn pulled into the chaotic Walmart parking lot in Rohnert Park, the two of them walked through the main doors.

"They're all the same." Sloane walked down the central aisle chuckling at the store's predictability. No matter the city, every Walmart had the same pedestrian feel with cheap products, stocked on flimsy displays, in narrow, disorganized aisles.

"I'll take your word for it." Finn scanned her surroundings.

"Walmart probably isn't in your wheelhouse anymore."

Finn stopped in her tracks and faced Sloane, hands on her hips. "What kind of crack was that?"

"I'm sorry." Sloane could have kicked herself. "But when you mentioned the trust fund, I assumed that—"

"You assumed what? That because I have money, I wouldn't lower myself to walk inside a Walmart?"

"No, I'm—"

"I don't know why I'm telling you this, but I've only dipped into my trust fund once, and that was to get into the condo. I needed to live close to work, and the city is so damned expensive. Otherwise, I live off my salary. And for your information, I'm a Target girl. It was closer to my old place."

"I'm truly sorry." The injured look in Finn's eyes made Sloane shrivel up like a raisin. In the last hour, she'd either acted like a hermit or a teenager without a filter. Finn must've thought she was unbalanced. "You've been nothing but kind, and I had no right to judge you. I'd like to think we are becoming friends again, and I hope I didn't torpedo that."

"We *are* friends." Finn scrunched her nose like she used to do when they were kids. "Apology accepted."

"Phew!" Sloane rubbed the length of Finn's arms. She didn't have to force a grin. "I'm a Target girl too."

"All right, my friend." Finn's smile went all the way to her eyes. "Let's go talk to the manager."

Sloane led the way to the back of the store, kicking herself for insulting Finn. Besides Eric and Dylan, Finn was her only friend and hurting her hurt herself.

I gotta work on that filter thing.

After a few raps on the store manager's open office door, a blond, slender woman in her forties popped her head out. "May I help you?" The woman stepped out, straightening her professional, yet sensible off-the-rack gray business suit.

Sloane and Finn each flashed their badges and credentials.

"Are you the manager?" Sloane continued after an affirmative nod. "I'm Sergeant Sloane of the San Francisco Police Department. This is Agent Harper of the DEA. We need information on a prepaid phone purchased from your store."

A glint materialized in the manager's eyes. "Of course, come in." She walked to her desk, her gait hampered by a considerable limp. "Anything I can do to help ladies in blue."

After Sloane provided the manufacturer and serial number of Diego's burner, the manager located the purchase record in the store's database. "I have it right here. Someone bought it almost four months ago."

"Who?" Finn asked.

"Sorry, Agent Harper, it was a cash purchase."

Not surprising. A cash transaction meshed with a desire to remain anonymous. In Sloane's experience, only an amateur would've left a paper trail a mile wide and these guys were no amateurs.

"What about security tapes?"

"Sorry again. With so many cameras, we only store sixty days of surveillance video."

"We're screwed." Finn sucked in her lower lip, but this was one dead end Sloane wouldn't accept. She'd conducted enough investigations to know how one lead could lead to another in a trail of breadcrumbs. Things that appeared insignificant often ended up solving the case. She just had to find that first crumb.

"It can't end here." Sloane's brain went into overdrive, prompting her to pace the room to help her think. Convinced Diego's phone would break this case wide open, she stopped in her tracks and snapped her fingers. "Can you look up the transaction and tell me what else was bought with it?"

"Sure, hold on." The manager hit a few keys and navigated to another screen in the store computer system. "It looks like this purchase included seven prepaid phones, and that's it."

"That's better than nothing. Can you print out the serial numbers for each of the phones?" A hint of hope laced Sloane's voice.

"Sure thing." The manager's face lit up as she drilled into the store system. "You know, I thought about becoming a police officer when I was younger."

"Why didn't you?" She'd have made a fine officer, Sloane thought.

"My parents thought it was too dangerous, so I started working here." The manager patted her left leg and laughed. "The real danger was that out-of-control forklift."

Sloane nodded. Every job had its risks. Avery's didn't include a gun and a badge as a target, yet she died doing it.

Moments later, a laser printer next to the computer came to life and spit out a single sheet of paper. The manager handed it to Sloane. "I hope you get whoever you're after."

"Thank you. I'm sorry. I never got your name."

"Alice, Alice Patterson."

"Thank you, Alice." Sloane shook her hand. "This may help us solve the case."

Back on the road, Finn glanced at Sloane and then focused on traffic. "I thought this case might be dead in the water, but we have six more leads because of you. No wonder Eric is always singing your praises."

"He taught me never to give up." Sloane tightened her jaw. "I just wish I'd learned that lesson before my parents died."

Finn slipped her hand off the steering wheel and squeezed Sloane's hand. "You would've died too."

"Maybe I should've." Sloane pulled her hand back and stared out her side window, the blurred landscape reminding her how fast life can pass by. "Avery might still be alive."

"Don't talk like that, Sloane."

Filter, you idiot.

"I'm sorry." Their eyes met for a second before Finn returned her focus to the road. She regretted the worry on Finn's face. "I didn't mean that. As long as I'm breathing, this case will never be dead in the water. I won't quit again."

* * *

Taking in the view from Finn's Market Street condo had become a guilty pleasure for Sloane, not only for the view but also for the company. Tonight marked her third indulgence. Staring out the window, she remembered what Finn asked her the last time she visited. *The view never gets old, does it?* It hadn't.

Since the first day she moved to Hunter's Point, the bay had a captivating and comforting quality. In twenty years, that feeling never faded. Sloane couldn't explain it, but she sensed it would always draw her in.

"Beautiful." Sloane accepted the glass of mint water Finn handed her. "Thank you."

Finn stared at her and added a wistful lilt, "Yes, beautiful."

The way those words rolled off her tongue, Sloane could tell Finn didn't mean the bay. When their gazes met, she whispered back, "Thank you," and thought *I'm not ready. You remind me of Avery. Or did Avery remind me of you?* The question confused her more. Did she fall in love with Avery or an echo of Finn? *If I weren't grieving, would I pursue you? Maybe someday, but not now. Not yet.*

Finn held her gaze and then shifted her attention to the city lights glowing outside the window. "Tell me, Sloane, do you still sing? You were the best mezzo-soprano in the entire choir."

"No, I gave that up years ago."

The question left her uneasy. She'd never explained to anyone why she'd stopped, coming close only once with Avery. Explaining, she feared, would open old wounds, something she wasn't willing to do.

"That's a shame. You had such a beautiful voice."

Sloane turned sharply on her heel, her voice just as intense. "We should get to work."

Finn followed her to her den without another word.

Sloane flipped the rocker switch on the wall inside, waking the lights. The stark contrast of the room's untidiness with the rest of the condo still bewildered Sloane. It made her think she and Finn had a lot in common. Each of them hid their real selves from the world.

Before she crossed the threshold, a gentle hand fell on her shoulder. Finn's soft voice telegraphed her concern. "Did I say something wrong again?"

"No, you didn't." Sloane's voice trailed off with a heavy sigh. Filter, she reminded herself. "We've been sitting on this for days, and I'm just eager to get to work on those leads."

While the limitations of working this off-book case on restricted duty frustrated Sloane, she walked away from Finn for a different reason. If anyone did something wrong, it had been her. For two decades, she'd lived with the painful truth about what her singing cost her. Laying on the charred embankment while metal melted into a molten mess, she'd vowed never to sing again. But that was the distant past. She had no interest in lingering there while the present needed her attention.

Once seated on the couch, she laid the phone records of all seven prepaid phones on the coffee table. The documents detailed sporadic activity but revealed an interesting pattern. Six of the phones showed only occasional incoming and outgoing calls and text messages to one phone. Sloane labeled that one burner number seven. Number seven also showed calls and texts from a different phone, not one from the batch purchased in Rohnert Park. That phone was a mystery.

"The seventh phone has to be Caco's burner." Finn circled the number corresponding to the phone at the center of things.

"Or that of someone close to him." Sloane sensed they were on the right track, but she didn't want to jump to conclusions. "I'll track down this unknown number tomorrow. In the meantime, let's dive deeper into these records."

Over the next few hours, they cataloged the cell tower location of each call and text for the last four months. They worked well as a team. Sloane read off the geo-coordinates and Finn entered the data into a spreadsheet. Occasionally they stole glances at each other.

Finn's mind wandered. *What if things were different? What if she wasn't grieving for the only woman she'd ever loved? Would she pursue me? Maybe someday, but not now. Not yet. She's not ready.*

When Sloane raised her head, Finn returned her focus to their next task: locate Caco or his labs. She entered each geo-coordinate into a map application on her iPad and retrieved their corresponding street locations. Sloane then used pushpins to mark each spot on a large paper map they'd tacked onto her office wall. Using a different color for each cell phone, Sloane annotated from where each phone had sent a text or made or received a call.

When they finished, they sat on the couch and studied the map. It had a story to tell; they just had to decipher it. The trick to making sense of a scatter diagram like the one they'd assembled, Finn knew, was to ignore anomalies and focus on clusters. This would tell them where their suspects spent most of their time and where to find them.

Their problem: there were no real clusters. Several phones pinged primarily in a single city, but in too many locations to track. The pins for the seventh phone, presumably Caco's, were even more scattered. This drug lord had designed his pill-making operation to be mobile and had each lab often moved to avoid detection. The result—nothing for Sloane and Finn to focus their attention on.

"This is a nightmare." Sloane rubbed her neck in clear frustration. "There's no telling where the labs are, and Caco's phone has pinged in every Bay Area county. It'll be impossible to find him."

Finn approached the map and studied it up close. "Diego Rojas told us labs were in the city, Oakland, Richmond, Vallejo, and San Jose. That accounts for five of the phones. What about this other one? Like Caco's phone, it's pinged in multiple cities."

"A lieutenant, maybe."

Finn cocked her head several times. "This proves Diego was telling the truth. Maybe we can use that."

"How?" Sloane joined Finn at the map. "He's dead. Diego can't tell us anything more."

"He can't, but I know someone who can."

"Who?"

"His brother. I think we need to take a road trip to Solano Prison."

"Yes, we do."

CHAPTER NINETEEN

Sloane slid herself into the passenger seat of Finn's car for another off-book field trip, feeling better about how things were going at home. She'd taken Finn's advice. Instead of trying to be the same mother Avery had been, she decided to trust the love she and Reagan shared would be enough to forge a stronger bond. Being able to put that concern behind her enabled her to focus on getting another step closer to Avery's killer.

Their route today took them across the Bay Bridge through the MacArthur Maze toward Vacaville. Sloane stared out the front window, forcing herself to stay engaged.

"What was your excuse for leaving work early today?" Sloane knew her monotone voice didn't make for an impressive start for idle chitchat, but it would have to do. "Mine was a parent-teacher conference."

"Dental appointment." Finn offered a toothy grin. "Works whenever I need a little time to myself."

"I'll weave that into my lineup of excuses." Sloane nodded with a forced grin, recalling the last time she played hooky from work.

Not long after their wedding, Avery had phoned. "I'm not feeling well," she said. "I think you may have to drive me home." When they jumped in the car in the parking garage, instead of buckling up, Avery had leaned over and said in a low, husky tone, "You better rush us home. I think I need to spend the rest of the day in bed." She then kissed Sloane on the lips. "With you."

Sloane's grin disappeared. She missed those tender moments.

Finn glanced at her. "Are you okay?"

"I'll be fine." Sloane shook her head, more at herself than at Finn. She had to break this cycle of grief and, for Finn's sake, get off the eggshells she'd been walking on around her. "I have to get used to my new reality, that's all."

She focused on the purpose of their field trip. She needed to find something that would lead them to Caco so she could stand face-to-face with her wife's killer. "I got a hit on that unknown number that Caco's phone called. It's another burner. The carrier should send me the records tomorrow."

Finn nodded.

Sloane remained quiet the rest of the drive. The radio was on, but news bulletins from local stations describing the growth of wildfires in the state melted into white noise as she focused on how to leverage Diego's brother.

Incarceration in a federal or state prison, no matter the facility, was never a pleasant experience, even in the medium-security wing Miguel Rojas currently called home. While Finn didn't consider Solano rough compared to other California prisons like San Quentin or Pelican Bay, it was designed just the same to take away an inmate's freedom and any sense of controlling his own life.

Miguel was keeping a low profile as he went through his five-year stretch behind the prison walls. His counselor gave Sloane and Finn insight into Miguel's state of mind, including how he'd received news of his brother's death. Distraught, he'd lashed out at another inmate in a dispute over what channel to watch on the community television. It was his only behavioral infraction.

"We can use his anger against him," suggested Finn as they waited for a guard to bring Miguel into the cold, gray prison interview room.

"Yes, we can. The need for revenge can be overpowering."

With each passing day, Sloane's eyes had grown colder. She was staring off now into the distance. Wherever she was, it wasn't in the small, dingy prison interview room.

Finn had to wonder how far Sloane would go if they zeroed in on Caco. "I understand that urge, Sloane, but it's unhealthy."

"What do you know about revenge?"

"The man who killed Izzy was high on cocaine. He deserved to die, but he was a diplomat, so our laws couldn't touch him. I followed him for weeks, thinking about the best way to make him pay. I failed a class and lost my internship at a law firm because of my obsession. But it didn't matter. His country recalled him, and as far as I know, he never served one day in prison."

Sloane turned toward Finn. The look in her eyes spoke to a mutual understanding.

Finn swallowed the lump in her throat, pushing back the sickening feeling that given a chance, Sloane would cross a line she couldn't cross with her.

"Sloane—"

Finn turned her head when the door swung open. Miguel and a guard entered.

Miguel, dressed in Solano blues, sat down at the table across from Sloane and Finn. The guard hadn't chained him. His single outburst apparently hadn't resulted in him being labeled a threat.

"I'll be right outside. Yell if you need me." The guard closed the door behind him on his way out.

Miguel leaned back in his chair and stared at Sloane and Finn, not asking why they'd brought him there.

"I'm Special Agent Harper, DEA. This is Sergeant Sloane, SFPD. We'd like to talk to you about your brother."

"He's dead." Miguel clenched his jaw. A man of few words, he wore his emotions about his brother's death on his sleeve.

"If you help us find Los Dorados and their leader, we can help you." Finn held out hope as she had with Diego, she'd find the right incentive for Miguel to cooperate.

"Why should I help you?"

Sloane drilled Miguel with her stare. Its steeliness made Finn suspect her fears about her crossing a line were closer to becoming a reality than she first thought.

"Let's cut through the crap. Caco killed your brother. He also killed my wife. Tell us everything you know about Los Dorados and your brother's operation, and we'll work on getting you into minimum security. As a bonus, when I find Caco, I'll put a bullet between his eyes."

Having gained Miguel's full attention, Sloane leaned in, as did he. They stared at each other for several beats as if gauging the other's response. The rage behind their narrowed eyes heated the room. *Yes*, Finn thought, *that line is getting closer*.

"What do you want to know?"

"The address of their headquarters in the Lower Bottoms for starters."

* * *

After Sloane opened the door leading in from the garage of her cozy townhouse, she trudged up the few steps to the main level. She cursed her clumsy walking boot on every step. Tomorrow, when she could finally toss the bulky contraption, couldn't come soon enough.

A strange silence wrapped the house. She expected Reagan to be in her downstairs bedroom, blasting music or the latest episode of a singing talent show. Instead, she found her on the living room couch with only a single lamp lit to illuminate the room. Through the dim light, Sloane could see her eyes were red and swollen from crying.

Sloane closed her eyes to what she'd created. Reagan had only wept a few times in front of her since the funeral, having fallen into the role of caretaker instead of a grieving daughter. She kicked herself for placing that burden on her. A good mother would never have done that, but she promised to make up for it.

If Reagan's grief resembled her own, Sloane suspected Reagan was riding out another wave. Anything could've triggered it. A favorite coffee cup found in the cabinet. A perfect score on a geometry test she wanted to share. A photograph from last year's birthday party. It didn't matter. Something would start the wave rolling. Sloane just needed to convince her she wasn't alone.

After she tossed her keys on the coffee table, her heart grew heavier until she sat next to Reagan and pulled her into a comforting hug. "I miss her too."

"That's not it." Reagan sniffled several times. "It's Grandma and Grandpa Santos."

What now? She sighed away her gut response, which was to blow her top. She pulled out her calmest tone. "What about them?"

"They were here."

Sloane sprung forward in her seat. "Here? In this house?" She took in a deep breath to quell her anger. Giving in to it would make matters worse.

"They came right after school before you usually come home from work, but I didn't let them in."

Sloane inhaled another deep breath. The Santoses knew her schedule and had used it to defy her before the judge's ruling. They'd never shown her one ounce of respect. Why should she expect any from them now? Her temper smoldered, but she dug deep to set the right example. "Tell me what happened."

"They said Mom wanted me to spend time with them." Tears welled up in Reagan's eyes. "Is it true? Did she want that?"

"I don't know, honey. She never told me she was in contact with them. I don't know what she talked to them about, but I'm positive she would have talked to me about something this important."

Damn it, Avery. Three phone calls. Why didn't you tell me? Sloane had thought they told each other everything, at least the important things. Then again, she never told Avery the details of her parents' accident nor about Finn. *I guess we both kept secrets.*

Reagan slumped back into the couch. "I don't know what to believe, but I know I'm afraid of them."

"Did they say something to scare you?"

"They said you don't have a right to keep me from them, no matter what the judge says."

The veins in Sloane's neck throbbed. No right? The law gave her the right. She rubbed her temples to curb a mounting headache. "That sounds like a threat."

"That's what I thought."

Sloane rubbed her face with both hands, thinking about what Avery would do. The moment called for a straightforward solution. Sloane clapped her hands before standing. "This calls for ice cream."

They shared a bowl of chocolate ice cream to cool off. When Reagan said good night before heading down to her bedroom, Sloane assured her she'd handle her grandparents. Later, she closed her bedroom door, flopped on the bed, almost spread-eagle, and stared at the ceiling.

"What did you talk to them about, Avery?" Whatever her wife had done, Sloane needed to do what she thought best for Reagan.

After fishing out her iPhone from her pants pocket, she blew out one more long breath and dialed. "Kadin, I have a problem. I need a restraining order against the Santoses."

After Sloane gave a few words of explanation, Kadin served as the voice of calm.

"A restraining order might not be the wisest option. Judge Gonzalez might consider it an unnecessary escalation. Let me contact their lawyer and have him warn them to cease all contact with Reagan until the judge hands down her decision."

"I can't trust they'll keep their distance."

"It should only be a few days, Sloane. I'll light a fire under the guy. After I'm done with him, I don't think the Santoses will risk it again. In the meantime, you might be right about them lying about Avery. I'll do a little digging."

Sloane didn't like her position, but she had to trust Kadin's advice. After agreeing to wait, she ended the call. Staring at the ceiling again, she sensed the emptiness of her bed. Everything rested on her shoulders and hers alone. "I hope I'm doing the right thing, baby."

CHAPTER TWENTY

Losing the walking boot in the morning gave Sloane a rush, but Lieutenant West quickly doused her new taste of freedom by insisting she ride a desk a few more days.

"No sense in rushing things. Monday will be soon enough," West had said.

Sloane had nothing more to do other than review old files, and concentrating on work proved a harder task than she expected. Her mind kept drifting to Miguel Rojas and the information he provided, but she'd have to wait until the end of the day to follow up on it. While Eric caught up on cases he'd worked on when she recuperated at home, Sloane turned on the radio, hoping music would help her focus. Wall-to-wall coverage of the mid-autumn wildfires plaguing northern California interrupted her favorite radio stations, though, highlighting how overnight fires had destroyed hundreds of structures and authorities had reported several casualties.

Hearing about death and destruction made passing the time harder. Her mind bounced back and forth between the Santoses and Caco. Both topics posed trouble. While West had her chained to a desk, Luiz could try to contact Reagan and Caco was running free. Both thoughts unnerved her, but Caco had her most on edge. She feared she was on a collision course with him and one of them wouldn't survive.

"I've had enough of this." Sloane pushed back her chair, stomped to the window, and turned off the radio.

Eric reached into his desk drawer, pulled out a Snickers bar, and underhanded it to Sloane.

"What's this for?"

"You get a little cranky when you're hungry."

Sloane forced a grin. "Very funny." She *was* hangry. She ripped open the package and gnawed off a big chunk of the candy bar. The sweet and salty combination occupied her mouth but did little to curb that edge she'd been teetering on all morning.

After returning to her desk, Sloane clicked on her official email for the twentieth time. The cellular provider had yet to forward her the records on the mystery burner phone, and her patience had worn thin. She did, however, open a new email from the SFPD personnel division.

Her chest tightened with a sharp intake of breath and twisted on each word as she read. *Our records show you listed Avery Santos as your sole beneficiary for your life insurance policy. Considering her recent passing, we recommend you review your policy and designate new beneficiaries at your earliest convenience.* Just when she started to heal, another reminder picked at the scab.

She sprang from her chair. With West and half the staff already suspecting she'd come back too soon, she couldn't fall apart in front of the entire division. She zoomed through the maze of crisscrossed desks and dozen detectives, hoping to hold it together until she reached the seclusion of the ladies' restroom.

The lingering tenderness and swelling in her foot made for a slight limp as she quickstepped down the hallway. At the sinks, she splashed away—four, five, or six times...she'd lost count—the heavy reminder of how the explosion had made her a widow. But the email was right. She needed to make Reagan a beneficiary and put the Tenneys in charge of the money. When her mind settled and she looked up at the mirror, she found the reflection of Lieutenant West standing several feet behind her in quiet concern.

"We gotta stop meeting like this, L-T." Sloane hoped her quip didn't sound forced. After pulling out several paper towels, she patted her face dry. Inspecting herself in the mirror, she dabbed the corners of her eyes to erase any evidence of tears.

Lieutenant West stepped forward and then leaned one hip against the sink counter. "You looked upset when you darted past my door. I need to know you're okay."

"I'll be fine. It was nothing."

"Look, Sloane." Lieutenant West's expression spoke more to compassion than her official duties. "There are only four female detectives in this entire building, and two of them are standing in this bathroom. I know from experience we made it to where we are by being tougher and better than any man in our orbit. This is a man's domain. To make it, the primary rule is never let them see you cry."

"I told you, it was nothing."

"We both know better." West's stern tone meant she had stood her ground and wouldn't accept Sloane's reflexive brush off. "I'd like to think the rule doesn't apply when it's just the two of us. I know how tough it is to keep it together when everything around me falls apart. Lord knows I've needed a shoulder a time or two on the job. I want you to know it's okay to let go in front of me. Hell, I might even join you."

Sloane had a friendly work relationship with Morgan West, sometimes discussing little tidbits about family, friends, and vacation plans, but they weren't close by any stretch. Finn was a puzzling exception—Sloane couldn't deny their connection and the pull she'd felt for days—but West's offer of friendship made her uncomfortable, as did every such proposal from a woman. Getting close and personal didn't come easily to Sloane. Friends wanted to know her past, something she refused to share. Good friends would make her love them, something she refused to risk. She'd just lose them if she let them in. "I hear you. Some days are rougher than the others." Sloane hoped that would be enough to get Morgan West off this track. Talking was the last thing she wanted. "Thank you, ma'am, but I'll be fine."

Lieutenant West's shoulders dropped at Sloane's rebuff. "Just know the offer stands. There're so few of us women in this division. We have to stick together. My door is always open." She placed a light hand on Sloane's shoulder and then walked out.

Time to get back to work. Sloane straightened her back and squared her shoulders. After patting her face a few more times with the paper towels, she threw the damp, crumpled paper in the trash. Her reflection in the mirror gave her one last burst of confidence. "You got this."

Back at her desk, Eric took a few moments to study her. "Everything okay?"

"It will be."

Easily said, but not easily believed. Working through her grief, dealing with the Santoses, and chasing a drug-dealing murderer posed a challenge, but she refused to explain every time emotion got the best of her.

When Sloane clicked her computer mouse to nudge the monitor awake, she had one new message. Her heart pumped harder when she opened it. The cellular provider had just moved her one step closer to finding Caco with records of the mystery burner.

Leads had come in fast, first the information Miguel provided, now this. Remembering Eric's words to her in the garage, "Promise you'll bring me in when you get close," she sensed that time had come.

"Can you meet me after work tonight? I need your take on that project I've been working on." Code, but Eric had caught Sloane's underlying message with a nod.

"Sure."

Sloane's iPhone buzzed. She pulled it out to read the incoming text message from Kadin. *Heller read Santoses the riot act. Don't want case thrown out, they'll keep distance.* Sloane's muscles relaxed with a deep exhale. Kadin had taken one worry off her shoulders…for now.

She typed a reply. *TY. Owe u dinner.*

* * *

Until Judge Gonzalez ruled on guardianship, Sloane balked at leaving Reagan alone longer than necessary. She'd like to think her former in-laws were smart enough not to risk their guardianship case, but so far, smart hadn't been their trademark. Her townhouse would have to suffice as a meeting place for Finn and Eric.

"Hey, kiddo." Eric's voice echoed up the stairs when Reagan opened the front door to let him in. "Your mom's expecting me."

"Hey, Eric. Her friend's already here." She walked up the interior steps. "What? No groceries?"

He laughed, resting a hand on her shoulder. "I spoiled you two."

"I liked it when you did the shopping when Mom was laid up. You brought me Doritos."

"For which you're not out of the doghouse yet, mister." Sloane carried in two glasses of mint water from the kitchen as she breezed past Eric. "I had a hard time weaning her off them."

Eric wagged a finger at Reagan. "I told you to hide those."

"Oops, sorry." Reagan shrugged before turning her attention to Sloane. "I'm heading downstairs to finish my homework."

"I'd appreciate it if you'd stay downstairs while we talk about a case. We shouldn't be more than an hour."

After Reagan retreated, Sloane handed Finn one of the glasses and filled Eric in on the leads they'd developed, their narrowed-down suspect pool for the leak, and their latest puzzle piece—the mystery burner phone. The records she collected from the service provider showed the phone had made only two outgoing calls to Caco's phone, both from the same location, one following the lab explosion and one on the day Diego was killed in lockup.

"You two have been busy. Looks like you may have found the leak." Eric familiarized himself with Sloane's documents.

"And it's time to get busy again." Finn whipped out her tablet. "Sloane, you want to read off those geo-coordinates?"

Finn entered the numbers of the cell tower into her mapping program and leaned back in her seat, a stunned look on her face. "This can't be a coincidence." She ran both hands through her dark blond hair as if trying to digest what she'd seen.

"What is it, Finn?" Sloane wrinkled her brow.

Finn flipped the tablet around. A tag marked the exact location of the cell tower on the map. Finn zoomed in, pointing to a specific building on the screen. "The cell tower is less than one block from the Federal Building right here in San Francisco. The leak has to be in my building."

Sloane grabbed the tablet and studied the area, which consisted of high-end offices, apartments, and government buildings. It wasn't a known hotbed for drug dealers, and that confirmed her and Finn's gut-wrenching suspicion.

"Now we know it has to be Prichard, Quintrell, or Carol." Finn shook her head, Sloane sharing her shock. Someone she worked with, someone in a position of trust, someone with a security clearance was the leak. Had contributed to Avery's death. "They were the only ones who had access to the files and knew about Diego."

"My money is on Prickhead." Sloane had never liked bureaucrats. Slapping cuffs on him would be extra sweet.

Eric chuckled to himself and then turned to Finn. "Remember what I told you at China Basin? We find the leak, we find Caco."

"Then we need to set a trap." Finn nodded.

Her energy amped up, Sloane paced the room. She went over all the players and pieces in her head. Diego…Miguel…Caco…Prichard…Quintrell…Carol…burner phones…mobile labs. There had to be a way to leverage the information they'd compiled.

Sloane snapped her fingers and stopped pacing. "Miguel told us the exact location where Diego first met Caco. He said it was a Los Dorados headquarters for his lieutenants. What if we fake a joint SF-Oakland raid?"

"A head fake." Eric nodded with a knowing grin.

"Right. As a 'courtesy,'" Sloane used air quotes to emphasize her point, "we brief our suspects minutes before it's scheduled. If we make it sound time-sensitive, our leak may try to tip off Caco."

"But if all three suspects are in the same place, how do we flush out the leak? How will we know who it is?" Finn's uncertain tone meant Sloane hadn't thought all of this through to her satisfaction. But the plan was perfect to Sloane. Caco was her target, not the leak.

"We separate them." Eric swirled an index finger in the air as if whipping a loose idea into shape. "Get them into different areas of the city at the same time. If someone makes a call from that burner, we'll know what tower it came from and who's the leak."

"The logistics would be a nightmare." Sloane let loose a theatrical sigh. Too many moving parts meant too many chances to get it wrong. "I don't care about the leak. They all work in the same building. Let's do it there so we can go after Caco."

Finn sucked in a deep breath and stiffened her back. "To do this case justice, we need to do both and do it by the book."

Sloane turned to meet Finn's eyes. "What does following the book have to do with justice?"

"If we want a conviction—"

"Conviction? You mean in a court of law? The law and justice aren't the same thing. Haven't you learned that by now? He'll just offer up someone else the DEA can go after, cut a deal, and get out before Reagan finishes college. That's not justice."

"But a bullet to the head is?" Finn squared off toe-to-toe with Sloane just as she had the day she had to bounce Diego Rojas. Sloane got the impression there'd be no negotiating.

"It's better than the alternative."

"Then I won't be part of this."

Finn's expression turned to something Sloane had seen before in Walmart, only this time much worse. Finn wasn't just feeling slighted; she wore a look of genuine hurt and disappointment. Under any other circumstance, that would've been enough for Sloane to drop it, or at least consider it. Finn was, after all, her friend with the possibility of becoming more, but this was not the day for reversing course. This was the day for revenge, not justice.

Her dilemma: she and Eric couldn't bait all the players on their own. She resorted to the solution Eric had taught her: Give the impression of cooperation, even if you have no intention of following through.

Sloane softened her expression. "I don't want to argue with you over this. Let's say we do it your way. What do you propose?"

"We bring in Lieutenant West and ADA Harris." Finn's tone signaled this wasn't negotiable. "Use them to bait Prichard and Quintrell while I work on Carol."

"Then what?"

"If we're lucky, one will take the bait, and we'll get the leak."

Sloane clenched her fist. "And if we're luckier, we'll get Caco."

CHAPTER TWENTY-ONE

"I'm not sure what disturbs me more. The fact that you did all this half-cocked or that you suspected us?" Morgan West crossed her arms in front of her body. Sloane's gaze turned to ADA Kyler Harris, who appeared to be fighting mad as well; her arms were crossed in the same manner.

Sloane bit her lower lip at her misstep, regretting the pained tone in her boss's voice. "This wasn't personal, L-T. We had to think like detectives and rule out anyone who had knowledge of Diego's deal."

West shifted in her office chair and straightened her suit coat. "At least we know where we stand with you two." Her words sharpened to a fine point.

Sloane glanced at Eric, lamenting the rift she'd caused between them and West. She'd have to back-burner the repair work, though. Given the mobility of Los Dorados' operation, they needed to strike while the intel was fresh. "I couldn't be more relieved that we cleared you and ADA Harris, but now we need to focus on what's important, and that's finding Caco."

"And who at the Federal level is feeding him information." Finn served as the conscience of the group, reminding Sloane there was more at play than just revenge.

"Right." Sloane glanced at Finn and registered her uncompromising look. "We have a plan and need your help to pull this off."

"What do you need from us?" West softened her tone but not as much as Sloane would've liked.

After detailing their plan, Sloane finished with, "Timing will be critical, but we think the leak will take the bait."

"And how did you come up with the three different locations?" West had yet to look convinced.

"The department tech center helped me. They figured out cell tower ranges, then we had to pick three locations far enough apart that would allow for triangulation and wouldn't raise suspicion."

"I get the Federal Building for Carol and my office for Quintrell, but Sally's Café?" Kyler Harris asked.

"Prichard likes pie. He never passes up an opportunity for a slice."

West pursed her lips after she received an affirmative nod from Kyler. "This might actually work. When do you want to do this?"

"Today."

Prichard was reliable—always on time, especially when the prospect of a high-profile case was involved. Taking into account the location of Sally's Café, though, Sloane counted on having a few extra minutes to start mending fences with Morgan West. No one ever planned on the limited parking in the area and the resulting four- or five-block hike it usually resulted in, particularly at the time of day when Sally was gearing up for the dinner crowd.

Sally's was a low-rent restaurant in a high-rent district. Wobbly Formica tables for two lined the wall opposite the cluttered service counter. A line of another six tables for four, all with mismatched, well-worn chairs, filled the center. Dozens of black and white framed photographs littered the walls in an irregular pattern, memorializing visits from famous patrons in years past. Chatter from the twenty or so guests barely drowned out the clacking of wall-mounted oscillating fans near the ceiling making repetitive arcs to circulate the grease-tinged air.

Sloane studied her boss from across the table. Besides the pleasantries with the waitress, including, "We'll have two coffees and two slices of pecan," West had yet to speak to Sloane. Crossed arms, stiff posture, and narrowed eyes didn't bode well.

After West thanked the perky brunette waitress for the refill, Sloane forked off another bite of her half-eaten slice of pie and calculated her chances of making any headway before Prichard arrived. She decided on slim. "I'm sorry, L-T."

"For suspecting me or for going rogue?"

"The former. It's not that I didn't trust you, it's that I don't know you."

"And whose fault is that?"

"Mine." Her boss served her a mouthful of regret. Kindness and a desire to mentor were all West had ever shown her, and Sloane repaid her with suspicion. "How do I fix this?"

West averted her eyes. "I don't know yet."

Sloane's phone buzzed to an incoming text. It was Finn. *Carol's trap set. Meet you at Bryant.*

"Sorry I'm late. Parking was a nightmare." Prichard wiped beads of sweat from his brow and cheek with a folded white handkerchief. His oversized belly was another sure sign the short walk likely served as his only cardio for the week.

Sloane had disliked this guy from the onset, judging him as a bureaucrat who cared little about the toes he stepped on, including hers. Proving he tipped off the man who killed her wife would taste sweet…very sweet.

"Thanks for coming, Nate." West gestured to the empty chair to her right. "Can I get you anything? Coffee?"

When his gaze went to her untouched slice of pie, West slid it along the tabletop. "Help yourself. I lost my appetite." She gave Sloane a sardonic expression that made Sloane squirm in her chair.

"Well…if you're not hungry." His chewing matched his personality—annoying. "Not that I don't mind the company, but what's so important we couldn't do this over the phone?"

"I wanted you to hear this personally from me. We've been working with the Oakland PD on a joint drug task force. Our team located what we think is a lab or headquarters of a drug ring in the Lower Bottoms of Oakland. That drug ring might be Los Dorados. Since our intel is time-sensitive, I'm here as a courtesy. Unless circumstances change, we set the raid to go off at five thirty."

Prichard's ears perked up. "What makes you think it's Los Dorados?"

"A snitch believes the drug Kiss, the one you briefed us on several months ago," West briefly pointed an index finger at him, "has been coming from that home."

"Five thirty? That's not enough time for me to get a team in place." Prichard waved his hands up and down as if Morgan had laid a hand grenade in his lap, not an olive branch.

Mumbling, he whipped out his phone, quickly thumbing through his contact list. "This is Special Agent Prichard. Do you know anything about a possible Los Dorados lab or headquarters in the Lower Bottoms of Oakland?… PD is planning a raid in…" He checked his watch, "fifteen minutes…I know it's not enough time…I'll let you know." Prichard redirected his attention back to the table. "I can have a team there in thirty?"

"Sorry, sir. You misunderstand." Sloane lined her statement with a little extra zest. "We're not here to invite you on this operation.   We're here to let you know it's happening." Throwing the words he'd uttered at their initial Kiss meeting back at him made one corner of her mouth draw up in a satisfied grin. *Prickhead.*

Sloane's phone pinged again. It was from Eric. *Quintrell trap set. Going to Bryant.* Everything was going as planned, she thought.

On her way out, Sloane texted Finn and Eric. *Prickhead's trap set. Meet you at Bryant.*

A throb formed in Sloane's head, willing her boss to weave their official sedan faster through Bryant's parking garage. Seconds before the car dipped between the concrete layers, her cell phone had alerted to an incoming email from the cellular company tracking Los Dorados' burner phones. *Damn wheel of death!* She considered pounding her iPhone against the dash to speed up the loading message, but with eight payments to go, she decided against it.

Once she and West stepped off the elevator on the sixth floor, the spinning circle stopped, and the screen lit up to the email. Her stomach churned as she scanned the message, skipping the filler words, focusing on the meat. "A call was made from one of the phones to Caco's."

"It worked?" West's question ended on an uptick.

Sloane read more of the email, absorbing its contents. "I'm not sure. It says the call was made at five twenty-two, but not from a tower we had them monitoring."

"Couldn't be Prichard. That was right around the time he was with us. How about the others?"

"Unknown."

"What about Caco? Did he answer? Did they trace his end of the call?"

The words in the final paragraph provided Sloane the information she'd wanted for weeks: the location of the man who killed her wife. But her plans for Caco didn't involve West, Finn, Eric, or handcuffs. She preferred to involve the business end of her Sig Sauer and didn't want either of them anywhere near her.

"The call went to voice mail," she lied.

"I'm sorry, Sloane. We may have our differences, but I know how important this is to you. I have the feeling you three are on the right track."

When West stepped toward the squad room, Sloane looked at her phone again and feigned concern over an incoming text message. "Hey, L-T, Reagan's having a rough go right now. Can you tell Harper and Decker I went home?"

"Is everything all right?"

"She'll be fine. I just need to go."

"Go. Take care of family. This can wait until tomorrow."

When the door closed and the elevator dropped to the parking level, Sloane's chest grew tight. Lying to West was another thing she'd have to apologize for when this was all over. Though she wasn't sure any apology would ever repair things between them.

She bolted through the garage, weaving through several aisles toward her SUV, where she ran head-on into Finn—the last thing she wanted.

"Whoa. Where's the fire?" Finn raised her hands chest high to slow Sloane down.

"I gotta go. Can you move?" Sloane's heart beat like a kettledrum. Sweat had dripped down her brow from that short jog. Her lack of exercise over the last two months was a significant factor. *Damn, I'm out of shape.*

Finn scanned the area behind Sloane and then narrowed her eyes. "Not until you tell me where West and Eric are and what's going on."

"I don't have time for this, Finn." Sloane reached for the handle of her car door, but Finn blocked her.

"I have all night, sweetheart." Finn deflected Sloane's attempts to go around her.

"Look—"

Before Sloane could complete that sentence, Finn gripped her arm. "I don't know what's going on or what you have in mind, but I'm not letting you do it alone. Wherever you're going, I'm going with you."

Sloane's frustration grew. She didn't have time to argue because Eric would soon figure out she'd left him behind. "Fine." She sharpened her words. "Jump in."

Moments later, Sloane navigated onto the surface streets of the city. Early evening meant heavy traffic. She calculated in her head the quickest way to get to the Golden Gate Bridge. After that, the route was hazy. "If you want to help, plug the address of Three Owls Vineyard in Santa Rosa into my GPS."

"You got a hit on Caco's phone, didn't you?"

"Yes." Sloane kept her eyes focused on the road like a laser. "Where's Eric?"

"Squad room, I guess. He's a good cop and an even better man. I can't have him be part of this."

Finn of all people should've understood what Sloane meant. Finn's own words persuaded Sloane of that. *He deserved to die*, Finn had said about the diplomat who killed her lover in a car accident. Caco deserved to die too. Sloane pounded her fist on the steering wheel to summon the determination to bring her over the finish line.

"Okay." Finn squirmed in her seat, her voice laced with caution. "What about West? Did you tell her?"

"No, I lied. I told West the call went to voice mail. I want her out of this too."

Finn released a breathy sigh, a sign she wasn't happy with Sloane's choices. "What about the outgoing call? Who made it? Who's the leak?"

"I don't know." Sloane twisted her fingers around the vinyl steering wheel. The leak was a distraction, one she didn't need at the moment. "The call triangulated to a tower on the Bay Bridge. Based on the time, there's no way Prichard made it."

"The bridge? So, the leak could be Quintrell or Carol."

"We'll figure that part out later."

Finn studied the route to the vineyard. "Have you been listening to the news? Santa Rosa is right in the path of the wildfires."

"I know." The only thing Sloane cared about was Caco's impending death. The thought had her rage on a steady boil; nothing would stop her from exacting her revenge.

Sloane's phone rang, alerting her to an incoming call from Eric, who was no doubt in a panic. She answered via the car's Bluetooth speaker.

"Where are you?" Eric asked. "West said you're going home. I'm not buying it at a time like this. You got a hit on Caco's phone, didn't you?"

Sloane recognized his alarmed tone and clipped words, concern mixed with anger. "I'm sorry, Eric, but I need to do this part without you."

"Please tell me you're not alone."

"I'm not. Finn's with me. I'll let you know when it's over."

"Damn it, Sloane. After all these years, if anything happens to you, I'll never forgive myself."

"I have her back, Eric." The nod Finn gave Sloane reassured her she meant it.

Sloane's mind drifted to Reagan. *What if I don't make it back?*

"Listen, Eric. All of this is on me. Promise me, if something happens, you'll get Reagan to the Tenneys."

"Sloane…" Eric's voice cracked and trailed off.

"Promise me, Eric."

Silence.

"I promise."

"Eric…" She choked at the thought of Reagan having no mother to come home to and the loneliness and anger that would follow. "Thank you. I gotta go."

She ended the call and thumbed the screen to make another. Her voice shook when it connected. "Reagan, honey. I'm out on a case, and I'm not sure what time I'll be home. Could you go to Deni's tonight? Can you do that for me?"

"Sure." Reagan paused. "Mom, is everything all right?"

"Everything will be fine after I get home. I have to take care of something first. If I'm not home by morning, go to school. I'll try to text and let you know when to expect me."

"Okay."

Sloane recognized apprehension in Reagan's voice, but she couldn't turn back now. She could almost feel Caco's throat between her hands. "Thank you, honey." Sloane cleared the emotion from her gravelly voice. She couldn't cry, not now. "I love you, Reagan."

"I love you too, Mom."

She ended the call, and focused on the road ahead, knowing that if she looked at Finn and saw sympathy there, she'd probably break down. Instead, in the silence, she mired herself in the reality that if things didn't go right, Reagan would be an orphan, a fate she'd hoped they wouldn't share.

CHAPTER TWENTY-TWO

Downtown Santa Rosa resembled a ghost town, but it didn't deter Sloane. A smoky haze hung in the empty streets like a dirty fog, and the only sign of life came from the two first-responder vehicles with flashing lights. They'd blown past Sloane's SUV, traveling in the opposite direction toward the safety of the barricaded checkpoint she and Finn had just passed. Their badges and the excuse of needing to transport a prisoner had earned them entry with a stern warning to hurry.

The sun had set an hour ago. If not for a spooky orange glow from the front lines of the fast-running wildfire several miles up the highway, the evening sky would have been black. That glow served as a beacon for Sloane as she drove toward a turnoff a few miles past the far side of town.

Both women focused on the road and the dangerous task ahead of them, an ominous silence filling the car. As they passed the last few buildings marking the end of the city limits, light-colored flakes began to fall on their windshield.

"What the hell?"

Sloane recognized Finn's nervous tone. "Ash." Sloane turned on the wipers as if it were nothing.

"This is crazy, Sloane. I bet he's gone by now."

"Police evacuated that area this morning, yet he was there an hour ago." Sloane refused to take her eyes off the road. Nothing would deter her from catching up with Caco. "He's riding it out or packing things he can't afford to lose. I'm betting he's still there."

"If the fire gets closer, we're leaving." Finn glanced at Sloane and then returned her attention to the road. "If I have to, I'll hit you over the head and throw you in the back."

Sloane refused to respond. Not even Finn could make her turn back now.

The ash fell faster, resembling a massive Sierra snowstorm. The wiper blades struggled to keep up, a sign the approaching fire had picked up speed. Sloane turned onto the access road to the Three Owls Vineyard. With no more streetlights to illuminate the rest of the route, she struggled to see through the falling ash.

The GPS showed they were still a good half-mile from the main house, so Sloane kept her headlights on as long as possible. As soon as she made out the silhouette of a building, she doused her lights and slowed the car to a crawl. Only the muted sound of the tires crunching pebbles on the pavement met her ears.

Finn pulled her Glock pistol from her shoulder holster and patted the attached ammo pouch, touching her two extra magazines.

After driving as close as she could without being detected, Sloane pulled over onto the gravel edge of the access road and parked. She reached across Finn, popped open the glove compartment, and retrieved her stash of jumbo zip ties. She handed a few to Finn and placed the rest in her back pocket. "Just in case."

Following Finn's lead, she prepared for a firefight, pulling her Sig Sauer from her shoulder holster and checking her ammo. A gut feeling told her they would soon be in battle. Locking eyes with Finn, she searched for signs of doubt but found none. "Ready?"

"Ready."

Sloane turned off the car's dome light so it wouldn't light up when they opened the doors. As soon as they did, ash and thick, pungent smoke hit them, but not so hard that they couldn't breathe. Sloane took the lead and crouched to minimize her silhouette; Finn was right on her heels, a step and a half behind. Both held their weapons in the low-ready position and weaved their way down the road's edge to a corner of the main house.

Both exterior and interior lights illuminated the Tuscan villa with its cream stucco, stone accents, and terracotta roof tiles, but Sloane saw no movement through its tall windows. Two unoccupied dark luxury SUVs sat idling in the circular driveway, one with its rear door up—all signs that whoever received that phone call hadn't left yet.

Sloane's pulse picked up. She was leaning forward, preparing to leave her hidden position behind the corner wall, when two men in suits emerged from the front door carrying a metal case the size of a small footlocker. She held her arm out and signaled Finn. They waited while the men grumbled and loaded the case into the back of the first SUV.

When the smaller man stopped to wipe sweat from his brow, he asked the other, "How many left?"

"Caco said just the last two from his study." The larger man wiped his forehead with the back of his hand. "He's filling them now."

Caco was so close. Sloane licked her lips at the prospect of putting a bullet into his skull.

The first man scanned the night sky, observing as Sloane had done minutes earlier that the wind had shifted and the rate of ash falling had picked up. Worse, the haunting orange glow over the next hill had brightened. "We need to leave."

"We leave when Caco says we do," said the larger man.

The two men returned inside, and Sloane whispered, "Flank the SUV. We'll take them by surprise when they load the next case."

Sloane and Finn assumed a crouched position at the front end of the first SUV. No time to plan. No time to discuss who would take whom. Once the men came back, there would be no time to think. They'd have to rely on their training and instincts.

A minute later, the men returned, carrying a similarly sized case. They lifted it up and into the rear compartment. Sloane approached from the passenger side, almost scraping her backside against the fenders, gun drawn, while Finn did the same from the driver's side. They reached the rear of the SUV, where the men concentrated on loading the case.

Sloane assessed the man on her side; he was bigger and stronger than the other and could easily overpower her. Without hesitation, she struck the back of his head as hard as she could with her pistol. The crack told her she'd split bone. He tumbled to the ground unconscious, followed by the heavy case.

In the meantime, Finn placed the muzzle of her pistol against the back of the smaller man's head. "Don't move."

Relieved they neutralized their first obstacles, Sloane slid her weapon into her holster and reached into her back pocket for the zip tie. She secured the hands of the man Finn had at gunpoint. When she clicked its grip extra tight, she whispered into his ear, "Do you want to live?"

The man shuddered. "Yes."

"Answer my question, or you get a bullet in the head."

He nodded faster.

"How many in the house?"

"Two."

"Is Caco there?"

"Yes."

Not taking the chance of him alerting the others, Sloane retrieved her gun and whacked him hard on the head too, knocking him out cold. Finn caught him before he fell and leaned him into the back of the SUV. Unable to lift the heavy man into the vehicle, they dragged him toward a row of bushes several feet away.

"You couldn't have knocked him out inside the car?" Finn struggled with one of his arms while Sloane struggled with the other.

"My timing was off."

At the bushes, they released their grip and rolled him into the dirt.

"Next time, push him into the car *before* he falls." Muffling a cough, Finn handed Sloane their remaining zip tie. "Here."

"Much better plan." As she bound the man's hands, the charry ash that had coated her throat caused her to cough up particles as well.

Leaving the second man tucked in the bushes, Sloane drew her gun again and led the way under the exterior lighting to a position outside the front door of the villa. Finn had her back, just as she'd promised Eric, even though she didn't have to be there. That meant more to Sloane than she'd realized.

Specs of glowing orange embers now mixed with the large ash flakes floating in the air, reminding Sloane they had to hurry. She took point. If anyone stuck her head inside that door first and risked taking a bullet, it would be her.

Her Sig Sauer in both hands, she took two deep, calming breaths. "This is for you, Avery."

After counting to three in her head, her heart thumping faster on each count, she breezed through the open door with Finn a split second behind. The well-lit living room they entered was decorated with crisp contemporary furnishings but empty of people.

Where is Caco?

Sloane slid along the smooth wall, deciding to search left first. The wide hallway, containing only a single wooden sofa table for decoration, led to the bedroom area. All three doors were open. Sloane cleared the first two guestrooms with ease before moving to the master bedroom. The high probability that Caco stood steps away had Sloane's pulse picking up pace. She wiped sweat beads from her forehead with her free arm and then rushed through the door, turning left, with Finn a step behind, turning right.

After Sloane determined the room was unoccupied, she relaxed her tense muscles. Dresser drawers hung half open and appeared empty as did the closet with the door wide open.

The room had been ransacked, perhaps by someone packing essentials for evacuation.

He'll be leaving soon.

Sloane used hand signals with Finn, telling her to reverse their route and search the other end of the single-story villa. She remembered one man saying earlier something about the study. The smell of smoke was stronger in the main room as they retraced their steps past the open front door—another sign the wildfire had picked up steam.

They entered the hallway leading to the other end of the house. Male voices speaking Spanish with a dash of English stopped Sloane in her tracks, Finn right behind her. She understood only parts of what they said, but she made out the words "fire," "hurry," "Oakland," and "Mazatlán." One of them had to be Caco.

The thirst for revenge grew thick in the back of her throat. She didn't expect Caco would be the one to draw on her first, but his soldier would likely be ready to respond quickly. She and Finn would need to neutralize him first.

Sloane glanced over her shoulder and held up two fingers, signaling the number of voices coming from the open double doors a few feet away. She used hand signals again to show she would take whichever man stood on the right, and Finn should take the one on the left.

Finn placed a hand on Sloane's shoulder and moved until they were side by side. She gave her one last reassuring nod that sent a clear message: "I got your back."

Both hands on her weapon, Sloane burst through the open door. One man stood behind the desk to the left and one in front to the right. She aimed right. "Police, freeze."

Finn stepped in behind her.

The man on the right turned toward them, drew a gun from the holster hidden beneath his blazer. When he raised it toward Sloane, she fired twice, center mass, hitting him in the chest. Blood spattered in a red cloud resembling fairy dust. He fell to the floor, the gun slipping from his hand.

Finn had trained her weapon at the man behind the desk but held her fire.

Sloane pivoted her aim from the lifeless man on the floor, blood oozing in a pool around his torso. She turned to the only remaining target.

He remained still, not a hair out of place nor a single bead of sweat running down the dark brown skin of his brow. His chiseled features and perfectly trimmed dark black hair likely made women swoon, while his tall, muscular frame probably intimidated most men. His custom-tailored European suit contrasted sharply with the cheaper off-the-rack suits worn by the men Sloane and Finn had taken down. He had to be the man in charge. He had to be Caco.

He posed no immediate threat with his hands poised in front of his belly and filled with a stack of documents. Sloane raised the barrel of her Sig Sauer and pointed it straight at his heart, the thudding in her ears deafening everything around her. She focused on his face. Thick lines between his brows mapped a lifetime of cruelty and heartlessness, which had cost her Avery. He had too much blood on his hands. Handing him over to a court of law came with no guarantees, but a bullet would serve swift justice.

The horrid image of Avery trapped beneath mounds of rubble minutes before her death ignited a fire in her gut. Her index finger slid back over the trigger, and her jaw clenched when she applied pressure.

Don't.

She lowered her aim, but her rage picked up steam. She felt every muscle in her face contort as the battle within her waged. She raised her pistol again and aimed straight at Caco's heart, the fail-safe shot even if he flinched. Her hands shook.

Reagan.

Caught in a battle between her rage and her conscience, she lowered and raised her weapon. If she pulled the trigger, she could never again wear her badge with pride. It would forever have the stain of blood.

Finn took her eyes off Caco and turned to Sloane. "Don't. Reagan needs you."

Sloane had already killed two men in pursuit of Kiss and Los Dorados, and both times, they gave her no good choice—kill or be killed. However, at this moment, she had a choice. For months, she'd wanted everyone who had a hand in killing Avery dead, but he had no weapon. If she pulled the trigger, she'd be a cold-blooded killer.

Reagan needs you echoed again in her head. Reagan would be alone if she sent that bullet toward her target. She closed her eyes and pictured herself when she lost both parents—angry, sad, and lonely with nothing but heartache for company. She couldn't pass that along.

"Reagan needs me," she repeated in a whisper and lowered her pistol.

Finn let out a long sigh of relief and turned back toward Caco. "Raise your hands."

The man complied but appeared unshaken, smug even. "You have no idea what you've gotten yourself into."

His arrogance grated on Sloane. She gritted her teeth and rolled her neck to stop herself from popping him in the mouth with the butt of her gun. "I know exactly what I've gotten myself into, Caco. That lab of yours on Ellis Street, the one you had rigged to blow. My wife was in there. You killed her."

"You must be Manhattan Sloane." He lowered his hands.

Of course, he knew her name after all the media coverage, but she didn't like it one bit. Sloane bit the inside of her cheek, the coppery taste of blood spreading in her mouth.

"Hands up," Finn warned. He raised his hands again, this time splaying his fingers.

"I know this is personal for you. If you kill me, you will make it personal to my family."

"Then don't give me a reason to kill you." Sloane's eyes narrowed when she tightened her grip.

"Either shoot me or arrest me, Sergeant Sloane." A crashing noise from somewhere in the house made Sloane flinch. "Or the fire will take us all."

"Fine." She holstered her gun. While Finn trained hers on Caco, Sloane circled him and cuffed his hands behind his back.

"You're under arrest for drug trafficking and for the murder of Avery Santos. You have the right to remain silent…"

When Sloane finished reading him his rights, he remained unfazed. "You have nothing on me."

She tightened his cuffs one more notch for good measure. "If we have nothing on you, how do you think we found you?"

While the logic left Caco without a witty response, Sloane feared the flimsy evidence they'd assembled wouldn't lead to a conviction. However, given time, she was confident she'd find it. "Let's go."

CHAPTER TWENTY-THREE

Finn, walking several steps ahead of Caco, led the way toward the front doors with Sloane in the rear. When she entered the hallway, thick smoke choked her lungs. The crackling of burning wood and vegetation stopped her in her tracks.

"Shit." Finn's eyes widened.

The wildfire had reached the house, and smoke was billowing from the master bedroom. They'd stayed too long. Sloane held on to Caco's cuffed hands and maneuvered him to the front door. Flames had cut off the driveway and engulfed the SUV into which they'd thrown the guard. Fire had trapped them.

The lights flickered, and then the room went dark.

"Out the back." Her heart thumping hard in her chest, Sloane pushed Caco toward the wall of windows leading to the backyard.

Once outside, a fierce heat-fueled wind whipped the flames into a frenzy around them. The unbearable heat meant they'd run out of time. Fire had cut off every visible avenue of escape.

"The pool!" Sloane pushed Caco toward a cabana stocked with swim towels. "Finn. Towels. We can use them for cover."

While Finn holstered her weapon and gathered the towels, Sloane pushed Caco toward the steps leading into the pool.

"We can beat the flames. I know a way." Caco's eyes darted about like those of a trapped animal.

A ploy? Some trick? With no safe route visible, Sloane couldn't be sure.

"On the other side of the trees, there's a garage made of cinder block," he yelled. "It should be safe. I have a truck there." He pointed with his chin toward a nearby path. "We can escape."

Unsure what to do, Sloane turned to Finn. "What do you think?"

The flames and heat grew stronger. No time to debate. Finn's eyes grew round. "If there's a way out, we should try."

Sloane pulled out her Sig Sauer as a show of force. "Show us."

Caco turned and pointed his shoulder. "It's past the pool. Come." He took off at a jog, hands cuffed behind his back, with Sloane and Finn right behind. When he reached the far corner at the deep end of the pool, he stopped, turned, and slammed Sloane with his shoulder, pushing her into the water.

A shivering cold coursed through Sloane's body as she sank deeper, still clinging to her weapon. She flapped and kicked, but her waterlogged sneakers acted as weights and slowed her effort to reach the surface. She needed to jettison the shoes or work ten times harder. Her legs, weak from the months she'd spent in recovery, sank deeper into the water. She could never hold her breath long, and she hadn't taken in much air before she fell in. Carbon dioxide built fast in her lungs, and a painful spasm formed in her diaphragm.

When the need to gulp air became unbearable, she kicked and flapped harder. Then an arm wrapped around her abdomen and pulled her up. The instant that warm, almost hot air tickled her face, she gasped hard. Air, beautiful smoke-tinged air. Coughing and spitting, she sucked in as much as she could.

"Thank God, Sloane."

Finn's voice was next to her ear. Finn had saved her, but what about Caco? Sloane shook the chlorine water from her eyes. "Caco? Where's Caco?"

With her arm still wrapped below Sloane's breasts, Finn kicked and pulled them toward the shallow end. "I don't know. The trees maybe."

"No, no, no, no, no." Sloane kicked to match Finn's legs and move them faster. "You let him escape?"

"I had to save you."

With the next kick, Sloane's feet touched the bottom of the pool. She stood, whipped her head around, water spraying in an arc from the tips of her long hair.

Flames surrounded them with debilitating heat and choking smoke. The high branches of the trees and the rest of the backyard vegetation burst into flames as the wind swirled more burning debris from the house. With nowhere to go and nowhere to take shelter, they had to remain in the pool.

Oven-like heat above the water scorched Sloane's face, and the charred taste of smoke overtook the chlorine in her mouth, forcing a cough.

"Coats," Sloane choked out and secured her Sig Sauer into her holster.

They struggled to keep their arms and shoulders below the waterline while they removed their wet coats, stacked them, one atop another, and, huddling together, draped the jackets over their heads. They formed a cocoon to block out as much of the heat and smoke as they could.

Seconds later, bloodcurdling screams came from the direction of the trees. Sloane had heard screams like that once before, only this time they were lower-pitched, unlike the ones her mother had uttered. Someone was in agonizing pain, hoping death would take them.

Sloane and Finn stared at each other in silence. Caco was being burned alive.

The screams stopped.

"Good." Tears of relief formed in the corners of Sloane's eyes. The man who killed her wife had suffered unimaginable agony at his death and not by Sloane's hands. Until she faced Caco, she had been sure that only putting a bullet in his head would give her satisfaction. She was wrong. He had met the same fate, and she had still cleaved to her oath. Justice was served just the same.

Minutes passed in silence, the only noise coming from the crackling of windswept flames burning everything around them. The heat continued to rise in their cocoon despite the damp layers of fabric. She swallowed hard at her fate. She had felt death chasing her all her life. It had caught up to Avery, and now it had her and Finn in its ugly grasp.

Finn released a hand from the trailing edge of the coats and splashed water on the fabric lining the top of their cocoon. "We need to keep the coats wet."

Sloane released one of her hands and grabbed Finn's with the other to stop her. "Let's dunk."

Finn agreed. The heat became bearable through the wet coats after they dipped below the surface and bobbed back up, but when they vented the cocoon, smoke-tinged the air more, making breathing difficult.

"We're going to die, aren't we? We're going to run out of oxygen." Finn's hands shook right below the water's edge.

We can't die. I can't leave Reagan all alone.

Sloane's mind flashed to her close brushes with death. She had walked away from the accident that killed her parents with only a few bruises and scratches. She survived the explosion that killed Avery with only a busted ankle.

"We won't die, you hear me? I've survived worse," she said, remembering the words of her grandmother as she worked her way back from a fourth stroke.

Time to dunk again. When they came back up, the smoke-filled air burned their eyes and mouths. Sloane sipped enough pool water to coat and soothe her throat. Finn followed her example. "Not too much," Sloane warned. "The chlorine will make you sick."

The sound of crackling flames whipped louder. They flinched and moved their faces and shaking bodies closer.

The grip Finn had on the edge of the coat shook an inch below the water level again. She forced a smile. "Twenty years ago, I would have given anything to be this close to you."

Their mouths were only inches apart. Sloane focused on Finn's lips, the ones she dreamed about kissing for years until she found the courage to kiss a girl for the first time. What if she kissed them now?

Sloane captured Finn's heat-chapped lips with a hunger that ensured if she died tonight, death would come with one less regret. Nothing about this kiss felt wrong. Pushing deeper, she dropped her hold on the water-soaked coattail and encircled Finn's torso with her arms. She didn't expect Finn's well-defined back muscles to feel so soft when she let her hands roam the soaked fabric. When she brought their breasts together, years of teenage fantasies came to life. The shivers that resulted shot up her arms and ended at the tips of her nipples in a sharp ache.

Sloane dragged her tongue across Finn's lips. They parted. Sloane needed to feel alive before the flames engulfed them. After Finn's tongue went searching, Sloane sucked it hard, as if chlorine would be the last taste she'd ever know. When she inhaled through her nose, a chemical odor overpowered the pungent smoke. Given her options, it was a much better final scent.

The moan that escaped Finn's throat was almost loud enough to drown out the crackling inferno. Sloane splayed her fingers along Finn's shoulder blades, feeling her lungs fill and empty as fast as her own heartbeat. All of her senses sparked alive. If they were to die tonight, she wanted it to be in this moment, with Finn in her arms, their lips and bodies pressed together.

A crash forced their lips apart. Sloane locked eyes with Finn, waiting for the flames to take them. Neither flinched. Neither blinked. Both waited for death.

She refused to break her gaze, those eyes hypnotizing her just as they had when they were teens. Every time she looked at them then, her heart would thump like a drum and she'd turn to mush, unable to speak a coherent word. Sloane was sure now.

She had chased those eyes through every woman she bedded, even her dead wife.

I love you, Finn Harper. I've always loved you.

Finn's eyes darted to one side, breaking the trance. "Do you hear that?"

"Huh?" Disappointed, Sloane dragged her mind back to the present.

"The crackling, it's not as loud."

Sloane reached up and tested the damp coat fabric. The temperature had dropped. "You stay underneath. I'll check."

She held her breath and dipped under the water. Once she moved several feet away, Sloane inched her head up and opened her eyes. Her skin didn't feel like it would melt from her bones, but the heat persisted. She inhaled. The air remained thick with smoke and tasted like a campfire. She turned and scanned her surroundings. An inferno had engulfed the house, but the trees and shrubs along the pathway now appeared passable.

She yelled out, "Finn, it's safe."

Finn slid the coats from her head, unveiling the hellish scene. "My God," she gasped.

While the worst of the flames and heat had passed, the smoke had not. They needed to get out of there. Sloane looked toward the trees. "I'll try to make it to the garage Caco mentioned and see if there's anything we can drive."

"I'm going with you." Finn dragged the coats along the top of the water as she lumbered closer to Sloane.

"You should stay."

"I told you earlier, wherever you go, I go. Now, don't argue." Finn moved past Sloane and toward the pool steps. As she did, Sloane shook her head, grinning through a deep sigh. Finn glanced over her shoulder. "Coming?"

Despite grumbling under her breath, Sloane preferred to have Finn staying in her sights. She grabbed Finn's hand before it moved out of reach. "We stick together."

Once they were out of the pool, Sloane's soaked clothes clung to her like heavy rags. She was leaving a trail of water in her wake; with each step she took, her toes squished inside her sneakers.

Pressing their dripping suit coats over their mouths and noses to protect them from the smoke, they trailed the edge of the pool, leaving the burning villa at their backs. The six-foot-wide walkway took them past the first line of trees. They remained careful not to disturb the smoldering brush along its edges as small flames lapped at their feet like serpents.

Still holding on to Finn's hand, Sloane took the lead when the path twisted. An orange glow from the fire remnants provided barely enough light to navigate. She stopped. Fallen branches from nearby trees were blocking the walkway, some of them still burning.

Sloane squeezed Finn's hand. "I'll clear it."

Dropping her coat from her face, she slid one arm into a sleeve, making sure some of the wet fabric covered her hand. Using a sizeable smoldering branch to push the others out of the way, she cleared several yards of the path.

When Sloane tired, Finn tapped her on the shoulder. Like Sloane, she was using her wet coat sleeve as a mask. "Let me take over."

Ten yards down, Finn came across a sizeable scorched pile on the walkway. It appeared human, but the extensive burns on it made it impossible to identify. Black char had replaced skin, leaving lumpy outlines of dark muscle. Whoever it was, it was someone who had their hands bound behind their back.

She and Finn stood over what must have been Caco's charred remains blocking the pathway. He appeared dead, and that put Sloane's mind more at peace. The flames had judged him and delivered the ultimate sentence: death to the wretched animal whose drugs took many of San Francisco's youth; death to the man who killed her wife.

Sloane had her revenge, but it didn't taste sweet. It had the bitter taste that nothing had changed. Avery was still gone. She gave the corpse one final look, and then smoke blanketed her lungs again. She wanted to rest, but she couldn't. Not yet. Fire and death still chased her and the woman she'd realized only minutes ago that she'd always loved. She had to get her to safety.

Sloane placed her hands on Finn's ash-smudged cheeks and peered into her eyes. "I won't let it take you too."

"Take me? What? Where?" Finn coughed through the smoke burning her throat.

"I couldn't save them, but I *will* save you." She took Finn's hand and gave a sharp tug toward the only means of escape down the pathway.

There was a loud crack.

She pitched her gaze toward the treetops. A large branch high above had broken off and was hurtling toward Finn. With only an instant to act, she pushed Finn to safety. She fell to the ground, buried beneath a portion of the splintered tree, as Finn tumbled to the pavement.

"No, no, no," Finn shrieked.

Dazed, Sloane made out Finn's voice and sensed somehow that she was clawing her way through the charred debris. An intense throb in Sloane's shoulder seemed to be her only injury—until she took inventory of the rest of her. A turn of her head was punctuated by a dull ache above her left ear, and her quick intake of smoke-tinged air forced her to cough.

"Thank God." Finn trembled as Sloane's head leaned into her palm. "I'll get you out."

Sloane latched onto Finn's hand. "You're alive." Even with a smudged face and flat, stringy hair, Finn was as beautiful as the day they met.

Finn rose and studied the large branch over Sloane. Moving toward the narrow end, she lifted and rotated it until the bulk of it cleared Sloane's body. Brushing Sloane's wet, chaotic hair from her face, she rested a palm on her cheek.

"You saved me," Finn said, shaking her head. "Can you walk?"

Sloane reassessed her injuries. Other than a sharp headache and a sore shoulder, she seemed unhurt. She maneuvered to her knees. "I think so."

Finn helped her to her feet. "Are you sure?"

"I'm good." Sloane winced at the pain she felt in her ankle when she tested her steadiness, but she hid it from Finn. She couldn't slow them down, not with death still chasing them.

"I'll clear the rest of the path."

Finn worked fast, shielding her nose and mouth from the smoke. Moments later, the end of the path came into view. It opened to a paved area and a small cinder-block building, its sides blackened by flames. It had to be the garage Caco was trying to reach.

"The garage. It's intact." Finn pointed in its direction.

Sloane nodded. If the building was there, Caco likely told the truth about a truck, and with it, they had a chance to escape.

As she had done on their last day at choir practice, Finn grabbed Sloane's hand and led the way. The side door was locked. Locating a rock the size of a baseball, she smashed out one of its small, square windowpanes, reached inside, and unlocked the door.

The dark garage provided a bit of shelter from the thick, choking smoke. Finn tried the light switch, but nothing happened.

In the darkness, the building seemed the size of a double garage, but Sloane couldn't be sure. She made out a mower, weed trimmer, blowers, and small garden tools. When she and Finn went further in, she made out the silhouette of a 1970s vintage Chevy pickup truck.

"Check for keys." Sloane slipped past the pickup. "I'll get the door open."

With no power, only the manual release would open the garage door. While Finn searched the old maintenance truck, Sloane ignored her various aches and moved multiple tools and equipment out of the way so she could reach the release handle dangling from the opener's middle rail. Once she clicked the lever, she grabbed the lower garage door handle and lifted it.

Finn flipped the driver's visor, and the keys tumbled down. "Got 'em."

When Sloane got the door over her head, she pushed as hard as she could, grunting in pain when the weight of the metal door stressed her tender ankle. The pain in her ankle sharpened as she slid the door the rest of the way on the overhead rails, forcing her to hobble to a stack of potting soil bags a few feet away.

"Sloane?" Finn jumped out of the driver's seat and found her through the dark, smoky air. "Are you all right?"

"My ankle. I felt something sharp." She rubbed it a few times. "I'll be okay." The pain was more excruciating than she let on.

Finn examined Sloane's ankle. "You're not okay. It's already swollen and discolored. You may have broken it again."

She rummaged through the workbench and returned with two pieces of wood scraps and a few old rags. The care she took in crafting the splint didn't go unnoticed. Tender and cautious, Finn had glanced up after she completed each step and asked if it hurt. "I wish I had something for the pain, but this should help until we get you to a hospital."

"Thank you." Sloane squeezed her hand. "Thank you for everything today."

Finn rose to her feet and hovered over her so their lips were inches apart. "You're welcome." She waited a few beats, inviting Sloane to kiss her again. Which she did.

The kiss had less hunger than their first, but she still filled it with passion. Sloane lifted a hand and stroked Finn's cheek, avoiding a patch of skin the heat had scorched. *Am I ready for this?* Whether she was, if they made it out alive, Sloane wasn't prepared to let Finn walk out of her life.

Finn pulled back first. The smile on her face hinted that she wanted more as well.

"Let me get the truck started, and then I'll come back for you," Finn's smile gave Sloane hope they would make it out alive.

Seconds later, Finn had the engine revving. She adjusted the rearview mirror. "Shit. There's fertilizer in the back. Give me a minute." A horrible thing to haul when fleeing a wildfire.

Finn emptied the truck bed and then eased Sloane into the passenger seat. She jumped behind the wheel and began the slow drive down the access road to the rear of the property. Neither of them familiar with the area and their phones were waterlogged; they'd have to go by memory and best guess to navigate their way out.

They agreed to get back to the main road and then reverse the route they'd taken to the winery. If fire had cut off that route, they'd wing it. Finn turned left into thick smoke and onto an access road. On either side, rows of grapevines burned brightly, embers blowing across their path in a spectacular light show.

Sloane couldn't see the edges of the dirt road in spots. Both sides dropped off toward deep ditches, giving Finn no room for error. Dropping their speed, Finn gripped the steering wheel so hard her knuckles turned white.

With each fraction of a mile, the tension in the truck thickened. Flames jumped across the road, forcing Finn's hands to shake. She appeared at the breaking point.

Sloane laid a hand on Finn's thigh. "You're doing fine."

"Talk to me about something. Anything." Finn twisted her palms on the vinyl wheel.

"Like what?"

Finn glanced at her. "Why did you stop singing? You had such a beautiful voice."

"The accident."

"Did you hurt your vocal cords?"

"No." Sloane shook her head. "My singing caused the accident."

Finn's brows drew together as she kept her eyes on the road.

Once Sloane started, she couldn't stop telling Finn the horrible truth of how her singing had distracted her father and caused him to lose control and crash. She stopped short of telling how her parents had told her to save herself, just as Avery had done. And she couldn't say how she witnessed her mother burn before the car exploded. Those parts were still too painful to tell.

"I haven't sung since."

"Sing with me, Sloane." Finn swallowed hard after wiping a few beads of sweat from her brow. "Your mother would want you to sing."

Finn was right. The accident had stolen too many things. Sloane couldn't get her parents or her innocence back, but she could recapture some joy from her youth. Memories of singing and laughing filled her head. Singing to KC and the Sunshine Band's "Boogie Shoes" in the kitchen while her mother made dinner and she set the table. Blasting Creedence's "Down On The Corner" every Saturday while they dusted and vacuumed. She wanted to get that feeling back and nodded.

Finn smiled and then began the verse, "If you change your mind, I'm the first in line…" She encouraged Sloane with a nod, "Come on, like in choir. You take background." She repeated, "If you change your mind, I'm the first in line…"

Sloane joined in. "Take a chance, take a chance…."

Finn continued to sing, as did Sloane. With each word, the pain of Sloane's childhood faded. By the time they came to the end of the song, Sloane sensed, through her streaming tears, that the happiness her mother had hoped for her was within reach.

Soon they arrived at the main highway leading into town. The wide lanes made the drive less dangerous, but the city resembled a war zone. In block after block, structures glowed an eerie orange with flames consuming the last bit of wood and other flammables.

Several miles on the other side of town, they spotted in the distance the distinctive flashing red and blue lights of a police barricade. It was several miles back from where it was when they'd crossed it coming in.

Finn slowed to a stop.

Sloane and Finn had faced the flames and survived. And their fight to stay alive had brought them closer than Sloane could've imagined. Finn had freed her from the shackles of guilt. And her quest for revenge had ended with justice being served, but not by her own hand.

Finn shifted and held Sloane in her gaze. "Sloane… I…"

"I know." Sloane met her eyes.

"What now?"

"I don't know if I'm ready."

"We'll take it slow." Finn squeezed Sloane's hand.

"It could take a long time," Sloane said, the memory of Avery tugging at her heart.

"I'll wait for you." Finn's voice contained not a hint of hesitation.

Moments later, Finn took her foot off the brake and drove.

CHAPTER TWENTY-FOUR

"Deep, steady breaths, Sergeant," the energetic thirty-something ebony-skinned emergency room nurse directed after placing the oxygen mask over Sloane's face for the third time that night. When her stethoscope caught on the trailing end of her long braids gathered at the back of her neck, she adjusted it. Now both ends rested evenly against her ample bosom and blue scrubs.

"You got it, Shari." Familiar with the routine, Sloane scooted further up the gurney to promote better oxygen flow, pulling her new walking boot along the mattress.

The minute Sloane and Finn's police escort pulled up to the emergency room receiving area, doctors and nurses had swarmed them. Shari, the wife of a firefighter, had pushed others out of the way and approached first. Word had spread through the hospital faster than the wildfire about the two officers who had ridden out the flames in a swimming pool, and she wanted to be the first to help.

"Once your O-two levels return to normal, we can send you and Agent Harper home."

Sloane lifted the mask a fraction, so it didn't muffle her voice. Though she usually had an aversion to it, she welcomed the antiseptic hospital smell over the thick smoke she'd inhaled for hours. She turned to the gurney on her left. "Home sounds good. Doesn't it, Finn?" When she replaced the mask, the plastic rubbed against the tender first-degree-burned skin on her cheek, forcing a wince.

Finn winked at Shari. "Now if I can get you to rest that ankle."

"Listen to Agent Harper." Shari checked Sloane's beeping monitors. "You're lucky it's only strained. A few weeks in the boot, and you should be good as new."

Sloane gave bossy Shari a salute. "Yes, ma'am."

"Pumpkin?" Chandler, dressed again in crisp golf attire, inched the privacy curtain open enough to peek his head around it.

"Daddy?" Finn mumbled through her oxygen mask.

He smiled. "You had me worried."

"I'll be back to check on you two." On her way out, Shari slid the curtain back to give them privacy.

The long, tight hug he gave Finn spoke to his relief that he hadn't lost his daughter overnight.

"I'm fine, Daddy." Finn ignored his concern. "Like I told you on the phone, it's only a few heat burns and smoke inhalation."

"I needed to see for myself that my little girl is okay." Chandler lifted a small shopping bag before glancing at Sloane. "Besides, I brought you a change of clothes. I'm sorry I didn't think about bringing two sets."

"I'll be fine, Mr. Harper." Sloane lowered her mask below her chin.

"Please, call me Chandler." He extended his arm to shake hands.

"Pleased to meet you, Chandler. I'm Manhattan Sloane." The resemblance between father and daughter caught Sloane's attention. They shared the same high cheekbones, cleft chin, and hazel eyes. She was sure if not for his age, they'd share the same dark blond hair.

His eyes widened at her name. "That reminds me, Kadin Hall has been trying to reach you. She said it's urgent." He pulled out and dialed his cell phone. "Kadin, I have Miss Sloane right here."

Sloane accepted the phone. "Can this wait, Kadin? I've had a rough night."

"I'm afraid not. Judge Gonzalez wants to reconvene this afternoon. If you need a continuance, I need to know now."

"I can't use any bad news today, Kadin. If this hearing doesn't go our way—"

"I did that digging, and when I present what I found, I'm confident the judge will rule in your favor."

"What did you find?"

"You were right when you suspected the Santoses weren't forthcoming. It seems their bakery hadn't been doing well for years, and their house is in foreclosure. If you check your wife's bank records, you'll see she gave her parents five thousand dollars right before her death."

"I had no idea."

"The check cleared the day Avery died, which is what I believe precipitated her last call with her parents minutes before the explosion. Avery was talking to her parents about money, not Reagan."

Sloane returned Chandler's phone, her head spinning. She ran back in her head the conversation she had with Avery before the explosion. *I can't deal with this*, Avery had said before Sloane entered the room. *I can't think straight*, Avery had told her.

It all made sense. Sloane didn't upset and distract Avery; her parents did. She could see it now.

"It wasn't my fault." A tidal wave of relief overwhelmed her. She fell back in her bed and curled up in a ball, shaking.

"Daddy, can you give us a moment?" Finn's voice was laced with concern.

"Sure, pumpkin." Chandler headed to the nurse's station, metal scraping as he closed the privacy curtain.

Finn threw the sheer hospital blanket off her legs and went to Sloane, sitting on the edge of her bed and wrapping her arms around her quaking frame.

"It wasn't my fault, Finn." Sloane buried her face into Finn's embrace. Tears escaped, soaking both their hospital gowns. "I didn't kill Avery."

"Why would you think you did?" Finn tightened her hold.

Sloane lifted her head, looked into Finn's eyes, and confessed the guilt she carried for months, detailing what Kadin had unearthed. "I've been miserable for months, thinking I was to blame. I was so afraid Reagan would hate me for it."

"She couldn't—"

The privacy curtain opened. Eric spoke with a brittle voice. "Sloane, I'm so glad you made it out alive."

* * *

Hobbling up to the front door of the townhouse following that long emotional night, Sloane craved a hot shower and a good night's sleep. Rest, however, would have to wait. She still had so much to do today.

Even though she could do it herself, Eric opened her front door.

"I'm fine. I can manage."

"I know you can, but you might as well get used to it. I plan to pamper you until you're out of that walking boot again." He glanced at his watch when Sloane stepped inside. "We should have about an hour before we have to leave for court."

At the bang of the door closing, Reagan ran from the living room and down the few steps to the entry. "Mom!" She leaped into Sloane's arms and sobbed.

The walking boot made Sloane wobble, and she strained to keep herself upright while she wrapped her arms around her daughter. "Reagan…"

"I almost lost you." Tears rolled down Reagan's cheeks.

Sloane tightened her hold, relieved the ordeal was finally over. She'd come close to losing everything. If not for thinking of Reagan, she would have pulled that trigger. Because of her, she could wear her badge with pride, as she did when Avery and her Nana were alive. On the other hand, worst of all, she came close to making Reagan an orphan. Thankful Reagan wouldn't share that fate, she pulled back and smoothed her hair. "I'm fine, honey." She sniffed one of her arms. "Correction. I will be after a hot shower and some clean clothes."

"You do smell bad." Reagan's unforced laugh reassured Sloane they were past the worst.

Sloane ascended the steps and turned the corner to the living room. To her surprise, they had company. "Janet. Caleb. What are you doing here?"

"Reagan called us last night and said you sounded odd on the phone." Janet gave Sloane a giant hug. "When she told us she was afraid something might happen to you, we dropped everything and drove down. After hearing about what you went through, I'm glad we did."

"I'd love to sit and chat, but Reagan and I have to leave in an hour."

"I know, sweetheart. Reagan filled us in." Janet rubbed Sloane's arms. "You get cleaned up, and I'll have a snack ready for you when you're done."

The generosity of Janet and Caleb never ended. She had the sense, no matter how this dispute with the Santoses turned out, the Tenneys would be the grandparents Reagan deserved and the parents Sloane had longed for.

In the shower, Sloane stood under the warm water, her palms propped against the opposite wall. Water cascaded over her neck and back and soothed her tight, aching muscles. The last twenty hours replayed in her head. One question bubbled to the top. If she'd made different choices along the way, would four men have lost their lives last night? Caco's death didn't bother her, nor that of the man she shot, but the two guards they tied up didn't have a chance.

She replayed the time in the pool. She had no idea how long they had taken refuge there, but those minutes or hours were seared into her memory. She and Finn had cheated death, and once they escaped out of the flames, she felt more alive than she had since Avery died.

And those kisses. She was still unsure if she was ready, but the promise of more made her hope she would be soon.

Once she toweled off, she stood at her closet, debating what shirt to wear to court. While Judge Gonzalez preferred things casual, Sloane wanted to put her best foot forward. She settled on a light blue button-down and slacks, an ensemble which both Avery and her grandmother would've given a thumbs-up. Right before she closed the closet door, her gaze went to the far end. She still hadn't cleared out Avery's things. *It's time.*

After dressing near the bed, she glanced at the alarm clock, the one Avery insisted on setting every day to wake her from her hard sleep. She shook her head. *I gotta replace that damn thing too.*

Sloane opted for no makeup because of her tender heat burns, which were not as severe as Finn's. She regretted that her quest for revenge had led to heat reddening Finn's beautiful face. She fixed her hair, tallying up the things for which she had to thank Finn. There were too many to count. She promised herself to thank her properly when she got the chance.

* * *

"In light of new evidence," Judge Gonzalez scanned both tables fronting her elevated bench, "I believe Avery Santos had not changed her mind regarding visitation. In addition, the petitioners have failed to provide convincing evidence that Sergeant Sloane has endangered Reagan's safety and wellbeing. I hereby deny the petitioners' request for guardianship and court-mandated visitation." She then turned her attention to Sloane and Reagan. "That decision I leave in your capable hands. I wish you both health and happiness."

Reagan fell into Sloane's arms with the weight of the world clearly lifted from her shoulders, and on the gallery bench lining the back wall, a smile formed on Finn's face. In the hospital, she hadn't had time to say it, but she would've told Sloane that Reagan could never hate her. She'd already become her mother in her eyes.

"Thank you, Kadin." Sloane shook her hand.

"I'm happy you and Reagan can finally get on with your lives."

On their way out of the courtroom, Sloane asked, "We're going home for a celebration of sorts. Would you like to join us?"

Kadin glanced at Finn as if searching for permission, but Finn didn't offer any. Their time had passed, and it was time to move on to the next chapter without a nagging reminder of their failed past. "I'd love to, but I have to get going. Don't be a stranger now."

"I won't." Sloane gave her a tender hug.

After Kadin escaped a few steps down the tiled hallway, Finn placed a hand on Sloane's forearm. "I'll be right back." She caught up to her ex. "Kadin, wait."

Kadin stopped and turned. Her eyes matched her soft smile.

It had only been days since Finn last saw her at the door of their old apartment, but it seemed a lifetime ago. She felt no sadness, no pain, only respect and love. "Thank you for helping Sloane. It means the world to me."

"I saw you two before the hearing." She rubbed Finn's arms. "It's obvious she's important to you."

"She's grieving." Finn lowered her eyes, torn between patience and desire.

"Give her time." She pulled Finn into a hug and kissed her on the cheek. "Take care of yourself, Finn Harper."

As Kadin walked away, Finn answered her ringing cell phone. "This is Agent Harper."

Feet away, Sloane placed a hand on Reagan's shoulder. "I need to tell you something, honey. But can we sit down for a minute? My ankle is killing me."

"Sure, Mom." Reagan helped Sloane to the bench positioned outside the courtroom doors.

Sloane cleared her throat, stalling to gather her thoughts.

"Last night, when I thought we might die, I was scared, not for myself, but for you. We're a lot alike, you and me. We both lost our mom and dad at a young age, and I know how sad and lonely it can get without a parent around. I didn't want that for you." Her voice cracked at the memory of her own childhood scars. "Your mom and I talked about it right before she died. Since it's just you and me now, I'd like to make this official and adopt you."

"Really?" Reagan's smile stretched to her eyes.

"Yes, really."

Reagan wrapped her arms around Sloane's neck. "I'd love that."

"Then it's settled." *It's official, Avery.*

"But no more dangerous stuff." Reagan pulled back. "I almost lost it."

"I'm so sorry I put you through that. A lot happened last night, and I promise I'll never scare you like that again."

"Good, because I don't think I can take it a second time."

Finn returned. "We have a problem." She turned to Reagan. "Do you mind if I talk to your mom alone for a minute?"

"Naw, that's cool. I'll go find Eric."

"I'll be right behind you." When Reagan disappeared around the corner, Sloane patted the empty part of the bench beside her. "Sit."

Finn sat, but not too close. "I got a call from the Sonoma County Sheriff. He had some interesting news about the crime scene at the winery. They checked the ashes and found only three bodies."

"Three? Which ones?"

"All they said was they found one inside the house and two outside."

"So, what do they think happened to the other one?"

"They're not sure, but odds are he didn't make it out."

Sloane considered the news. She'd had enough of the case that had cost her too much. She was eager to be a mother and see what might happen with the woman sitting next to her.

"You know what? It will wait until tomorrow. The only thing I want to know right now is if you'd like to join us for a celebration dinner. I'm adopting Reagan." Sloane stood and held out her hand, inviting Finn to come with her.

"That's great news, but you know, we still haven't figured out who is the leak."

"That can wait too." She continued to hold out her hand. "Coming?"

"Absolutely."

When Sloane wrapped a hand around Finn's, her pulse quickened, just as it had twenty years ago. They had completed the connection between them, only this time, it went deeper. Neither of them was a little girl anymore. Sloane knew what love looked like, and this had all the makings. An unspoken promise floated in the air as they walked hand in hand down the corridor. A sign of much more to come. A promise born out of the flames.

EPILOGUE

This uncanny ability to consistently choose the wrong path was becoming worrisome. The drug operation Los Dorados and the cartel had spent years setting up was in jeopardy of falling apart, and today's news meant a crossroads had been reached. There was another choice to be made: do nothing or make the phone call El Padrino would expect. Either way, a noose was tightening. The call would restart the cycle of self-loathing, but doing nothing was something El Padrino could never forgive. The path that would avoid receiving a bullet to the head, for now, posed the best option.

"Yes." The voice on the other end of the phone was not cold and distant, which meant news of the wildfire had yet to reach the feared cartel leader.

"I have news."

It was easy to imagine El Padrino in his white three-piece suit sitting behind a stately, oversized dark oak desk in a wood-lined study, the very image of a cartel drug lord. This call to his private number had likely forced him to choose which item to put down, his smoldering Montecristo No. 2 or the tumbler of his favorite Osocalis.

"When you bring me news, it usually means I'm about to lose money." Padrino's tone remained light.

"Three Owls burned to the ground in the wildfire."

"So, Caco was right, but why isn't he telling me these things."

"Officers raided the compound. He and his men were killed or trapped by the fire. Authorities found only one injured survivor."

"I see." The chill now evident in Padrino's voice caused shivers of dread. "Who survived?"

"I don't know, which is why I'm calling. You should send a man to find out."

"And what of the officers?"

"They survived."

The silence on the other end of the phone meant another crossroad was on the horizon. Padrino would want to know who had put his son in a hospital bed or a grave. Until now, he had only been fed information that furthered the drug business. This was different. This was revenge. If Padrino wanted that, there would be no going back.

I would be a killer too.

Maybe if Padrino got only half of what he wanted, it wouldn't be so bad. A single name would probably suffice, but which one?

Padrino finally broke the unnerving silence. "Who is responsible for this?"

"Manhattan Sloane."

Bella Books, Inc.

Women. Books. Even Better Together.

P.O. Box 10543
Tallahassee, FL 32302

Phone: 800-729-4992
www.bellabooks.com